# A DARLING HEIR

## DARLING MEN
## BOOK FOUR

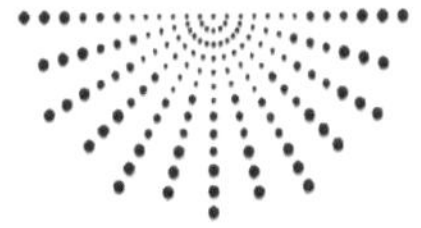

## LARK HOLIDAY

GLASS ELEPHANT PRESS

*To remembering who you are.*

# CHAPTER ONE

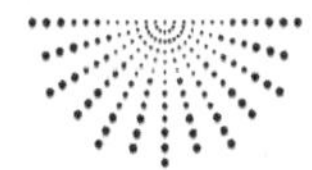

VIVIAN

Vivian Locke stared at the perfect four-layer chocolate cake she had spent all morning working on. Or at least, it had been perfect until she had tripped en route to the table and dropped the dessert.

She had the absolute worst luck.

"Is everything okay? It sounded like something..." Her mom stepped into the kitchen, her graying hair swaying as she looked between Vivian and the ruined cake. "Oh, honey. Let me help you."

"I've got it, Mom." Vivian knelt down, scraping up handfuls of fluffy buttercream frosting. It was bad enough that she was almost thirty and still couldn't do anything right. She didn't need her mom's help cleaning up the mess. "Sorry I ruined dessert."

"There's nothing to be sorry about. I can run down to the store and grab something. Any requests?"

"Whatever you want is fine with me." That was one benefit of owning and operating the only grocery store in

Darling. It was easy to restock at a moment's notice, a true luxury on an island in Alaska.

"Be right back. Maybe I'll grab some Neapolitan ice cream. That's Robert's favorite." Her mom headed downstairs. They lived on the second story of the building, directly over Locke Grocery.

Vivian stiffened. Her uncle was the reason she'd been on edge all day. No wonder she dropped the cake. Her parents always rolled out the red carpet for Uncle Robert, but Vivian dreaded his appearance. He had last been in Darling eight months ago for Thanksgiving, and that was not long enough in between visits, in Vivian's opinion.

As she tossed the cake into the trash, Vivian's throat grew tight. If this wasn't a metaphor for her life, she didn't know what was. In the trash went the cake, where her dreams of being a pastry chef had long since gone too.

Her eyes burned, and she blinked furiously. Vivian refused to cry. She wasn't upset about the cake, not really. Sure, it had taken hours, but it was a break from working at the store, a never-ending job she shared with her parents.

It was the fact that Vivian was in nowhere Alaska, scraping chocolate cake off the floor, and her ex-boyfriend was off in New York City, living the life *she* should be living. Thank goodness Philippe couldn't see her now, or he'd probably laugh himself into a coma.

After washing her hands, Vivian sprayed cleaner on the floor and wiped up the frosting smudges with paper towels. She had done this to herself. She should've never looked at his social media before dinner. Why make a bad situation worse?

But she had already been on a downward spiral since Uncle Robert announced his impromptu visit. The man was a plotter, a planner. If he took a break from running his beloved empire in Anchorage to visit Darling at the last minute, something was up. Her uncle owned a ton of commercial real estate, including the building for Locke Grocery. Without him, there was no way her parents could've afforded this store, a fact he loved to remind them of at every opportunity.

It was definitely *not* the time to torture herself with her ex's success. It wasn't like Philippe was a full-fledged celebrity or anything. But a handsome, charismatic French chef who had just opened his third, and supposedly best yet, restaurant didn't go completely unnoticed by the world. There was enough publicity online for her to keep tabs on him anytime she was stupid enough to look. It helped that Philippe was addicted to attention and never missed an opportunity to have the spotlight on him.

Vivian washed her hands again and put the cleaner away. Yeah, he loved attention so much that when she had come back to Darling for a family emergency, Philippe had found himself a new girlfriend *and* a new pastry chef almost immediately. And if that wasn't bad enough, he had also cut her out of the New York City restaurant they had invested in together. Vivian should've never mixed business with pleasure. But she had been young and naive, and it had never occurred to her to ask her boyfriend for a contract until after everything had fallen apart.

She pressed the back of her hand to her forehead. Vivian would be the first to admit she had been dazzled senseless by his French accent and good looks. After working under him in his first restaurant for six months, she was a total goner. And he had used it to every advantage.

But Philippe hadn't just stopped at breaking her heart. No, he obliterated it. And once he had stolen her happiness, he took her dreams too.

Everyone had a horrible ex. That didn't make Vivian special. But it was something special to have a horrible ex that had a golden touch. Especially when everything Vivian touched turned into trash. For example, chocolate cakes.

She took a deep breath. Whatever. That was seven years ago. Vivian had accepted that this was her life now, plain and simple. Even if it wasn't her dream, it was better than losing everything. The things she wanted came at a price that she wasn't willing to pay.

And the fact that she was still finding her groove in Darling? A minor hurdle.

Not that it mattered. Vivian wouldn't have left if her parents begged her. Leaving last time had almost destroyed her family, and Vivian swore it would be the last selfish thing she ever did.

Her mom came back to the kitchen, Neapolitan ice cream in hand. "Do you mind getting your dad and uncle from the living room while I scoop this up?"

Vivian tied off the trash and heaved the bag up. "Not at all. I'm going to take this out to the dumpster. I'll be back in a minute."

A throat cleared, and they turned to see Vivian's dad standing in the doorway. "Uncle Robert has something he wants to talk to us about."

Her mom held up the gallon of ice cream. "Sure thing. We can discuss it over dessert."

Her dad glanced over his shoulder. "He asked if we could talk now."

Vivian clenched her jaw as she lowered the trash bag to the floor. Her dad adored his older brother, and Uncle Robert always took advantage of that to get what he wanted. She didn't know what her dad saw in him, but maybe she would be the same way if she weren't an only child. Vivian had always wanted a sister, but that was just another dream that wasn't meant to be. "Let me wash my hands. I'll meet you there."

Vivian was the last to join the other three in the living room. Her parents sat on the couch, and Uncle Robert leaned back in the recliner.

She took a seat on the tufted stool in the corner. Hopefully, her uncle wouldn't hassle her about ruining the cake. If he wanted it so bad, he was welcome to paw through the trash.

Uncle Robert looked them each in the eye. "I have exciting news. Something that will be good for all of us."

Dinner turned to a rock in her stomach. Suddenly, Vivian wished this *was* about the cake. The only thing Uncle Robert thought was exciting was money. How it would affect them all, she couldn't guess. Her uncle was many things, but generous wasn't one of them.

He beamed, his green eyes glittering. "I've decided to sell the store."

The room swam in front of her. There was no way he had just said that. No way. This had to be a bad dream. She'd wake up in a cold sweat any minute now.

But the nightmare wasn't over. Uncle Robert kept talking, telling them the details of the deal, including the amount the buyer was willing to pay for the store. Vivian had never seen her uncle smile so big.

Her throat burned. She was going to be sick. How could he be happy about this? Didn't he realize that her parents weren't rich? That they would have to get new jobs? At their age? And what about Vivian? This store, this place, was her entire life. And if she knew her uncle at all, he would take the money and leave them to figure out the rest. All rich people were the same. They cared about themselves and only themselves.

Her dad stared at his brother wide-eyed. "Is it worth that much?"

"Not nearly." Uncle Robert laughed. Vivian didn't get the

joke. Maybe it was only funny to people with fat bank accounts and no morals. "If the number wasn't so intriguing, I'd wonder what they saw in this place that I didn't."

"So you think we should take the deal?" Her dad's graying brows pinched together.

"I do," Uncle Robert said, a subtle reminder of who made the decisions. "It makes sense. You two can't run this place forever. Then there's Vivian to think of."

All eyes turned towards her as if she held the secrets to the universe. Vivian blinked. "What about me?"

Uncle Robert smiled. "This is good for you. You can't possibly want to stay here forever. You had a career in front of you, your entire life—"

"I'm the one who chose to come back." Vivian stuck her chin out. "I'm perfectly happy here. This is what I want."

Uncle Robert's smile disappeared. "Trust me. You'll thank me later."

Yeah, right. As if she'd ever trust him. She looked at her parents. "Mom, Dad, what do you think? You're part owners, after all."

"Minority owners," Uncle Robert said. "Your parents sold back shares to me a few years ago."

Vivian pressed her lips together. She knew exactly what that money had gone to. She just hadn't known at the time where her parents had gotten the funds to help her out with her business venture. That made it all the more sickening that Philippe wouldn't give back her investment in the restaurant. He did not actually need the money she so desperately did.

"If you think it's a good idea, then I'm sure it is," her dad said.

Uncle Robert nodded. "I've thought about it a lot. You can't run the store forever, and it's not good for Vivian to waste her life in Darling. I thought eventually she would get up the courage to move away again, but clearly, she needs a little push."

Vivian clenched her teeth. She was a grown woman, not a baby bird clinging to the nest.

Before she could tell her uncle exactly where to shove it, her dad spoke up again. "Vivian is doing just fine—"

Uncle Robert let out a deep sigh, as if he had one minute of patience and his brother better use it wisely. "She's not fine, Henry. She's stuck. You made your choices, and look how it's affected your daughter."

Vivian's face burned as they talked about her as if she weren't sitting right there. This was mortifying. Not only was she an adult, fully capable of doing whatever she liked with her life, but the last thing she wanted to discuss after dinner was her dad's affair.

Her dad paled. "That was years ago. We've moved on."

Uncle Robert waved his hand. "You can't blame yourself. Even successful people fail as parents. Look at Charlotte's cousin, Stefan Becker. He's one of the most respected people in my industry. A billionaire, for Christ's sake. His kids had every advantage, and they've hardly done anything worthwhile. I still can't believe they even come to hang out in this town."

Vivian cringed. She wasn't exactly close with the Beckers. She had seen them around town, and they had come into the store a few times. But they were Charlotte's family, and Charlotte *was* her friend.

She had to hand it to Uncle Robert. Only he could insult so many people and the town they loved in just one sentence.

Her dad shook his head. "I'm just not sure, Robert. It would be a big change for all of us. Why can't I buy the store from you? We can set up a payment plan. On your terms, of course."

Her stomach twisted tighter at the clear desperation in

her dad's voice. Even if Vivian hadn't forgiven him completely, she also didn't doubt that her father loved his family.

But Uncle Robert only looked bored. "Listen, Henry, this is for your own good. It's clear from past actions you don't know what's best for your family. Well, I do. I may not have kids of my own, but I know it's not good for Vivian to stay here forever. Her life came to a halt when you screwed up." Her father paled at that.

One more word and Vivian wouldn't be able to hold her tongue any longer. She had been raised not to say anything at all if she couldn't say anything nice. Around her uncle, that quickly turned into a vow of silence.

The stool scraped against the floor as she stood suddenly. "I'm going to take the trash out. Be right back."

She left the living room, breezing past the kitchen and the trash bag. Vivian went downstairs to the store instead of outside to the dumpster. She doubted Uncle Robert would know the difference or care. He didn't actually care about her family. He probably just wanted the money from the store for some other investment, not to mention he would no longer have to make visits to Darling.

Her chest constricted. That last part was more than fine with her. She was so sick of rich jerks. Between her uncle and Philippe, she'd known enough to last her a lifetime. They all sucked.

Her eyes burned as she picked her way down the steps in the dark. She should've turned a light on, but Vivian didn't want people to peep in the window of the store and see her crying. Outside, dusk had already fallen over Main Street as the early April day shifted into night.

Vivian wiped at her nose. Once upon a time, she dreamed about a different career, a different life. But after what happened with her parents, Vivian had vowed to do anything and everything to keep her family together. She had fought and sacrificed more than anyone would ever know. The fact that Uncle Robert could make it all disappear in an instant was an unpleasant reminder that some things were out of her control. Her bad luck had followed her all the way home. She wasn't just useless. She was worthless.

The staircase creaked. "Vivian, are you down here?"

Her heart pounded. The last thing she wanted was for her mom to see her having a breakdown. This news affected them all. Vivian couldn't be the only one upset. "I'm fine, Mom."

The light flicked on, and footsteps grew louder on the wooden stairs. Vivian cursed herself. She should've just taken the trash out if she wanted a moment to herself. "I know it's a big change, sweetheart."

Vivian swallowed. Big didn't begin to cover it. It wasn't just big. Her entire life would be different. All their lives. "This can't be happening."

Her mom sighed as she reached the bottom step. "Maybe this is for the best. We can't run this place forever. And your uncle is right. You're so young. It can't be good for you to stay here, day after day. You never meet anyone new. You don't do anything. If we sold, you could go back to—"

"So what?" Vivian threw her hands in the air. "Is there something wrong with me if I don't mind any of that? Is there some rule that I have to be married with kids by thirty and have some great career?"

Her mom reached for Vivian and pulled her close. "Of course not, honey. The only thing I want for you is to be happy. That's all parents want for their children."

Vivian sniffed as she buried her face in her mom's familiar salmon-pink cardigan. "It's going to happen, isn't it? Uncle Robert is going to sell."

"I think so." Her mom gave Vivian a squeeze. "I promise

everything will be okay. Have you thought about opening up a restaurant again?"

Vivian pulled away. She thought about it all the time. But she wouldn't be stupid enough to ever actually try it. Vivian had accepted that dream was one of the many sacrifices she'd made for her family. The threat of everything disappearing if Uncle Robert really did sell the store only made the truth more obvious. Her career didn't matter as much as her family. Nothing did. "I'm afraid."

"Oh, honey. What happened before, well, that was a mistake. It won't happen again."

Vivian's throat tightened up. She wished she could get over her dad's infidelity as easily as her mom did. But she still couldn't believe he could betray their family, her wonderful mother, like that. Vivian had been trying to forgive him for years, and she wasn't even sure that she was halfway there. "Enough about me. How do you feel about it? What will you do?"

"Maybe it'll be a nice change. It's always so hard to get away with the store. Now we could do some of the things we wanted. Take a vacation or something."

"Will you stay here? In Darling?"

"I suppose we don't need to." Her mom lifted a shoulder. "Maybe we would move. I've always wanted to go to Minneapolis."

A laugh bubbled up in Vivian's chest. "Minneapolis? Why? Most people want to move somewhere warmer when they leave Alaska. Not colder."

Her mom giggled. "I really don't know."

"Can I come with you?"

"I'd be sad if you didn't." Her mom gave her a warm smile. "Just remember, honey. Sometimes the life you plan doesn't happen. Instead, you get the life you were meant to live."

With one last hug, her mom went back upstairs, leaving Vivian alone with her thoughts.

She rubbed at her eyes, torn between bursting into tears and throwing a full-on temper tantrum.

Vivian didn't know who she was madder at.

Uncle Robert for selling the store.

Her ex for stomping all over her heart.

Or herself for falling for the idiot in the first place.

If it hadn't been for Philippe and the restaurant, she might have had the money to buy the store from Uncle Robert. At the very least, her parents would've had equal shares in the business.

Her failed career as a pastry chef was proof Vivian wasn't meant to venture outside life in Darling. Her parents had taken a bet on her and lost.

She massaged her forehead. Last time disaster struck, Vivian had been able to fix everything by coming back to Darling and staying here. Her personal and professional life had fallen apart, but she had been able to keep her family together. That was worth it. That was what mattered.

Vivian was determined to do it again. She had to find a way to keep their store.

She took a deep breath. She was going to figure out a way to fix this. And once she did, Vivian would finally have complete control of her life once and for all. No man would ever take her away from Darling ever again.

# CHAPTER TWO

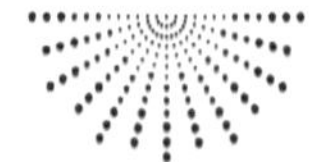

THOMAS

Thomas Becker didn't know what to do when someone was nice to him.

"Are you sure there's nothing else I can get you?" his cousin Charlotte asked again, her blue eyes rounded. Her German accent only seemed to emphasize her apparent concern.

Thomas looked down at the breakfast platter she had set in front of him. It was the same every time he visited Darling. Charlotte doted on him nonstop, and for someone not used to human empathy, it was overwhelming. "I'm sure."

She patted his shoulder. "Just let me know if you need anything at all."

Thomas watched her walk away, her petite form disappearing through the swinging doors that led to the kitchen of the Buckwild Bar and Grill. He didn't deserve Charlotte. Didn't she know that he was a disappointment? In his family, success was practically guaranteed. But Thomas had still managed to screw up.

He picked up his fork with a sigh. The hearty breakfast was a feast compared to the protein shake he normally downed before heading to the gym every morning back home in New York. Staying in shape was one of the few things in his own life that he could control, and he did so with a vengeance.

But Alaska was a million miles away from the real world. Might as well live it up.

He cut into an over-easy egg and dunked a slice of sourdough toast into the golden yolk. The combination of the tangy bread and sweet butter practically made his eyes roll back into his head. It sure beat the hell out of a chalky protein drink. If there was one thing Thomas could appreciate in life, it was good food.

"Should I give you and your toast some privacy?" Marina slid into the bench seat across from him, her dark eyes dancing with laughter.

Thomas gave his younger sister a look. "You're up early."

"I'm here to support you, remember? Your emotional support human."

"You make me sound like a robot."

Marina snatched a piece of bacon off his plate. "That honor belongs to Dad. I'm pretty sure he just plugs in at night."

He swatted at her hand. "Get your own breakfast."

With a grin, she caught Wolfie's eye and pointed at Thomas's plate.

Thomas lifted an eyebrow. Ever since their first visit to Darling a little over a year ago, Marina acted right at home at the Buck. Charlotte owned and operated the restaurant with her husband, Wolfie. They had run the business since they moved from Germany to Alaska close to three decades ago. "You're sure getting comfortable here."

Marina stuck out her tongue. "Maybe you should do the

same. Hell, consider moving here. You realize they're not going to forget, right?"

Thomas lifted a shoulder, even though his stomach clenched at the unnecessary reminder of why they were in Alaska right now. "I don't see why not. It was only a three-hundred-person wedding. I gave everyone twenty-four hours' notice. That's all they require at the dentist."

Appropriately, the idea of marrying his ex-fiancée was about as appealing as a root canal. On every single tooth.

Marina nodded. "I'm sure that's how Dad saw it too. I bet he didn't even notice the fact that you ruined a merger that would've doubled his net worth."

"A marriage disguised as a business deal. How are our parents from this century?" Thomas grumbled into his coffee.

"You made a lot of bachelors happy, at least. Your fiancée is one of the most eligible women on the market again."

"Ex-fiancée. And besides, you didn't even like her."

"Not one bit." Marina grinned. "But I wasn't the one who was going to marry her."

Thomas set down his coffee cup. "Why don't *you* almost get married so we can discuss your canceled wedding instead?"

His sister barked a laugh. "Not likely. You know I don't do relationships."

"Good morning." Wolfie's gray mustache parted into a smile as he walked up to their table, a breakfast platter in one hand and a coffeepot in the other. He barely came to a stop as he dropped off Marina's food, poured her a cup of coffee, and refilled Thomas's mug before moving on to the next table. The breakfast rush was in full swing.

Once Wolfie was out of earshot, Thomas looked back at Marina. "No relationships, huh? I would bet money I heard you sneak back in this morning while I was doing sit-ups."

"Only a psychopath does sit-ups at four in the morning. And mind your own business."

"Come on. Who is he?"

"We were discussing your life, remember?" She drizzled maple syrup over her pancakes. "Why did you cancel the wedding, anyway? Besides the fact that Celeste is a class A bitch."

"Mind your own business," he mimicked Marina.

She rolled her eyes. "Whatever. I was just trying to help."

"I know." Thomas leaned back in the booth. But no matter which way he looked at it, the situation was beyond help. "Any chance they'll change the conditions of the trust and let me off the hook?"

Marina wrinkled her nose. "And break with generations of tradition? I doubt it. You either get married by thirty and get your money, or you don't. It's pretty simple."

"Yeah. I guess." He rubbed the back of his neck. Except it was anything but simple. Thomas had lived his life for this family, for all that stupid money. He worked a job he hated, killed himself trying to meet his dad's impossible standards, and never once managed to measure up. All those years of waking up every day to realize he still hated himself, that he still wasn't good enough, had taken their toll. Now, he had *finally* found something he cared about, and it was going to take everything he had not to lose it.

God, his life sucked. And no one knew.

Marina nibbled a piece of bacon. "Assuming Mom and Dad don't rewrite the rules for you, what's the backup plan for money?"

Thomas pushed away his half-eaten breakfast. Unlike his sister, his appetite had disappeared, along with any hope he had for the future. "No idea."

"Me neither. We'll just have to be penniless together. But I think it might be pretty cozy in that one-bedroom of yours.

Any chance you would spring for a bigger place? You have to have some money saved from working for Dad all these years."

Thomas shifted in his seat. "About that. You know the restaurant?"

She snorted. "Hell, I think all of Manhattan does. I'm pretty sure the whole island heard you and Dad arguing about it the day you bought the place. He called it proof you were an idiot."

"Thanks for the reminder." Thomas winced. "But Dad is going to be the one who looks like an idiot. It's going to work, Marina."

"You don't think that maybe our father—who is a billion-aire, in case you forgot, and in the real estate business—knows a good investment when he sees one? Or is the restaurant just your way of pissing him off?"

Thomas clenched his jaw. Maybe that's how it had started, though he'd never admit it. The restaurant was a chance to do something different, sure. Something that had nothing to do with his father. But the more Thomas had thought about it, the more he had liked the idea.

He had a good head for business. Why not use it for something he enjoyed? Something that was just his? For the first time in years, he was actually excited about something. Even though it was exhausting balancing two careers, Thomas was already restless to get back to work at the restaurant after just a few days in Alaska. "It has nothing to do with the investment or sticking it to Dad. I was the prob-lem, and you know it. He never lets me off easy."

Marina slurped her coffee. "Dad sucks. That isn't news."

Thomas sighed. Truer words had never been spoken. "The point is that this venture is turning out to be a little more expensive than I realized."

"You're telling me that a French restaurant with a killer

location in the East Village is turning out to be more expensive than you thought?" She blew air through her lips. "Shocker."

"Hey, I knew it wasn't going to be cheap, okay? I'm a project manager for Becker Commercial Properties. I am aware of the market." He rubbed the back of his neck. Thomas didn't just know the market. The market knew him. It was why he had asked to be a silent partner, even though he held majority ownership.

Thomas had been judged by his last name his entire life. He didn't want special treatment. For once, he wanted to earn respect for his work ethic and skill, not his family's reputation. Luckily, his celebrity chef was more than happy to hog the spotlight when it came to the restaurant. Unluckily, celebrity chefs weren't cheap. "It's doing well. The place has already gotten fantastic reviews. It'll just take a while for me to earn back my investment, is all. Assuming I can keep it open and operating until then, which requires a certain amount of capital. Hence, not a lot of savings right now."

"Sounds like we're going to be sharing a one-bedroom." Marina stabbed a forkful of pancake and chased syrup around the plate. "Let's talk about something less depressing. Like what do you want to do today?"

"Change our plane tickets to go back earlier?"

"Thomas!"

He gave her a look. "Come on, Marina. I love visiting Charlotte, but this place is boring as hell after two days, and we've been here for five. I am not sure how everyone in this town hasn't lost their goddamned minds. Or maybe they have. Maybe we have."

She tapped on her chin. "Funny, I seem to remember it was you who suggested coming here."

"I had to get away. Alaska seemed like the answer."

"It sure made Charlotte's day."

Thomas smiled as he remembered how excited their cousin had been to see them. Until Thomas and Marina had visited her for the first time last year, they had barely spent any time with their much older cousin. Charlotte wasn't exactly tight with their parents, even though she was closer to their ages than Thomas and Marina. There had to be a story there, but no one had bothered to fill him in on the details.

Now that they had reconnected, Thomas and Marina made regular, albeit short, visits. Their parents never came along, another reason why Alaska seemed like the obvious choice after canceling the wedding and royally pissing off his dad. It was a safe space, where nothing ever happened and no one bothered him. Unfortunately, *safe* had quickly morphed into *boring*. "So stick around and hang out with her? It's not like there's anything else to do."

"You really hate this place so much? I love it here."

Thomas's jaw dropped. "Are you kidding? You're the life of the party. There's no way you can like it that much. No clubs. No bars. No nothing."

"That's not fair. We're in a bar right now."

"The one bar, and restaurant, in the whole town." He frowned. "God, it sounds even sadder when I say it out loud."

"How about going for a walk? Enjoy the scenery? People dream of Alaskan vacations their entire lives. Might as well make the most of ours."

Thomas looked out the window. Even though it was technically spring, the April weather looked abysmal. The sky was blanketed in gray clouds, and a steady mist fell over Main Street. It was the same bleak picture that had greeted him every single morning of every single visit to Darling. This wasn't his dream.

No, his dream was to make his own money. Run his own show. And finally prove he was more than a privileged last name. After years of waiting for the chance to do that, of biding his time until he could be the person he wanted to be, he was so close. If only he wasn't a little bit closer to losing it all.

The trust wasn't just money. It was freedom. Freedom to be whoever he wanted to be.

He looked back at Marina. "I don't care what we do. I just don't want to think about Dad, the wedding, or the fact that we're both likely screwed."

"Isn't that why we came to Alaska in the first place?" Marina flashed him a teasing smile. "Besides, if you're nice to me, I might not even make you pay rent in my penthouse."

"I thought you weren't getting married? No marriage, no money."

She lifted her hands in the air. "I have another three years until I'm thirty. I may change my mind between now and then."

Thomas chuckled. "As long as we're speaking in theoreticals, can I be your maid of honor?"

"Man of honor. And that goes without saying. I don't have any friends who want the job. Mom and Dad will probably have to hire people."

Thomas shook his head. He didn't buy it. Of course his sister had friends. She was always going out. He was the one who worked all the time. "If you say so. I'll be your man of honor and your ring guy. We can get me a fake mustache to slap on halfway through so no one knows the difference."

Marina giggled. "I don't know what I'd do without you."

"Don't worry about it. I'm not going anywhere."

She leaned back in the booth and rested her hands on her stomach. "After that feast, I'm definitely in the mood for a walk. You coming or not?"

"I'll be ready to head out in a minute." Thomas raised his coffee cup. "Just going to finish this."

"I'll go grab our rain jackets." Marina stood and headed for the stairs. The second story of the large building held Charlotte and Wolfie's home. It was also where the Becker siblings stayed when they visited. There was a lodge in Darling too, but Charlotte wouldn't hear of her family staying anywhere other than her own home.

Once Marina left, Thomas was alone with his least favorite person.

Himself.

He slumped in his seat. Thomas should check in with the restaurant. That would be better than letting the anger in his stomach fester and grow more bitter. Reminding himself over and over of all the reasons he had called off the wedding.

The rub was none of it mattered. He couldn't marry Celeste, not after what she had done. Even if he could bring himself to forgive her, it wasn't like she had actually cared about Thomas beyond his family's legacy and net worth. And without his trust, neither of those held much weight anymore.

Not to mention that marriage didn't interest Thomas in general. Why would it? It wasn't like his parents had a great relationship. He wasn't even sure how they tolerated each other.

If it wasn't for the terms of the trust, Thomas doubted he'd ever get married. Even with that carrot dangling in front of him, he still couldn't bring himself to do it. If he ever did get married to gain access to his trust, not that he had much time left with only three months until his thirtieth birthday, he wanted it to be to someone he could at least respect. A feeling he hoped would be mutual.

Thomas tipped up his coffee cup, the last few drops as bitter as his mood. He just had to hope the restaurant was everything he thought it could be. When Thomas had invested the majority of his savings in the restaurant, he had thought he'd be liquid in less than a year, whether the business turned a profit or not. But that was before he called off the wedding and, with it, kissed any hopes of accessing his trust fund goodbye.

Now, he had nothing except a new restaurant in a prime location and the belief it could be something incredible.

Thomas rubbed his eyes. If it failed, maybe he *should* just move to Alaska. At least here, no one knew how worthless he actually was.

"You ready?"

He looked up to see Marina holding his jacket. "Yep, let's go."

A walk wasn't the most thrilling way to spend his day, but maybe it would be a good distraction from thinking about his problems. No matter how much he tortured himself, he never came any closer to solving them. At this point, it would take a miracle.

He had spent his life keeping his head down and biding his time. Now, Thomas only had three months before he lost everything he never had.

# CHAPTER THREE

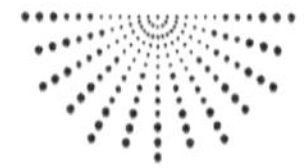

VIVIAN

How many pies would it take to earn enough money to buy the store back? A million?

Vivian stretched plastic wrap over the banana cream pie, careful not to smash the thoughtfully placed banana wheels nestled in the whipped cream. She should've gotten these to the Buck earlier, but she was running behind. Vivian had taken orders for both the Driftwood Coffee Company and the Buck today. Any other time, she would've rescheduled one order for tomorrow. But she needed all the business she could get.

It had been two days since Uncle Robert had broken the news about selling the store and turned their lives upside down. He had gone back to Anchorage yesterday. After going back and forth about it countless times, Vivian had finally gotten up the courage to call Uncle Robert earlier today and ask about buying the store herself. He was family, after all. There was nothing scary about that, right?

*Wrong.* Blood may be thicker than water, but for Uncle Robert, nothing was thicker than cold, hard cash.

He was willing to sell the store to Vivian, alright. For double what the other buyer had offered. And she had to have the money by the end of the sixty-day escrow, which officially started today. That gave her until June to come up with more than a million dollars. It was so ridiculous that she would have started laughing if she hadn't been busy crying.

Once again, Uncle Robert had told her that he was doing her a favor. Her parents might not realize that Darling wasn't a good place for Vivian, but he did.

Vivian packaged up the last pie and tucked the plastic wrap back into the cabinet. No one knew about the store. Not yet. Though it wouldn't take long for the Darling gossip mill to get a hold of the news, Vivian had begged her parents not to say anything to anyone.

The fewer people who knew, the better. Because the sale wasn't going to happen. Vivian only had to bake about a million more pies, minus five.

She chewed the inside of her cheek. If only Philippe would pay her back what she had invested in the restaurant. But wishing for that was just wasting her time. She'd never see a penny of that money again. At least he had given her one very important thing, a lesson she'd never forget: don't trust men, especially rich, handsome men.

"Are you sure you don't want any help?" Her mom walked into the kitchen, empty wineglasses in hand.

"No, thanks. Enjoy your evening with Dad. I've got this." Vivian loaded the pies into a flat. They saved all the boxes from the store's inventory. People in town didn't use grocery bags a lot of the time. Boxes were easier to load into a truck bed. "I'm going to drop these off, and I'll be right back."

Her mom reached for the bottle of cabernet, refilling the

glasses. "I hope you sleep in tomorrow, sweetheart. You've been going nonstop."

"You know I can't sleep in." Not to mention, Vivian couldn't afford to take a break. She needed every dollar. If she couldn't save the store, then the money from her baking would help her family get settled somewhere new, wherever that was. Vivian picked up the box and headed for the front door. "Be back soon."

Balancing the pies, Vivian paused at the entryway and slipped on her rain boots. While it wasn't exactly pouring outside, Darling was always kind of wet. The town had a permanent mist that only went away a few rare days out of the year.

The windows of the Buck glowed, a welcoming beacon in the dusk of the early spring evening. Inside, people shuffled around, and music could be heard from outside the building. It was Friday night, after all. Most people were at the bar kicking up their heels, not at home, frantically baking pies to save their lives.

Avoiding the crowd, Vivian walked around the building and let herself in the back door. The kitchen was about twenty degrees hotter than the temperature outside. She slipped off her jacket before tucking the pies into the fridge.

Charlotte came into the kitchen. "Vivian, there you are!"

Vivian closed the fridge. "Sorry, I'm behind schedule. I meant to have these over to you earlier."

"The only thing I am sorry about is that you're working so late." Charlotte shook her head. "Our order could've waited."

Vivian wiped her hands on her jeans. If things had been different, she would have suggested that herself. But she needed all the business she could get. "I was happy to do it. I'll bring by the chocolate cream tomorrow."

"The citizens of Darling thank you." Charlotte's blue eyes

crinkled. "Now, don't you want to come out and have a drink? On the house."

Vivian smiled. Charlotte and her husband, Wolfie, never charged anyone. The menu didn't even list prices. Darling wasn't exactly a thriving metropolis, and some people truly scraped by. The Buck was a refuge for anyone and everyone, regardless of the size of a person's bank account. People paid what they could, sometimes more, and somehow, it all evened out enough to keep the place in business.

Vivian had often wondered what the heck had happened in Wolfie and Charlotte's lives that they had so much compassion for others. It must've been something significant. But she never asked, and they didn't offer to tell her. "It's always on the house."

"Which means you should have no trouble accepting my invitation." Before she could come up with another excuse, Charlotte hooked her plump arm around Vivian's own, guiding her through the swinging door that led to the restaurant.

Most of the tables had been pushed to the side to create room for the makeshift dance floor. Vivian spotted her friend Grace, the owner of the Driftwood Coffee Company, dancing with her husband, Hunter. Grace had been single when she moved to Darling two years ago, but she and her estranged husband had reconnected when he'd visited her in Alaska.

She used to invite Vivian out to the Buck, but Grace had finally gotten the message that Vivian was a hermit and intended to stay that way. Besides, Grace had Hunter back in her life now to keep her company. At least her love story had a happy ending.

Charlotte dropped Vivian off at the bar, where she ordered a glass of white wine from Wolfie.

He tipped the bottle over a glass, passing it to her with a wink. "Nice to see you out. Enjoy."

"Thanks, Wolfie." Vivian took a small sip. He had given her the sweet kind she liked. The only kind she liked. Vivian wasn't a big drinker. She preferred a cup of hot chocolate to a cocktail any day of the week.

Vivian found a free spot along the wall and stationed herself there. There was no way she was getting out on the dance floor. Vivian would rather watch. It was safer.

She took in the crowd. Vivian had known almost everyone here all her life. Heck, she'd been in Darling almost all her life, except for those few years she'd gone to school and then worked on the East Coast. At that time, Vivian had thought she'd never move back to Alaska. She had loved her life in New York. It felt like she had finally become the person she was meant to be. But that was years ago, and now she was back to being the same old Vivian. At this rate, it seemed like things would be the same forever.

But there were at least a few people in the room who were new to town. Marina Becker, Charlotte's much younger cousin, stood in the middle of the dance floor, moving with the kind of grace that a person was either born with or not. Vivian definitely fell into the second category.

Both Marina and her brother, Thomas, had come into the store a couple of times. Marina seemed nice enough. Thomas, however, had barely said two words to Vivian. Girls like her probably didn't even register on his radar.

She glanced around the room. Where was Thomas, anyway? Vivian shook her head. Who cared? Like his sister, he was filthy rich. Strike one. But he was also handsome. Strike two.

However, in searching the room, Vivian was interested to note that someone else was watching Marina. Another newcomer, the retired firefighter from California, Ransom, who had moved to town last year.

His eyes never once left Marina. Vivian didn't even see him blink. And she suspected Marina knew she was being watched. Vivian wished the two of them the best. She never had much luck when it came to romance. Heck, she never had much luck at all.

She took another sip of her white wine, which had already started to turn warm. Her eyes grew heavy. Just a dropper full of alcohol was practically a sleeping pill for her. It gave her a homing device for her bed.

Her ex had known all about wine. Philippe had promised that when they went to France, he would teach Vivian everything about it. He had told her she needed to know all about wine for their restaurant.

She had insisted that all she needed to know about booze was how much to put in rum cake. Vivian wasn't one for drinking back then either.

Philippe had laughed and kissed her on the forehead. "But we're partners, babe. We're doing this together."

At the time, the words had warmed her like the sweet white wine. Now, the memory made her feel sick. It was one of a million empty promises that her life had been built on. No wonder it had all come tumbling down. If Vivian ever dated again, which was unlikely, she wanted the truth from day one.

The song changed, and the dancers shifted places. Vivian peered at her wineglass, still almost full. She hated to waste it, but Vivian wasn't in the mood to party. She was tired. She was stressed. Her stomach churned, a mix of anxiety about what was to come and the bad memories of what had already happened.

As she turned to drop off her wineglass at the bar and

head home, Vivian bumped into someone. The wine sloshed over the edge of the glass, plastering her top to her skin.

Marina's dark eyes grew wide. "I'm so sorry."

"It's fine." Vivian plucked at her shirt, peeling it away from her stomach. "It was probably my fault."

"Have you had three shots of whiskey?"

"Um, no?" Vivian hadn't even had one shot of whiskey in her entire life.

"Then it was definitely my fault. Let me get you a new shirt."

Vivian shook her head. She wanted to get out of there, not socialize. All she had to do was cross the street to go home. The wine-soaked shirt wasn't a problem. "It's fine. Really."

"Please. I insist. I packed too much anyway." Marina clamped a hand around Vivian's wrist and led her upstairs. For the second time that night, Vivian found herself being dragged around the Buck. Was this some kind of bizarre family trait?

Marina led them to a room on the second floor and flung open the door.

Vivian's jaw dropped. The woman hadn't been exaggerating. There had to be a room here, somewhere. Clothes were flung on the floor, the bed, and what may have been a chair in the corner. Colorful fabric covered every square inch of the room. It was like being inside a circus tent, if the circus tent happened to be made out of haute couture.

Marina quickly sorted through a few tops before holding one up to Vivian. "This is your color. It'll make your eyes pop."

Vivian pushed the plum-colored shirt back towards her. "It's fine. Really."

"Nonsense." Marina turned around. "Don't worry. I won't look. Anyway, it's just us girls."

Vivian sighed. Marina was as stubborn as Charlotte and clearly wouldn't take no for an answer. It'd be easier just to change. Vivian shimmied out of her damp shirt and tugged on the new one. "Done."

Marina turned around, and her eyes lit up. "I knew it. It looks way better on you. You have to keep it. "

Vivian shifted to her other foot. The top was a tighter fit than she usually wore. It wasn't her style at all. That was one thing she had loved about her old chef whites. They were far from formfitting. "I couldn't."

"You can, and you will. You're doing me a favor. Packing is going to be a nightmare."

Now that Vivian could agree on. Once again deciding that resistance was futile, she gave Marina a small smile. "Thank you. That is really nice of you."

Marina studied her. "Any chance you're single? You'd be perfect for my brother."

Vivian shook her head. Surely Marina couldn't mean Thomas? Maybe she had another brother. "I'm not looking to date right now."

"Too bad. You'd be good for him. You're pretty, and you're actually nice. His last girlfriend was a real bitch." Marina's face soured. "Thank God Thomas called off the wedding."

Vivian made a mental note to never do three shots of whiskey. She preferred to keep private matters private.

"Alrighty, back to the party." Marina grabbed Vivian's hand and led the charge downstairs.

Vivian couldn't help but smile again, despite the fact that the last thing she wanted to do was party. Marina was impossible not to like. Thomas was lucky to have her as a sister. Some days, Vivian felt like she had no one at all.

Once they were downstairs, Marina disappeared back onto the dance floor, and Vivian made a beeline for the door.

She was halfway across the street when she realized she had forgotten her jacket.

With a groan, Vivian stomped back to the Buck. She was beyond ready to be home. It had been a long day. Her feet ached. Her head ached. Her heart ached.

Remembering that she had taken her jacket off when she first arrived, Vivian made her way to the kitchen.

That's when she saw him. Thomas Becker was eating one of the banana cream pies straight from the pan. His eyes were closed as he chewed. A fork was stuck in the middle of the pie, probably turning one of the banana wheels into a shish kebab.

She let out a huff and grabbed her jacket. Sure, she was annoyed. But there was no point in saying anything. Who cared about the stupid pie? Charlotte paid her either way.

Thomas blinked his eyes open. "Oh, hello."

"Goodbye," she muttered. It was so typical of a man like Thomas. He was no different from her Uncle Robert or Philippe. Men like that thought having money made any behavior okay, no matter how rude. Handsome men with money were even worse.

Her chest grew tight. Men like that had also left Vivian without savings. Without options. Without the life she had always known. And she was sick of it.

Strike three.

Vivian turned on her heel, stabbing a finger at Thomas. "Actually, no. Not goodbye. I made those pies. It was a lot of work. And you're just sitting there eating it like an animal."

He blinked at her. "You made this?"

"Yes, I made it. With my own two hands. With no help from anyone." Her voice cracked, and she pressed her lips together. Just because she was a loser didn't mean she had to go around making that obvious to everyone else.

"This is the single best thing I have ever tasted in my life."

He looked down at the pie. "I have had a lot to drink, though."

Vivian shook her head. Him and Marina both. Another family trait, perhaps. Whatever. Not her family, not her problem. "Enjoy it. Tomorrow, it'll be chocolate cream."

Thomas's dark gaze roamed across her face, and a shiver ran down her back. Even though she was annoyed with him, Vivian could see that he was heartbreak in human form. Luckily, she wasn't stupid enough to get that close. Not anymore. "You're way too hot to be a baker. A woman like you shouldn't be hidden in the kitchen."

She bristled. Just like she suspected. A rich jerk. So why was he making her feel all tingly at the same time? "Don't tell me what I should or shouldn't do."

He took a step towards her, balancing the pie in one hand. "And you have the most incredible eyes. When I saw you at the store before, they were light green. But they're darker now, the color of a forest."

Her breath hitched. It wasn't *her* eyes that Vivian was thinking about. It was his eyes. His full brows. His sculpted chin. And what all of those things were doing to her insides. Dangerous things that set off every warning alarm in her body.

A smile spread across his face, slow and confident. "Have a drink with me?"

Vivian looked away, trying to break whatever hot guy trance he had put her in. She didn't trust herself. She was getting dangerously close to staying here, to wasting time she didn't have. "I should go home."

"*Should* doesn't count." He set a hand on her arm, and a zing traveled up under the plum-colored sleeve straight to her heart. "Do you *want* to have a drink with me?"

The scent of sandalwood tickled her nose. Vivian swallowed. "What does what I want have to do with anything?"

He held her gaze. "Isn't that the point of life? To do things because you want? Don't those unnecessary things make life more delicious?"

Vivian's chest tightened. Thomas had no idea what he was talking about. He couldn't know about Uncle Robert selling the store. He couldn't know what happened the last time she left. He couldn't know how she yearned for something different but was too afraid that doing something else would change everything for the worse.

The music drifted into the kitchen. Faint vibrations traveled up her legs, created by the dancers as they stomped around the wooden floor. Vivian had to be strong before. And she would have to be strong again. Surely one tiny moment of weakness won't cause everything to fall apart? Life wasn't as delicate as a banana cream pie, was it? "Fine. Because I want to. Not because I like you."

His grin widened, and her heart thawed another degree. "Sweet-talk like that, and you'll never get rid of me."

# CHAPTER FOUR

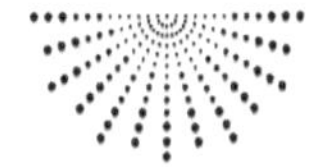



It had practically taken an act of God to convince Thomas to leave the pie behind. But Vivian didn't want to attract any extra attention. Or at least not any more than they already were. She couldn't shake the feeling that all eyes were on them the minute they walked into the dining room.

Vivian perched on a barstool, adjusting her shirt. Between the change in clothes and having a drink with Thomas, she was giving the citizens of Darling a lot to talk about.

If Wolfie was surprised to see her back at the bar, he didn't show it. "The usual?"

She nodded. "Thanks, Wolfie."

Thomas held up his hand. "I'll take the same."

Wolfie's mustache twitched, but he didn't say anything as he poured two glasses of the sweet white wine. As he passed them across the bar, he caught Vivian's eye and gave her a wink. "Enjoy."

Thomas held up his glass, inspecting it. "So, this is the usual? A favorite of yours?"

"It's okay." She took a sip, the second glass going down easier than the first.

"*Okay.* The gold standard in Alaska, I suppose." He took a gulp, gagging. "Oh my God. You actually like that?"

Vivian bit back a laugh at his pained expression. "Like I said, it's okay. I'm not much of a drinker. This is the least of all evils."

"The least of all evils, huh? I can relate to that." He took another sip of the wine, his mouth pinching together. "Nope. It doesn't get better. You sure I can't get you something else to drink?"

She shook her head. "But I won't be offended if you want something else."

"I'm good. Once I make a choice, I commit." Vivian raised an eyebrow. Not exactly the kind of character she expected for a guy with a bottomless bank account. He probably never had to put up with anything if he didn't want to.

Thomas flashed her a smile before forcing another sip. "Besides, wasting it would be alcohol abuse."

She sighed. Now, *that* sounded more like it. "Charming."

He set his drink down, resting his chin on his hand. "So if you're not much of a drinker, what do you do for fun around here?"

"There *is* more to life than drinking, you know."

"That's why I'm asking. Enlighten me."

Vivian shifted on the barstool. The wooden seat was uncomfortable. Heck, this whole situation was uncomfortable. Including the direction of this conversation.

When was the last time someone had even asked her a question like that? The fact that the answer might actually be *never* was more painful than the wooden stool. "Is that what people come to Darling for? Fun? Is that why you came here, Mr. Fun Police?"

He barked a laugh. "Definitely not."

Her shoulders hunched together. Darling might not be her first pick of places to live, but she didn't like Thomas trash-talking her hometown. She'd heard enough of that from Robert the other night. Thomas basically saying the same thing just confirmed everything she knew about him. He was no different from any other rich jerk. "You can leave whenever you want."

Thomas looked her in the eye, his expression sober. "Sorry. That was rude. It's not an excuse, but for what it's worth, I'm not in a good headspace right now. "

Caught off guard, Vivian took another sip of wine. The last thing she had expected was an apology. Then she remembered what Marina had said about Thomas canceling his wedding, and suddenly, Vivian felt like she was the one who should apologize. Even though his sister was openly relieved, the situation must be hard on Thomas. "I get it. Darling isn't everyone's cup of tea."

"But you must like it, right? That's why you're here?"

Her stomach twisted. That was the logical conclusion. It was her hometown. She had family here and, if not a career, at least a job. She should like it, right? But then why was Vivian so uncomfortable sitting in this bar right now? Or anywhere in Darling? Why did she never feel like she fit in? "It's okay."

Thomas gave her a small smile. "There you go with *okay* again. I'm starting to detect a pattern."

Vivian lifted her wineglass before immediately setting it down again. Empty. Her eyebrows squished together. Was that why she felt light-headed? Maybe she was just dehydrated. Vivian *had* drunk more than usual.

Not that the drink had done a darn thing to cool her off.

She tugged at the shirt again. The room was sweltering, more like a sauna than a bar in Alaska. The open windows didn't seem to be doing much either.

People kept coming through the front door of the Buck. Vivian didn't know which was more unbelievable: that there were people left in town who weren't already at the bar or that they somehow were able to fit. The place was packed more tightly than the cans of smoked salmon that they sold at the store.

Regardless, Vivian knew one thing for sure. The way she was feeling definitely had nothing to do with the man next to her. Even if he was the definition of tall, dark, and handsome.

Thomas said something else to her, but she didn't catch it. Vivian shook her head and pointed at her ear. The room had grown louder as the crowd swelled. Between the stomping of the dancers and the jukebox blaring, she could barely hear her own thoughts anymore, let alone Thomas.

"What?" she shouted.

He leaned in, his warm breath tickling her neck. Vivian gulped and forced herself to focus on what he was saying. This wasn't the time to lose her head. "Wanna go outside?"

Her gaze drifted over his shoulder, and Vivian spotted Grace passing by. Her friend gave Vivian an exaggerated wink. Vivian's face turned hot, and she felt like she might die from embarrassment. Suddenly, nothing seemed more important than getting out of the public eye. "Yeah. Definitely. Let's go outside."

"Meet you out there. I'll grab us another drink."

Another drink was the last thing Vivian wanted, but she didn't bother saying so. He probably wouldn't hear her, and she was desperate to get out of there.

She hopped off the barstool and made her way outside, hoping that some fresh air would clear her head.

The back door of the Buck led to a small dirt area mostly

used by smokers, dotted with plastic chairs, a free-standing ashtray, and a firepit that was currently cold. A lone flood-light illuminated the space. There was no one else out there right now.

Vivian took a deep breath of the cool night air. What was she even still doing here? She should just go home, but she felt bad about ditching him. Even if he was a rich jerk, no one deserved that.

She chewed on her lip. Unless he had ditched her. He was pretty hammered. He'd eaten a pie straight from the pan, for goodness' sake. She'd give him ten minutes. If he didn't show up, she'd make her escape guilt-free.

The back door swung open with a squeak, and Thomas stepped outside holding two pint glasses, each filled with clear liquor and garnished with a neon-colored straw.

Her stomach turned over, and Vivian pressed her lips together to keep from gagging. Hard liquor was definitely not what she wanted right now.

Thomas smiled as he handed her one of the drinks, looking so proud of himself that she couldn't bring herself to tell him that she didn't want it.

Vivian held the straw in between her fingers, forcing a sip and hoping she didn't actually gag. Her eyebrows shot up her forehead at the refreshing lemon-lime flavor. "It's soda."

Thomas lifted a shoulder. "Figured you didn't want another drink. Since you're not generally a fan of alcohol." He smiled, looking obnoxiously handsome. "Mine, however, is vodka. Sorry, but no more *Vivian usuals* for me."

She took another sip, her mouth suddenly dry. She wasn't sure what to think. Even after she had surprised herself and agreed to a drink, Vivian had expected to hate every single thing about Thomas Becker. He was rich, he was handsome, and he was drunk. Any one of those alone would've been reason enough not to like him. But all three together? Now, that was a recipe for disaster.

Despite all those things, he had actually listened to her. He *heard* her. He might not be an angel, but maybe he wasn't quite the bad guy she had thought either. "Thank you."

He nodded. "And to answer your question about what I'm doing in Darling even though it's not fun, I just needed to get away from some family drama."

She gave him a sympathetic smile. Vivian could definitely relate to family drama. "I'm sorry."

He looked out towards the forest. "I was supposed to get married last week."

Vivian shifted her feet. "Yeah. Marina, uh, mentioned that."

The corners of his mouth tugged down. "This is what happens when my sister drinks whiskey."

Vivian bit back a smile that Thomas was complaining about his sister's drinking when he was far from sober himself. "So, do you want to talk about it? What happened?"

His shoulders hunched up. "Not really. Getting cheated on was bad enough. I don't want to think about it anymore."

Her heart squeezed. The last thing she expected was to have something in common with Thomas. But it didn't matter what kind of a bank account a person had. Getting cheated on sucked, and Vivian had more than one reason to hate cheaters. Not to mention, she knew firsthand exactly what it was like to feel less than. She knew what it was like to wish to be someone different. Someone who mattered enough to inspire loyalty. "I'm so sorry, Thomas. That's awful."

He took a gulp of his drink, treating the glass of vodka like mountain spring water. "Nothing to be sorry about. Saved me from a huge mistake."

Vivian licked her lips, knowing the next thing she said

would make her vulnerable. But maybe, just maybe, it would make Thomas feel less alone. A feeling she knew all too well. "But I understand what that's like. Something like that happened to me too."

His eyes widened. "Someone cheated on you? In this town? What an idiot."

She smiled in spite of herself. "Not in this town. But yes, definitely an idiot."

He ran a hand through his hair, and a lock flopped over his eye. Vivian's pulse quickened. How did he look better the less put together he was? It made no sense. It had to be that second glass of wine talking. Yes, that was it. She wasn't actually attracted to him. "I'm not exactly a genius myself. Canceling the wedding was the right thing to do, I have no doubt about that. But it messed up a lot more than monogrammed towels."

"It's the worst, isn't it? That you can do everything right, and you still end up screwed."

He smiled, but it didn't quite reach his eyes. "Couldn't have said it better myself."

With a sigh, Thomas leaned against the building and looked out at the shadows of the forest.

Vivian sipped her soda. When was the last time she stayed up this late? Shouldn't she be exhausted? But instead, Vivian felt light. Awake. Happy.

Misery really did love company. Especially good-looking, admittedly charming company.

But it was more than that. It was more than the fact that Thomas was easy to talk to. That he listened. It was that he *heard* her. When was the last time someone had really heard her?

And it terrified her. Moments like this were never real. Not for Vivian. Things never went her way for very long.

Thomas finished his drink with a gurgle, setting the glass

on the ground. "I've been here a week, did you know that? And I still don't know what to do."

"A week, huh? Your parents must miss you."

He snorted. "My mom, maybe. If my dad notices I'm gone, it's only because I'm not at work."

She bit her lip. Thomas might be a spoiled brat, but that didn't mean that he was a happy spoiled brat. "I'm sure they notice."

He shifted, and she could feel his eyes on her. Her face warmed, and she was thankful for the dark of the night. She didn't want him to think the color in her cheeks had anything to do with him. Because it totally did not. "I don't want to talk about my parents. Or anything back home, really."

Vivian swallowed, her heart beating faster. She had been here before. About to tip over the edge. About to find someone more interesting than not. And she refused to fall again. "What do you want to talk about?"

"Your pies."

She barked a laugh. "My pies? What about them? How there's one less, thanks to you?"

Thomas let out a throaty chuckle, and a tingle traveled down her back. "You are an incredible baker, you know. I'll think about that pie for the rest of my life."

She turned to face him, studying the outline of his face in the glow of the moonlight. The curve of his chin, the shadows that highlighted his cheekbones.

Maybe she had drunk more than she realized. Maybe the exhaustion and booze and stress had created some kind of temporary insanity.

But in that moment, all Vivian could think about was the fact that even though she had no reason in the world to ever talk to Thomas again, maybe they weren't so different after all.

The cool night air wrapped around her, tugging her closer to him like a deep, dark velvet blanket. Her foot crunched against the ground as she took a step in his direction. It was so perfectly quiet out here. The breeze stilled, and the forest trees had stopped shivering. She was certain he could hear her heart pounding in her chest.

Thomas placed a hand on one side of the wall next to her, his muscled arm curved protectively around her. He looked down at her mouth and then up at her eyes. Vivian knew exactly what he was thinking. Because she was thinking it too.

Her heart slammed against her ribs. Vivian had dedicated her life to her family. She knew what every single day for the rest of time looked like. What was wrong with one last selfish act? A final goodbye to all the things she had ever wanted and would never have?

Her gaze dropped to his mouth, and she swallowed. If for one night, she wanted to be someone else, someone who did what she wanted, what harm did that do?

*Just this once.*

Before she could talk herself out of it, Vivian closed the gap between them, pressing her lips to his. She held her breath, certain that Thomas would tell her she had the wrong idea. That a guy like him could never be with a girl like her.

But then he kissed her back, and every doubt in her mind went silent.

Her heart swelled. Just this once, she wasn't such a loser after all.

# CHAPTER FIVE

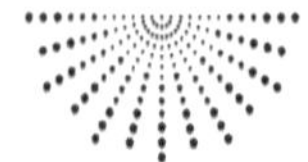



She should have never stayed.

Never gone back to give Thomas a piece of her mind. Definitely said no to that second glass of wine. And without a shadow of a doubt, she should've never ever kissed Thomas Becker.

Vivian groaned. As if she didn't have enough problems.

She tried to focus on restocking the inventory. It was a never-ending task. At least that's one thing she wouldn't miss if her uncle sold the store. A thought that was immediately followed by guilt.

Vivian shook her head. That was precisely why she shouldn't go around kissing handsome heirs. It distracted her from what really mattered. A distraction she couldn't afford with only fifty-nine days left until escrow closed. Not exactly a lot of time to keep her world from falling apart.

That was the last time she would ever do something like that. Something so completely stupid. So totally irresponsible. So…delicious.

Vivian gritted her teeth. *No*, she told her brain. She hadn't enjoyed it. Not at all.

Well. Maybe a little bit.

And why shouldn't she? It had been years since someone looked at her that way. Heck, it had been years since *she* had looked at someone at all. Vivian had thought she was done with romance. Until Thomas.

Vivian paused in front of the body wash, tempted to knock all the sandalwood bottles off the shelf. She didn't need any reminders of last night, nor of Thomas's seductive woodsy scent.

She had woken up after just a few hours of sleep. Her heart had pounded, and she was wide-awake. Realizing she still wore her clothes from last night, Vivian had pulled off the shirt and turned on her bedside lamp to read the tag.

*Dry clean only.*

Vivian's head had sagged against the pillow. So much for washing and returning the shirt. But she would return it all the same. She could even offer Marina money for the dry cleaning bill. Marina definitely didn't need the cash, but it was the right thing to do. Even though Vivian didn't own a single item from that brand, she recognized it as a luxury label. The shirt probably cost more than Vivian's entire wardrobe combined.

But returning the shirt would have to wait for a bit. It was the wee hours of the morning, and Vivian was probably the only person in town who was awake. Not even Grace would be up yet, and the coffee shop opened at five in the morning.

The same way she had snuck back in the night before, Vivian had tiptoed past her parents' closed door and went downstairs to the store. If she couldn't sleep, she might as well get some work done. As soon as she could, she would march straight over to the Buck and give Marina her shirt back. That would be the end of Vivian's involvement with the Becker family for the rest of time. Except for Charlotte, of course.

Vivian chewed on her lip. And what if she saw Thomas? What exactly would she say? The truth?

*Thank you for the kiss, but it was a onetime thing. I prefer to live as a hermit.*

Except for the fact that some teeny, tiny little part of her *did* want it to happen again.

It was all his fault, really. He had to be so fun. So handsome. And such a good listener. She hadn't solved a single problem last night. If anything, she had created more. But Vivian hadn't felt so alone for a change either.

Her stomach churned with embarrassment as she recalled the kiss, and she covered her face with her hands. Vivian wished she had drunk more for once. At least then she would have an excuse. Or, even better, she might not remember kissing Thomas at all.

A tapping sound interrupted her thoughts. Vivian peeked through her fingers and dropped her hands. Her eyebrows shot up her forehead when she saw Natasha smiling at her through the window. It was still dark outside, her face half-hidden in shadow, half-illuminated by the lights inside the store.

Everyone in Darling knew of Natasha, Darling's rumored psychic, whether or not they had ever actually spoken to her. She lived outside of town, and Vivian's mom delivered grocery orders to Natasha's trailer, saving the woman a drive to the store in her ancient stick shift. Vivian had gone a few times but always stayed in the car. Until now, her conversations with Natasha had consisted of a wave and a smile.

Vivian opened the door, grateful for a distraction even at this odd hour. "Morning."

"Good morning. Are you open?" Natasha asked in that lilting voice of hers. Though the older woman had lived in

Alaska for decades, she had been born in Russia. Along with her supposed psychic abilities, her accent only added to her mystique.

"Um. Sure. Come in." They didn't usually open quite this early, but that was how things were in Darling. If the light was on, it was fair game. Business hours were merely a suggestion.

"It must be my lucky day." The petite older woman stepped inside the store, shrugging off her hood. Wisps of fine, graying blonde hair floated around her head like a halo. "I woke up in the middle of the night with a craving that would not leave me alone. "

*How ironic.* It was Vivian's unlucky day. Or, to be more precise, an unlucky life. "Can I help you find something in particular?"

"Actually, I know exactly what I'm looking for." Natasha walked to the freezer, plucking out a strawberry ice cream bar.

Vivian shuddered. Ice cream at this time of day? Even she didn't like sweets *that* much. She punched the buttons on the old-fashioned cash register. "Two dollars, please."

Natasha pulled her wallet out of her embroidered purse and handed two crisp bills to Vivian.

Placing the money in the cash register, Vivian was left holding a tarot card. "I think you gave this to me by accident."

"That's for you. That's the Wheel of Fortune."

Vivian studied the illustration. "What does it mean?"

"Good things, of course! That's one of the luckiest cards you can get. And that's what it's about. Luck."

Vivian's shoulders sagged. Luck? When it came to her and luck, it was never good news. "Any chance it means my luck is changing?"

Natasha's blue eyes lit up. "Now you've got the idea. The

wheel comes up, and the wheel goes down. If you don't like the way things are right now, don't fret. They will change again."

A shiver snaked down Vivian's back. As far as she knew, her parents hadn't mentioned the store being sold to anyone yet. So why did it sound like that was exactly what Natasha was talking about? Unless, of course, she really was psychic.

But in that case, Natasha should know that Vivian had always had bad luck, and that wasn't going to change anytime soon. She held the card out to Natasha. "That's, uh, interesting, but I don't think this card is for me."

"Of course it is. You make your own luck, you know." With a wink, Natasha opened the wrapper and took a bite of the ice cream. "Some things you are never too old for. Good memories are one of them."

Vivian smiled. She had no idea what Natasha meant, but she wasn't going to ask her to stick around. It would probably only result in more unsettling messages. "Have a nice day."

"You too, dear." Natasha had one foot out the door when she glanced back at Vivian. "By the way, Grace just opened up. She's a good listener, don't you think?"

After Natasha left, Vivian looked back down at the card. It was pretty, but that was all she could say about it. Make her own luck? Yeah, right. Not to mention that change always made things *worse*, not better, regardless of what Natasha had said. Still, Natasha's message seemed eerily relevant to the situation with Uncle Robert selling the store.

Vivian slipped the card in her back pocket. It didn't matter. Everyone knew that stuff wasn't real. Besides, Vivian had bigger problems than a tarot card.

Like kissing Thomas.

Vivian cringed. *No.* She did not, could not, want more. Thomas was the son of a billionaire. He had more money than she could wrap her head around. He was spoiled and overly confident and annoying.

*But you like him.*

Vivian took a deep breath. She needed to get her head on straight. This was real life.

Which left the other problem. The bigger problem. The one that would decide if her life would stay the same or change forever.

Which dragon did she want to slay first?

Vivian slipped on her jacket. Natasha had one good suggestion this morning. Maybe Grace would have an idea that Vivian hadn't thought of yet. No matter what she came up with, it definitely couldn't make the situation worse.

* * *

GRACE GASPED as she set a hot chocolate in front of Vivian. "Did I hear you right? Double?"

Vivian nodded. "Double. But he did give me the sixty-day escrow to raise the funds. Which started yesterday."

"A prince amongst men." Grace snorted. "What the hell are you going to do?"

"I have no idea." Vivian massaged her forehead, the anxiety she'd felt since that morning morphing into a migraine. "This is so embarrassing. Please don't tell anyone."

It was just her and Grace at the Driftwood right now. Vivian had arrived just as Mac was leaving, and no one had come in since. But it wouldn't last. From her view at the store, Vivian saw a steady stream of people go into the coffee shop all day, every day, that the Driftwood was open. Before Grace moved to town, the only options for coffee were drip at the Buck or making it at home. Darling had quickly adjusted to life with lattes and cappuccinos.

"You know you can trust me." Grace gave her a sympathetic smile. "But you're the victim here. I don't see what you have to be embarrassed about."

Vivian dropped her gaze to the mug in front of her. Not even hot chocolate sounded good to her right now, a sign of just how bad things really were. "I don't know. I just am."

Ah. But she did know, and it wasn't because of the store. It was the kiss. The kiss that she wasn't ready to tell anyone about. The kiss that should've never happened. The kiss that added even more complications to her life.

Vivian should be focused, in problem-solving mode. So why did her mind keep tugging her back in the direction of Thomas? Hadn't she had enough of rich, handsome jerks to last her a lifetime?

She should tell Grace about Thomas. Grace was trustworthy. But Vivian was still trying to make sense of it in her own mind and failing miserably.

Grace took a sip of her Americano. "I wish there was something I could do. I could ask Hunter for money…"

"Please don't." Vivian shook her head. Grace's husband was a famous lifestyle photographer. But the last thing Vivian wanted to do was drag Grace, and Hunter, down with her. Her parents had helped Vivian with the restaurant, and it had cost them the store. She didn't want to ruin Grace's life too. Vivian couldn't stand the idea of hurting anyone else that she cared about.

"I appreciate it. I really do. But I didn't tell you thinking that I would get a handout. I just felt like my head would explode if I didn't talk to someone."

Grace nodded in apparent understanding. "Whatever you want. I just wish there was something more I could do. I can't imagine this place without you."

Vivian's eyes burned. How had she ended up here again? About to lose everything? "Me neither."

Ruby, Grace's miniature Australian shepherd, sat by

Vivian's feet and nuzzled her leg. Vivian dug her hands into the dog's plush fur. She wished she had a dog. Dogs never carried out sneaky business deals or ruthlessly broke hearts.

"Maybe there is a silver lining." Grace set her mug down. "My whole life changed when I came to Alaska, and it turned out pretty well."

Vivian tilted her head. "That's because your extremely attractive, talented, famous photographer husband followed you here. So I don't think that's exactly comparing apples to apples."

Grace barked a laugh. "You make a good point. But you never know. Maybe there is a rich, handsome man in your future."

One came to mind instantly, but Vivian shoved the idea away. Rich or not, she wasn't in the place for romance right now. "Yeah, right. Even if I were interested, which I'm not, there's no one like that in Darling."

"What about Thomas?" Grace waggled her eyebrows.

Heat crawled up Vivian's neck, and she ran her finger under her shirt collar. Had this thing gotten tighter in the last ten seconds? "What about him?"

"He couldn't keep his eyes off you at the Buck on Friday night. I saw you talking to him. And then you disappeared out back together."

Vivian's underarms prickled with sweat. No one had seen her kiss Thomas. So why did she feel like the whole world knew about her huge mistake? "Where approximately nothing happened, and then I went home."

Grace sipped her coffee calmly, apparently not picking up on Vivian's paranoia. "All I'm saying is that you're wrong. There *is* someone handsome and rich right here in town. Someone I think has a crush on you."

"Okay, let's say you're right. You're not, but let's pretend.

So I should just walk right up to him and ask for a couple million, no strings attached?"

Grace shrugged. "Do you have any better ideas?"

"No." Vivian sighed. "But I don't think I have the moxie for that one either."

"What about a small-business loan?"

Vivian straightened. "Now, there's an idea."

Grace bit her lip. "It's just…are you sure this is what you want?"

"What do you mean? The business loan?"

Grace shook her head. "The store. This life. You're so young and smart, and the store would be a huge commitment." Grace looked her in her eye. "Please talk to your parents first. I would hate for you to make this huge sacrifice and realize afterwards that it wasn't what any of you actually wanted."

Vivian swallowed. Grace couldn't know the sacrifices that Vivian had made for the life she had now. A business loan was nothing compared to what she had already given up. "This is what I want. I like things just the way they are."

Grace clapped her hands together. "I feel like we need booze. A mimosa?"

Vivian's stomach turned over. "No, thanks. I don't know how people can go to the Buck every week. I'm never drinking again."

*And definitely not with Thomas.*

"Famous last words." Grace chuckled. "Now, is there anything I can do to help? Need help with the business loan application?"

"I think I've got it. How hard can it be?"

"You're taking this really well. I think I'd be flipping out. Definitely not calmly thinking about solutions while I drink hot chocolate."

Vivian giggled. "Maybe I should be flipping out. Who knows the right way to handle this situation?"

"I'll tell you this much. There is no right way to live life. Trust me. I've tried. Failed. Given up. And now I think I can finally say I am happy."

Guilt slammed into Vivian, and she shifted in her seat. She should be happy for her friend. When Grace had arrived, she'd seemed so quiet. So sad. Over time, she and Vivian had grown close, despite the fact that they were very private people and the decade age difference between them.

It had been years since Vivian had a close friend in Darling. Her childhood friend Sarah had moved away from the island for years and, when she had finally returned, was almost instantly busy with a new husband, a new baby, and running her family's lodge. Vivian understood that, as adults, it was natural for people's lives to go in different directions. But that didn't mean she wasn't lonely. With Grace next door, Vivian had thought she finally had someone in town who understood her. Someone who would always be there.

But then Hunter came back. Things were rocky between him and Grace at first, but they both seemed genuinely happy now.

And once again, Vivian was the third wheel. The only spare wheel in a town full of pairs. It didn't used to bother her so much until she knew the difference. Having Grace as someone she could always talk to, always depend upon, was more important to Vivian than she had realized. And it was another reason she could never ask for help from Grace or anyone else that she cared about. Vivian wouldn't risk her bad luck rubbing off on someone she cared about again. If she was going to drive through life as a worthless spare tire, she could at least protect the people she loved.

"Thanks for the hot chocolate. And the advice." Vivian stood. Not only did she want to get started on the possible solution right away, but she wanted to get out of here before another customer came in and maybe overheard something. She hadn't given up hope that she could solve the problem before the Darling gossip mill ever got wind of Uncle Robert selling the store. "I'm going to go back home and start researching business loans."

"Anytime." Grace gave her a hug. "I'm always here for you."

Vivian's chest grew tight. She wasn't worried if Grace would be around in the near future. It was whether Vivian herself would still be in Darling. And she was willing to do whatever it took to stay. Anything except ask someone for help.

# CHAPTER SIX

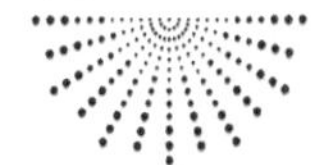

THOMAS

The first sunny day since he'd been in Alaska, and it had to be the worst hangover of his life.

Thomas pulled his pillow over his head with a moan. Surprisingly, he hadn't been this trashed after Friday night's party at the Buck four days ago. Thomas didn't even remember how that night had ended. But he had been drinking mostly beer then. Whatever he drank last night was an entirely different category.

He only had himself to blame. Though it seemed impossible, Thomas was somehow both bored out of his mind in Darling while at the same time anxious about the problems waiting for him back home. As much as he dreaded facing his parents after the canceled wedding, he couldn't wait to get back to his restaurant. Thomas didn't know what to do, so he had decided alcohol was the answer. It helped with the boredom, at least.

After a couple of beers with dinner, Thomas slipped a bottle from behind the bar. One sip told him that this wasn't the average liquor. He kept sipping until the bottle was empty, falling into a deep sleep.

The room glowed with rare Alaskan sun. It must be late. And although spring days weren't nearly as long as summer in Darling, he wouldn't get a break from the bright light for several hours yet.

Thomas ran a hand down his face. His tongue was glued to the roof of his mouth. A glance to the side revealed that he had indeed drunk the entire bottle of whatever the hell it was.

After a long, scalding shower, he changed into clean clothes and brushed his teeth. Wiping the fog off the mirror, he confirmed that he did actually look like shit. Made sense. He felt like it too.

Thomas checked the time. Hopefully, most of the morning crowd would have cleared out by now.

He walked into the dining room, and his shoulders drooped. Luck was not on his side. The restaurant was packed. Wolfie hustled around the dining room, his long legs carrying him between tables quickly. The murmur of conversation and clanking of silverware sounded like a high school marching band, and not a very in-tune one.

Thomas took a deep breath and made his way to the lone empty booth against the wall. On the other side, a woman with long, stick-straight brown hair sat in the neighboring booth. Even from the back, he recognized her immediately.

His stomach sank. No, he was not having any luck at all.

Deliberating as he walked across the restaurant, Thomas decided to take the seat with his back to Vivian. Maybe she wouldn't notice him. Her head was tucked down as she picked at what looked like chocolate chip pancakes. Interesting choice.

He let out a deep breath as he slid into the booth. She hadn't noticed him after all. Conversation avoided.

Flirting with Vivian the other night had been a mistake, even if she did bake the best pie he had ever tasted. At least nothing had happened between them. This town was too small for bad blood.

Wolfie appeared at the booth with a coffeepot in hand. The old man took one look at Thomas and let out a low whistle. "I think I figured out what happened to that bottle of schnapps last night."

Thomas squinted, the throbbing behind his eyes getting worse with each passing minute. "Schnapps, huh? Never again."

"That's what they all say." Wolfie chuckled. "Be right back."

Thomas opened his mouth, tempted to call out and beg for a cup of coffee. His body screamed for caffeine. But he closed his mouth again, deciding he would have to live in pain. The last thing he wanted was to draw attention to himself in such a sorry state.

Wolfie returned a few minutes later, a full coffee cup in hand.

"Thank you." Thomas lifted the cup, taking a tentative sip of the hot drink.

"Careful. That's not just coffee."

The sour taste of alcohol hit Thomas's tongue, and his stomach lurched. Holy cow. Couldn't a guy get a break? "Oh, God."

Wolfie rested a hand on Thomas's shoulder. "Hair of the dog. You'll thank me soon enough. Breakfast?"

Thomas shook his head and pressed his lips together. Bile rose in the back of his throat. His appetite had vanished as his hangover grew worse. The idea of eating anything was nauseating.

"I'll bring you something." Wolfie walked away.

Gripping his coffee cup, Thomas took another small sip.

He willed himself to not be sick right here in the restaurant. Slowly but surely, the booze in the brew eased some symptoms of his hangover.

"Good morning, sunshine." Marina smirked as she sat across from him.

"Morning," he muttered.

She peered at him. "You look awful."

"Thanks. Means a lot coming from the queen of hangovers."

"Seriously. What the hell did you do last night?"

Thomas scratched his head with a sigh. It was stupid. Embarrassing even. "I called Celeste."

Marina's dark eyes grew wide. "Thomas. Holy hell. Getting married for money? Now you're sounding like your father's son. You can't seriously be considering this."

"Can't I? I'll tell you what I can't do. I can't keep living this life. It's killing me. We're talking millions, Marina. It's my chance."

His only chance to finally be free from all the obligations that came with being a member of the Becker family, including putting up with his father's impossible expectations. Every other penny Thomas had was tied up in the restaurant.

Marina's eyes rounded in apparent sympathy. "I know. You've worked hard for a long time. But you can't marry someone just for money. Not even millions."

"It doesn't have to be Celeste."

"It shouldn't be just *anyone*, Thomas." She shook her head. "Besides, if not Celeste, then who? Who is randomly going to be available for you to marry in the next few months? Who would even be crazy enough to agree to it?"

His stomach sank. If he thought he felt bad from the hangover, he had another thing coming. The truth of Marina's words hit him like a ton of bricks. He had his chance, and he chose not to take it. Now, he had the rest of his life to figure out what the hell to do. "Any better ideas?"

She lifted a shoulder. "Are you sure you don't want a roommate? Because I think it's time to accept that we can't count on getting our trusts."

Thomas took a gulp of his coffee. He wished Wolfie had filled the whole thing up with booze at this point. It couldn't make things worse. "This whole situation is impossible, isn't it?"

"You got it, roomie. So what did Celeste have to say?"

Thomas glanced away. "I, uh, don't remember."

Marina laughed. "You must be hurting this morning."

"Don't remind me." Thomas winced. "Can we please discuss your love life for a change? Just this once?"

"No way. You know I'm a confirmed single lady."

"Not all men are losers."

Marina blew air through her lips. "Agree to disagree."

Wolfie returned and slid two breakfast platters onto the table. "Hope you don't mind, Marina. Brought you the same thing."

"It's perfect, thank you." Marina smiled up at him.

Thomas practically teared up at the sight of the food. He loved gourmet eating, but on a day like today, nothing beat a huge greasy breakfast. "I've decided you're an angel."

"Remind Charlotte of that next time you talk. Some days, she isn't sure." Wolfie winked before walking away.

As he ate, Thomas tried to figure out what the hell he was going to do. For better or for worse, he had the restaurant. While most of his money was tied up in the venture, it also provided Thomas with the potential for income outside of working for his father. Except the restaurant had just barely opened, and it could be years before it was liquid. If it even lasted that long. There were tons of other restaurants out there with talented chefs and great locations that failed.

But how long could Thomas hold down two careers? It was already starting to wear thin.

And then there was the trust to think about. No, he couldn't get married just for money. But it was tempting with millions of dollars dangling in front of him. Money that promised a way out from under his father's thumb.

At the same time, Marina was right. Who could Thomas hope to meet in just a few months? Who would understand that the marriage would be more of a business deal than a romance? And even if he found someone who agreed to all that, wouldn't that make him no better than his dad?

His head throbbed. Maybe he should just give up. If he hadn't been successful in the last thirty years, he wasn't feeling that hopeful about the next thirty being much different.

A throat cleared. Thomas turned to see Vivian standing beside him. "I can help you."

He knit his brows together. "You can help me? With what? This monster of a hangover?"

Vivian shook her head. "With the money."

He blinked. Shit. "How much did you hear?"

"Millions. Getting married. Not all men are losers." The way she said the last part made him think Vivian sided with his sister on that topic.

Thomas sighed. He should've known she was nuts. Pretty girl like that in the middle of nowhere? She was bound to go crazy. "Are you stalking me or something?"

"Don't flatter yourself. I came to return this." She held out a shirt to Marina. The garment was so precisely folded it looked like it had come from a factory line. "Thanks again."

"I told you to keep it." Marina smiled. "It was a gift."

"I don't need any help." If Thomas had learned one thing in life, it was that no one could help him with his problems.

"Take a seat." Marina patted the bench next to her. "I apologize for my brother being so rude."

Thomas almost stuck his tongue out at his sister, but he realized that would just prove her point. He shoved a piece of bacon in his mouth instead, making a mental note to invite his sister's date, whoever it was, to brunch next time. Then he'd see how Marina liked the tables being turned.

Vivian sat down next to his sister and held his gaze. "I am telling you, I can help."

Thomas chased the bacon with a sip of coffee. "Sweetheart, this isn't going to work. You don't know what you're getting into."

"You need a wife. Well, here I am."

Thomas almost spit out his coffee. The most impressive part of her offer was that she said it with a straight face. She couldn't be serious. "I'm not marrying you. I don't like you that way."

Her nose wrinkled. "And what makes you think I like you like that?"

"So then, why did you get out of your booth, walk over here, and interrupt my breakfast with a marriage proposal? Sounds like someone who has more than friendly feelings."

Vivian flattened her hands on the table. "Because from what I heard, you just need to get married. Not be in love."

"So?"

A smug look passed across her face. "So who has to know if it's all fake?"

# CHAPTER SEVEN

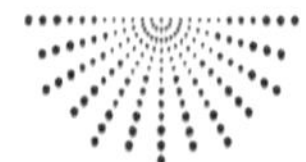

VIVIAN

*Denied.*

There had been more than that in the email from the bank, of course. But that was the only part that mattered. Her loan application had been denied.

Vivian had applied for the business loan the day after she had spoken with Grace. It had only taken another two days after that for the bank in Anchorage to decide that Vivian wasn't worth the risk.

If she hadn't felt like a loser before, she definitely would've now. But with only fifty-six days until escrow closed, she didn't have time for a pity party. Instead, she settled on taking a short break to eat breakfast and regroup. Maybe a full stomach would help her think of a new idea.

Going to the Buck also gave her a chance to return Marina's shirt. That was the only thing standing between her and never having anything to do with the Becker siblings ever again.

Wolfie set the chocolate chip pancakes on the table.

Vivian looked down at the plate to see cherry eyes and a whipped cream smile.

It warmed her heart, but the feeling quickly morphed into melancholy. How much longer would the Buck be in her life? She looked up at Wolfie. "You didn't have to do this."

"You used to love these when you were a kid. But if you prefer plain pancakes…" He reached for the plate.

She grabbed the plate and moved it out of his grasp. "Don't you dare. I'm going to eat every bite."

Wolfie chuckled and gave her a pat on the shoulder before heading to the next table.

Vivian cut into the pancakes, dipping a fluffy chocolate chip bite into a dollop of whipped cream. As she chewed, she closed her eyes and wished she were a kid again. Back before she knew what real problems were.

Ignorance really was bliss.

When she opened her eyes, Thomas stood on the other side of the room.

Vivian swallowed, glancing around only to confirm what she already knew. The only empty booth was right next to hers. Dang it.

Thomas walked her way. Her heart pounded, and she trained her gaze on her food. Maybe he wouldn't notice her. What would she say if he did? What if he mentioned the kiss? She couldn't deal with both the rejection of her loan application and Thomas confronting her about their kiss today.

But he walked past her without so much as a sideways glance.

She let out a deep breath, not sure if she felt disappointed or relieved. But at this point, perhaps she shouldn't borrow trouble. She had enough problems without Thomas in the picture.

The booth shifted slightly as he sat behind her, and she caught a whiff of his sandalwood cologne. Her heart did a flip-flop, and she tightened her grip on her fork. Maybe Thomas had the right idea after all. It was best if they ignored each other. She really couldn't afford a distraction right now.

She was halfway through her short stack when Marina walked across the restaurant, joining her brother at the booth next to Vivian.

Glancing to her side, Vivian eyed the neatly folded blouse. She didn't want to ambush Marina before the woman even had a cup of coffee. It would also give Vivian a chance to finish her own breakfast.

She wasn't trying to eavesdrop. Not at first. All Vivian wanted was to eat her pancakes, return the shirt, and then get back to solving the impossible. It wasn't like she could hear every word of their conversation anyway. The Buck was far from quiet, the hum of other diners chatting and the clink of silverware filling the restaurant.

Then she caught the word *millions*. Millions of what? Dollars? Vivian stabbed another forkful of fluffy pancake. Of course they were talking about money. What else could the children of a billionaire talk about? They had all the money in the world.

Vivian sat up straighter.

*What am I supposed to do? Just stroll up and casually ask for a spare couple million?*

It seemed so ridiculous when Grace had said it three days ago. But not today. After too many dead ends and too many nos, it suddenly was the best idea Vivian had. The only idea left.

She couldn't ask Grace for help. She couldn't ask her parents. She didn't want to ask anyone that she actually cared about. What if she ruined their lives too?

But Thomas? Vivian didn't give two hoots about him,

even if he was a good kisser. And besides, he was *rich*. She couldn't ruin his life if she tried.

Vivian strained her ear as she finished her food. She wasn't quite ready to go and beg for money just yet. Maybe if she could catch more of the conversation, there would be a good opening. As if there was a good time to ask someone for a seven-figure favor.

Then the clouds parted. It couldn't have gone more perfectly if Vivian had planned it with the Fates themselves. She had finished her pancakes, and her rear end was numb from sitting in the wooden booth for so long. But it had paid off. Vivian wouldn't have to ask for a favor. Because she had something Thomas needed.

A wife.

Before she could chicken out, Vivian stepped out of her booth and told him as much.

Her heart slammed into her ribs as she slid into the bench seat across from him. Vivian didn't think of herself as conniving. She left that to people like her uncle. But here she was, about to jump out of the frying pan and into the fire.

*You make your own luck.*

Or her own stupid decisions. That remained to be seen.

He studied her. "You want to get married? What do you get out of this?"

Vivian focused on keeping her voice low. The empty booth behind them provided some privacy, but she didn't want to risk anyone overhearing. "My uncle is selling my family's store. I want you to buy it."

Thomas leaned back against the booth. "This is how I know you're not serious. Why would I do that? It's my money."

She crossed her arms. "Which you won't get without my help."

He lifted a shoulder. "I don't need you."

"If that were true, we wouldn't be having this conversation."

Marina laughed. "She's got you there."

Thomas's face turned the bright pink color of fireweed. He glared at his sister before looking back at Vivian. "That money is mine."

She clenched her jaw. If only Vivian could explain that she, too, had paid a high cost for the store. Even if she told him, she doubted he would understand. Thomas had probably gotten whatever he wanted his entire life. Until now. "Just hear me out."

"Fine," he muttered. "How exactly would this work?"

Vivian glanced over Thomas's shoulder to make sure no one was within earshot. "It's a business deal, plain and simple. There is no risk of things getting complicated. And because it's a business deal, I'm going to need something in writing."

"Then we have a problem." He punctuated his words with a tap on the table. "The kind of prenup we would need would take too long. Ask me how I know."

Vivian folded her hands in her lap, trying to keep them from shaking. As much as she didn't want to repeat history and enter any kind of deal without a contract in place, it wasn't unbelievable that Thomas was telling the truth. He had almost gotten married, after all, and his assets were probably a lot more complex than the savings from her pie sales. "Then I need you to promise you'll buy the store regardless of what happens. And give me the deed when you do. Marina can be the witness."

"Happy to." Marina smiled in between a bite of toast.

Thomas shot his sister another dirty look. "And just how much is the store?"

Vivian named the price her uncle wanted.

Thomas's jaw dropped. "Now I know you're crazy. I don't intend to spend all my money on charity cases."

She bristled. "So I'm a charity case now?"

"You know what I mean. The way I see it, you're getting the better deal."

Vivian fought to keep her voice down as her body turned hot with anger. Typical rich jerk, always thinking of himself. "I am guessing whatever you stand to get out of this is millions—well and above the offer on the store. Don't make it complicated. If we pull this off, we both get what we want."

"I'm way too hungover for this." Thomas rested his forehead on his hands. "This is not the day for these kinds of decisions."

Vivian sighed. Yeah, she and him both. She might not be hungover, but she didn't want to be dealing with this right now either. If only any of it was in her control. "Unfortunately, we don't get to pick and choose when we deal with life's little inconveniences."

Thomas looked up at her, and Vivian held his gaze. Let him size her up if he wanted. He would find her a worthy opponent. It took a special kind of person to not give up after a million nos in life. "How about my word? Or is that worthless?"

She shook her head. "I'd feel better with a contract."

"Come on, sweetheart. You want this or not? You're going to have to trust me. I'm putting myself on the line here too." He reached out his hand.

Vivian hesitated. She was out of the habit of being brave. But that was about to change.

She clasped his hand, and a zing traveled up her arm. Vivian tried to jerk her hand away, but Thomas tightened his grip.

His dark gaze held hers. "I'm trusting you too."

She gulped as he let go of her hand. Suddenly, Vivian

wasn't so sure about this anymore. But she couldn't back down now. This could change everything.

Vivian would be safe. Her family would be safe. No more risk. No more pain. Everything would stay the same forever, a thought that was almost as unnerving as it was comforting. "When do we get married?"

Marina cleared her throat. "Uh, guys? Not to ruin your budding romance, but do you want to take this conversation somewhere a little more private? Breakfast is almost over."

Vivian looked up to see a few tables had already cleared out. Soon enough, it'd be quiet enough to hear a pin drop in here. Which meant anyone else who happened to be at the Buck would hear their conversation.

"Good point." Thomas stood from the table. "Shall we finish this discussion in private?"

Vivian looked up at him. "Now? I told my parents I'd be back at the store after I finished breakfast."

"What was that thing you said about life's little inconveniences?" He cocked a dark brow. "Take the day off if you have to. I don't exactly have time to waste."

She swallowed. Neither did she. "There's one more thing you should know. The store is already in escrow. We only have two months to buy it from my uncle instead. Well, fifty-six days, actually."

Thomas rubbed his chin. "I never thought I'd say this about this situation, but that actually works out. I only have three months to get married by my thirtieth birthday, or I don't get a cent. Which means we need to be husband and wife before July."

Her eyebrows shot up her forehead. Maybe they had more in common than a ticking clock and a drunken kiss. "So, uh, what's the plan, then?"

He looked up at the ceiling. "The best bet for privacy is probably going for a walk. I'm thinking down by the water."

"I'm coming too," Marina piped up.

Thomas frowned at his sister. "Why?"

"Duh. So I can mediate." She looked at Vivian. "Does that work for you?"

Vivian nodded, even though the confidence she had felt when she first approached Thomas was a distant memory. "Sounds good to me. I just have to let my parents know I'm going to be out for the rest of the morning. Maybe longer."

"Whatever you have to do. I'll meet you in front of the Buck in ten minutes." He walked across the restaurant to the staircase that led upstairs. With a wave over her shoulder, Marina followed behind him.

Vivian slumped in the booth, suddenly exhausted. The last few days of too much stress and not enough sleep had caught up to her just as the sugar crash from the pancakes kicked in.

But she couldn't rest yet. She still had so much to do. After Vivian checked in with her parents, she had to finish the conversation with Thomas.

About the details of their marriage.

Vivian gulped. No, she was far from done. Things were just beginning.

# CHAPTER EIGHT

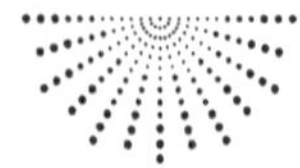

THOMAS

"You're supposed to be helping." Thomas scowled at his sister.

Marina held up her hands. "I *am* helping. It's a completely reasonable question."

He ran his hand through his hair. Thomas had perfected his game face over the years. How could he not have? The Becker household was less touchy-feely, more baptism by fire. But between the hangover and his impromptu engagement, he was struggling to hold himself together today.

Thomas turned to Vivian. "Fine. What happens if we have kids?"

"No chance of that." Vivian shook her head.

He frowned. "You don't like kids?"

"It has nothing to do with my feelings about kids. I just don't see us engaging in the required pre-kids activity."

Thomas let out a huff. This was what he got for waiting until the last minute. Who exactly did he think would be available to get married? His dream girl? "So that's another rule, then? No sleeping together? This marriage just keeps getting better and better."

"I definitely wasn't planning on it." Her face pinched together, and Thomas tried not to take it personally that she looked horrified at the idea of being intimate with him. Did it even matter? It wasn't like Thomas ever planned on getting married for love anyway.

He looked out at the water. Wasn't nature supposed to be relaxing? If so, he should be practically catatonic after more than a week in Alaska. Even now, they were surrounded by the stuff. Dark waves lapped at the rocky beach, and thick forest trees stood behind them. Heck, he had even spotted a bald eagle enjoying the rare sunny day. If Thomas looked away from Main Street, he could almost believe he was in the middle of nowhere. Then again, that wasn't really a stretch. Darling *was* basically in the middle of nowhere.

But his head ached, his back ached, and he felt far from relaxed. It didn't help that Marina seemed to be enjoying herself in equal proportion to his misery. Seriously, whenever she did get in a relationship, he was going to give her so much crap.

Thomas turned back to Vivian. "What about dating other people?"

"Do whatever you want. I don't care. As long as it doesn't mess up you getting the trust and me getting the store." She arched a dark brow. "Think you can control yourself that long?"

Thomas worked his jaw. Control himself that long? She obviously had no idea what his life had been like. Oh, she probably thought she knew. Everyone did. They thought he was rich and spoiled rotten. No one had any idea that he'd been patiently waiting for decades to be happy. That he was *still* waiting. Because while agreeing to this marriage meant he could actually get his trust, it would also keep him away from the restaurant that much longer. "For the record, I was offering if you wanted to. I'm not interested in dating around."

Something that may have been surprise passed across her face, and Thomas couldn't help but feel a little smug. Vivian thought she knew what kind of guy he was? She had another thing coming.

Marina cleared her throat. "And Thomas? How often do you plan on visiting Vivian?"

It took everything Thomas had not to actually growl and bare his teeth at his sister, especially when he saw the laughter dancing in her eyes.

Then it occurred to Thomas he couldn't remember the last time he had seen Marina so happy. Lately, he only saw that side of her when they visited Alaska.

He took a deep breath. At least one of them was having fun. "I suppose whenever we come back to visit Charlotte."

"Two for one. Very efficient." Marina nodded.

Vivian wrinkled her forehead. "Maybe visiting me won't even be an issue. How long do we have to stay married anyway?"

Thomas barked a laugh, startling a raven from a nearby tree. The large bird let out an angry cry as it flew away. "My wife, a true romantic."

"Isn't that why you fell for me in the first place?" Vivian's mouth turned up slightly at the corners.

Thomas found himself smiling back. So there was a sense of humor hiding beneath that oversized rain jacket, huh? "I honestly don't know. I'll double-check the exact wording of the trust and get back to you."

"So we've covered kids, the impending divorce, and buying the store for Vivian." Marina counted off on her fingers. "What about the actual marriage? Can I do the honors? I heard it takes like ten seconds to get ordained online."

"You're enjoying this a little too much." Thomas narrowed his eyes. "But that seems easiest. No need to make a big deal out of it. And the sooner, the better for both of us."

Vivian twisted her hands. "Speaking of soon, I understand why we're doing this, but my parents won't. Don't you think we should at least get to know each other a little? So they don't, you know, worry I've lost my marbles?"

"Good idea." Marina tapped her temple.

Thomas shot her a look. "And you still need to be here, why?"

"To help you keep the facts straight, duh. You know Dad isn't going to like this. He's going to ask questions. *Lots* of questions."

He frowned. She was right. Their dad could sniff out a scheme with the most innocuous clue. Not that it would stop Thomas and Vivian from getting married, but he would at least like to keep the bloodshed to a minimum. "Fine, I'll start. Where did you go to school, Vivian? Studies of Arctic Housekeeping?"

Her lips twitched. "I went out of state."

"Now, that is the smartest thing I've ever heard you say."

She stuck her chin out. "Hey. It's not that bad here."

Thomas waved his hand. "Maybe not for whatever you've got going on. But there's no way I could live here."

She rolled her eyes. "Shocker. I know your type."

"You know my type." He let out a dry laugh. "Oh God, this is going to be good. What's my type? Please, tell me."

"With pleasure." Vivian crossed her arms. "You only date blondes. You sign Christmas cards with just your name. You order wine by the year, and you think that makes you better than everyone."

Marina bit back a laugh that turned into a snort.

Thomas glared at her again before turning back to Vivian. The irony was that he didn't think he was better than everyone. In fact, Thomas had the opposite problem. But he'd never tell her that. No, Thomas gave as good as he got. "Fascinating coming from a gold digger."

Vivian's cheeks turned pink. "I'm not a gold digger! We have a deal. If anyone is a gold digger here, it's you. You stand to gain the most from this."

Thomas took a deep breath of the crisp sea air. This wasn't the time to lose his head, even if her words hit home. How many times had his dad accused Thomas of being obsessed with money? And maybe he was, but that money meant the independence to finally be himself. "Let's agree to disagree. Besides, we have more important things to discuss. Like selling this story, remember? Eye on the prize."

"Fine." She stuck her chin out. "What else?"

Thomas took in her baggy rain jacket, faded jeans, and tall rain boots. Even if he had been drunk when he flirted with her the other night, he remembered that a gorgeous figure hid beneath those tired clothes. "You're definitely pretty enough to be my type, but this whole prairie girl look has to go. How do you feel about a new hairstyle? And dear God, some new clothes. Do you know how to do makeup?"

"Thomas!" Marina chided, but he ignored her.

"I don't know if I should be flattered or offended." Vivian pressed her lips into a thin line.

He looked her in the eye. "What you're going to be is thankful when my family doesn't eat you alive."

She held his gaze, her chin still stuck in the air. He could respect that she never backed down. He knew from experience it took a strong person to do that. A person who had a lot of practice being pushed. "My mom cuts my hair. I don't have makeup, but I can grab a few things from the store. And

I order my clothes by catalog. Once in a while, I might pick something up in Ketchikan."

Thomas let out a groan. He didn't even know catalogs existed anymore. "God. My fiancée is from the 1800s."

"Shut up," Vivian hissed. "It's not that bad."

"I can help." Marina held up her hand, putting a stop to their argument. Maybe they should keep her around. So far, Vivian and Thomas didn't have a great track record of getting along on their own. "You can start by keeping that shirt from the other night. We can see what else I have that'll work."

"Thank you." Vivian gave his sister a small smile. At least she seemed to like one of the Becker siblings, even if it wasn't her fiancé. "But I still don't get why it even matters. Your parents aren't here."

Thomas cracked his neck. Of course Vivian didn't get it. In Darling, no one cared about looks. But in the rest of the world? Appearances mattered. "They will be. There is no way my dad is signing over a penny without seeing this with his own eyes first. If we have the marriage certificate before July, I get the money either way. But that doesn't mean they're going to be nice about it."

Vivian glared at him. "Fine. Anything else I should know about you? Besides your total lack of manners?"

Thomas chuckled, and her scowl deepened. "I think our lessons here are done. You already sound like my mom. You'll fit right in. When in doubt, let me do the talking. Got any plans tomorrow?"

"Yeah. To work."

He lifted an eyebrow. She might be the one person on earth who worked more than him. It seemed every time he passed by the store, he spotted her through the window. And he thought he was bad at relaxing. "Can you at least free up an hour for a date?"

Now she looked like the one with a hangover, her face twisted. "I feel like we've already had more than enough time together."

"Well, sweetheart, get used to it. We're getting married in less than two months. Your idea, remember? It'll give us a chance to get to know each other, and this whole thing will be more convincing if people see us together."

"You're right." Her shoulders sagged, as if admitting that he wasn't a complete moron caused her physical pain. "I can take a break for an hour. I'll meet you at the Driftwood at ten."

They walked back to town together, their feet crunching on the gravel road.

Thomas wasn't sure there was a right way to feel about a fake fiancée, especially when it was leading to a very real marriage. But there was one thing he knew for sure.

Even if he and Vivian didn't see eye to eye on everything, he already felt better about this match after just a few hours than he did after knowing Celeste for years. Looking back, he couldn't ever remember Celeste laughing, let alone making a joke.

At least he and Vivian shared a similar sense of humor. Fake or not, who didn't want to laugh for their entire marriage? Not to mention, she was an incredible baker, something that was worth a lot in his book. If she enjoyed food too, that might be another thing they had in common.

Thomas glanced to the side. A rare gust of wind blew across the beach, whipping Vivian's dark hair around her face.

Sensing his gaze, she gave him a small smile. She looked as unsettled as he felt. Who wouldn't be in their situation?

Thomas faced forward again. But there was something else in her smile. Something he could respect.

Courage.

# CHAPTER NINE

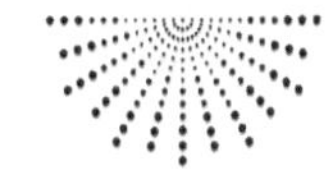

VIVIAN

"I thought you weren't into rich, handsome men?"

Vivian lifted a shoulder. "Maybe I was too quick to judge Thomas. He's pretty nice."

"Good for you." Grace smiled as she stacked clean mugs next to the espresso machine. It was just the two of them in the coffee shop again, and if Grace wasn't enjoying a coffee herself, she often multitasked while they chatted. "Who knows what could happen?"

"Yeah. Totally." Vivian shifted her feet. Except she did know. She knew exactly what could, what *would*, happen because it was all planned out. She felt horrible keeping it from her friend. After all, the whole scheme had started as Grace's idea. Not to mention, Vivian hated lying. She had been lied to enough to never want to do that to anyone herself.

Grace wasn't the only one she was lying to, though. Vivian hadn't told her mom the truth yet either. The whole thing was too complicated without keeping it from her parents. But she hadn't been able to get the words out. Not after she had seen the look on her mom's face when Vivian mentioned having a date. Her mom had looked so *happy.*

Vivian hadn't dated since Philippe. Seven years later, it still hurt to even think about everything that had happened in her last relationship. But what harm did it do to let her mom believe that her daughter actually had a life? Hadn't the poor woman been through enough? Didn't she deserve some good news for a change?

As far as what would happen once Thomas left Darling? Vivian would deal with that when the time came. By then, the store would be hers, and she'd have more brainpower available to devote to explaining the situation to her mom. Right now, she could only handle one problem at a time.

The bell over the door of the Driftwood Coffee Company chimed, and Vivian turned to see Thomas step inside, flashing her a dazzling smile.

She swallowed. He had the kind of smile that would be so easy to fall for. But for better or for worse, Vivian had learned the hard way that real feelings were for fools. "You're late."

"Sorry, gorgeous. I had to check into that *thing* I told you about yesterday." He came up to her, brushing a kiss against her cheek. Her heart, traitor that it was, skipped a beat.

"Of course." Vivian nodded. Thomas had said he was going to double-check into the particulars of the trust. Not that they were going to discuss that topic at all in the presence of other people. Not even Vivian's closest friend.

Grace glanced between them, looking like a proud mama bear. Grace was about ten years older than Vivian and tended to take on the big sister role. Her obvious happiness caused Vivian's guilt to multiply. "What can I get you two to drink?"

Once they had their drinks in hand, Thomas and Vivian

headed down towards the waterfront. Grace had invited them to stick around the Driftwood three separate times, and each time, they had declined. Luckily, the coffee shop picked up in business, and Thomas and Vivian had slipped out quietly.

Outside, the sky was its usual shade of gray. The rain had lightened into a mist that gathered silently on their plastic jackets. The only sound was the occasional car driving by and the crunch of the gravel beneath their feet as they walked to the end of Main Street and down to the water. It was perfectly quiet and perfectly awkward.

She snuck a sideways glance at Thomas. Had she really agreed to marry this guy? If they weren't discussing their scheme, they didn't even have anything to talk about. Why did Vivian think it was a good idea to marry someone she had almost nothing in common with?

But she knew the answer already. She had one very good reason. And as the time ticked down to escrow closing, Vivian had no other options. Even though she never intended to trust a man again, she was doing exactly that. A man she barely knew. And what she knew of him, she didn't like.

*You liked him enough to kiss him.*

Her mouth soured. Once Vivian got through this, she was going straight back to her no-dating policy. Not even the occasional kiss with handsome men who turned out to be very annoying. She wanted to live her life in peace, without any pressure or expectations from other people ever again.

Hopefully, fifty-five days was enough time to make it happen.

"So." Thomas finally broke the silence. "A tea person. No coffee? Ever?"

"Never ever. Just don't like the taste. Besides, it makes me hot and sweaty."

"Talk dirty to me."

Vivian sighed. That was at least one thing she didn't have to worry about. There was no way her feelings about Thomas could get complicated. Her heart would be perfectly safe in his annoying hands.

They left Main Street behind and walked down to the water, standing a few feet away from the softly lapping waves. No one would overhear their conversation out here, unless they counted the bald eagle watching them from its perch in a Sitka spruce.

Vivian turned to face him. "So? How long do we have to stay married?"

"Good news. There isn't actually a rule about that."

She felt strangely like laughing. The fact that was actually good news said a lot about their situation. In what topsy-turvy world do two people enter a marriage together with a plan to leave it? This world, apparently. "Okay. A divorce after six months, then?"

"Can't wait to get rid of me, huh?" His mouth quirked up at the corner. "It's really up to you. If you say six months, then six months it is."

"That sounds good to me." It was longer than she ever intended to be married anyway. A quickie divorce was no skin off her nose. Vivian had no intentions of ever dating again, so she'd never have to explain her brief first marriage to a future husband either. "So what now?"

He smirked. "We are on a date. Which I know is hard for you to pretend since you've probably never been on one. There's like five people in this town."

She narrowed her eyes. "I know what a date is like, okay? I wasn't raised under a rock."

Thomas scratched his chin. "I imagine if I picked up a rock, the underside would look very much like Darling."

Vivian felt a headache coming on, the distinct dull pain

behind her eyes. Maybe she was allergic to rich jerks. "Luckily, this is temporary, and you don't actually have to live here."

"To each their own." Thomas shrugged. "It's no New York."

She took a sip of her tea to stop herself from saying more. From telling Thomas she knew exactly what New York was like. They might be getting married, but she wasn't getting any more personal than necessary to pull this scheme off. "I have a question for you since you're the dating expert between the two of us. Is it normal to spend the whole thing feeling insulted?"

His shoulders sagged. "No. I'm sorry. It's not your fault."

"So whose fault is it? You're the only other one that I see here."

He cracked his neck. "It's my dad. If he's involved, it puts me on edge."

"But you work for him."

Thomas dropped his gaze, dragging the toe of his shoe through the rocky shore. "Yep."

"Why? If you hate it so much."

He looked out at the water. "It's not exactly a topic for the first date. Let's just leave it at I don't plan on working with him forever, or I wouldn't be here with you right now."

"Interesting."

Thomas looked back at her. "What's interesting?"

She took a long sip of tea, amused at the twitch in his jaw. It was nice to know she could get under his skin the same way he got under hers.

Maybe this fake relationship thing wouldn't be so bad after all, especially because her heart wasn't involved. Not having real feelings for someone took a certain amount of pressure out of a relationship. "You ask me to trust you, but you hold all the cards. You aren't even willing to let me peek at them. How can I trust someone who doesn't trust me? Who doesn't give me a reason to trust him?"

He laughed. "You sure don't mince words, do you?"

"Nope." She checked the time on her phone. Her mom had probably been keeping a vigil at the front door since Vivian had left. This date was the most exciting thing to happen in her life since she had come back to Darling all those years ago. "I should be getting back soon."

"Not until we figure out what we're doing next."

She shoved her phone back into her pocket. "Let me guess. You have it all figured out."

"You can blame it on my sister."

Vivian lifted an eyebrow. This was going to be rich. How predictable that Thomas would shift the blame to someone else. "What does Marina have to do with this?"

"Marina said you are, and I quote, *too damn skinny* to wear any of her clothes."

Vivian frowned. "But she loaned me some things yesterday. She said they'd be fine."

"As soon as you left, she made me promise to buy you stuff that actually fits. She's quite the clotheshorse, my sister. You want to talk about someone who could never live in Darling, it's her."

Vivian fought the urge to roll her eyes. "Seriously, Thomas. No one here cares. We could be standing here naked, and all anyone would be talking about was that I was on a date. That's the real news."

The corner of his mouth lifted. "As intriguing as that image is, I promised Marina I would take you shopping."

"Did you forget my family owns the one store in town? The only place to go shopping for clothes around here is in your own closet."

He leaned forward, bringing with him his sandalwood scent. Her pulse quickened, and she gritted her teeth. *Hell no.*

There was nothing about this man she found attractive. "That's why I'm taking you to Juneau."

She shifted to her other foot. It wasn't just the idea of being alone with Thomas for that long that made her squirm. Vivian didn't have good memories of Alaska's capital city. "Juneau?"

"I'll be a gentleman, I promise." He splayed his hand against his chest. "Separate hotel rooms."

"I hate to ruin your plans, but I don't have the money for a shopping spree in Juneau right now."

"Don't worry about that. Your future father-in-law is treating you. He's the one who put me in this situation. He can pay the credit card bill."

She snorted. "And you're spoiled too. I'm a lucky lady."

Vivian braced herself for his comeback. If she had learned anything about Thomas, it's that he gave as good as he got. Something she could *almost* admire. Instead, his eyes turned down, his voice quiet. "I'm not spoiled. If you were in my shoes, you'd know that."

She chewed on the inside of his cheek. Maybe Thomas really didn't lead the charmed life she believed. After all, why would he be trying to escape it? "I'll go to Juneau. Is Marina coming?"

"Nope." He took a sip of his latte. "She doesn't want to be a third wheel."

In Vivian's opinion, the more wheels, the better. "And when—"

"Tomorrow."

She shook her head. "I have to work. I can't ask my parents to cover for me all the time."

"Then close the store." His face hardened, his relaxed demeanor disappearing faster than Alaskan summer. "Do whatever you have to do. Because if we don't make this happen, you'll have nothing but free time to go to Juneau. Do you want to pull this off or what?"

Vivian hunched her shoulders. She hated how he put the burden on her and how easily she took it. She reminded herself that Thomas had skin in the game too. No one was doing anyone any favors here. She didn't owe him anything.

She needed to remember this. That behind the sad eyes and handsome smile, there was someone ruthless. Someone willing to leverage her guilt against her to get what he wanted. Someone she could never trust. "I'll figure it out."

Thomas ran a hand through his hair. "Thank God. Too much about this situation is unbelievable. The fact that I fell in love with someone who looks like they live in a little house on the prairie is going to be the giveaway that something isn't right."

"And it's so believable that I would be into you?"

"Why not?" He gestured to himself. "If only you knew what was underneath this raincoat, baby."

Vivian fixed a sneer on her face, hoping he wouldn't sense the flip-flops her stomach was doing at the idea of Thomas without any clothes on. "I know what's underneath there. Someone who is selfish and clever. Someone who would leave me hanging the minute he found someone better to collude with."

He pinned her with his dark gaze. "Then, sweetheart, you don't really know me at all. Because if you did, you would know that loyalty is everything to me. All I ask is that you return the favor."

Vivian wanted to ask him how it was possible, then, that loyalty required so many lies. Maybe if he explained himself, she would know which way was up. But getting to know him would be a waste. Vivian knew what she needed to know. She knew what she would get from this. And Thomas would be gone before she knew it. "You don't think I'm serious about this? I'll prove to you how serious I am."

*You make your own luck.*

Natasha had gotten the part about change right. But Vivian still wasn't sure they were good ones.

She pulled her phone from her pocket. Hopefully, Thomas didn't notice her hand shaking as she tapped the screen. "Hello, Uncle Robert. I wanted to let you know that I will have the money for the store before escrow closes. Yes. I promise."

Not only was Vivian serious, but she didn't have time to waste. She would find out soon enough if Thomas was a man of his word.

# CHAPTER TEN

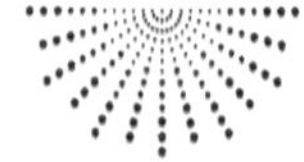

THOMAS

The ferry pulled into the harbor at Juneau, inching closer to the dock while a crew member waited, holding a rope as thick as Thomas's arm. Once the ferry was close enough to touch, the man threw the rope like a lasso and secured the boat to the dock. A flurry of motion followed as preparations were made to disembark.

It was impressive the first time Thomas had seen it. But that was several islands ago. He hadn't realized before this trip that the ferry would stop at every tiny town it passed, even when there didn't seem to be a town at all. One stop was nothing more than a dock. But still, people had gotten off the ferry. Where did they even live?

He cracked his neck as he watched the ferry creep closer to Juneau. Dear God, were they moving in slow motion? As if a few hours on a boat with the most prim and proper woman in Alaska weren't enough, there wasn't a drop of alcohol on board.

Back home, Thomas barely drank. He was too busy

working, keeping his head down until he could finally live the life he wanted. But in Alaska, there wasn't much to keep himself busy. It gave Thomas too much time to think about what waited for him at home.

He had been emailing regularly with the restaurant manager. Thomas wished he were there in person. But he still hadn't answered the last email from his dad, asking when Thomas would be back at work.

Not back at *home*. Back at *work*. That said it all.

His shoulders sagged. His dad always said Thomas was spoiled. Maybe there was some truth to that. Here he was, sailing through islands that had more wildlife than people, something that was a once-in-a-lifetime opportunity for most, and all he could think about was stopping at the first bar he saw in Juneau to quiet the worries in his mind.

Thomas frowned as he took in the shore. Except that didn't seem like it was an option either. There was nothing but a few other ferries, metal ramps, and a building. "This is the capital of Alaska?"

Vivian let out a huff. She did that when he annoyed her. Which seemed to happen a lot. Even though they had just gotten engaged yesterday, they already had perfected the role of an old married couple who had spent the last several decades barely tolerating each other. "This is the ferry terminal. We have to drive into the city."

"Ah. I see now why Charlotte insisted I take the van."

Vivian turned back to look at the men on the dock, either interested in what they were doing or doing a great job of pretending to be so that she didn't have to talk to him.

But Thomas wasn't looking at what was happening on the dock. He was looking at Vivian. She really did have the most remarkable eyes, ever shifting between different shades of green. Out here under the cloudy sky, they appeared to be emerald. The rest of her face wasn't half-bad either. Beautiful even, with a long, straight nose and full lips. "You know, you are kind of attractive, under the whole prairie girl look."

Vivian kept her gaze trained ahead. "How I look is something you shouldn't waste time thinking about. The only thing that matters is the next fifty-four days."

Thomas bit the inside of his cheek, holding in a retort. He was so used to fighting back all the time. But if they were going to get through this weekend—hell, this marriage—maybe he shouldn't take every shot.

After all, how stressful must it be for her to have this deadline looming over her head? Not that the countdown wasn't on for Thomas either. He had less than three months until his thirtieth birthday. Three months until he finally got to live the life he had been dreaming of or lose that chance forever.

But for better or for worse, Thomas had a slightly higher-than-average immunity to deadlines. He had lived his entire life under some imaginary deadline, unspoken pressure, and impossible expectations. Without realizing it, his family had trained him to be a fighter. But Thomas was fighting for something different. And Vivian was fighting for everything to stay the same.

Finally, the boat tapped against the side of the dock with an almost imperceptible bump, not even enough force to bruise a peach. As the crew secured it to the dock, Thomas turned to Vivian and offered her his hand. "Shall we?"

Rolling her eyes, she placed her hand in his. His body warmed at her touch, and Thomas swallowed. Did she feel it too? Or was he just that starved for affection? Either way, the last thing this fake relationship needed was real feelings. This arrangement was complicated enough already.

Other drivers gathered in their vehicles, engines idling as they waited to drive off the ferry. Vivian broke away from Thomas, walking to the passenger door. He shivered as he made his way to the driver's door. It was a chilly day, that was all. It had nothing to do with Vivian suddenly not being by his side.

He got behind the wheel and clicked on his seat belt. "Ready?"

"Let's just get this over with."

He glanced at Vivian. Her face was strained, and she looked anything but ready. Thomas understood that she wasn't excited about this whole arrangement, but did she have to look so completely miserable at the idea of spending time together? "You okay?"

"Perfectly fine," she snapped. "Just focus on the road."

Thomas tightened his grip on the steering wheel, staring straight ahead. He was suddenly a lot less worried about developing feelings. Vivian might be beautiful on the outside, but her personality wasn't nearly as appealing.

They drove off the ferry, the metal ramp letting out a loud *clunk* as they crossed over to land. Vivian deigned to speak to Thomas again, giving him directions to town.

They stopped at a mall first. At least that's what Vivian said it was. Thomas had seen gas stations that were bigger, and he told her as much.

Vivian undid her seat belt. "Unless you want my wardrobe to be nothing but T-shirts that say *Alaska*, this is the place. You can't get this stuff downtown."

Thomas shook his head. "I can see why you order from a catalog."

There was a surprising amount of people in the mall, and it was much livelier than he had expected from the outside. They started at one end and worked their way to the other, stopping at any store that appeared it might have something for Vivian.

She was shy and made him leave the store when she tried on the clothes. He would stand in the middle of the mall, looking like one of those sad puppy dog husbands he always pitied, and eventually, Vivian would come out with a bag of whatever clothes she deemed good enough to buy. Thomas insisted he carry them so he didn't feel totally useless.

They were halfway through the mall when a display window caught Thomas's eye. He paused and nodded towards the window. "Vivian. You need to try that dress on."

Vivian's eyes grew wide. "No way. It's way too tight. And short. And…what are you doing?"

Thomas dropped the bags he had been carrying to the ground and riffled through them. "I want to make sure I didn't pay for any bonnets or other prairie clothes. Good God, Vivian. It's a perfectly modest dress."

"What do you know about women's clothes?"

He flashed a cocky smile. "I'm a connoisseur of all things related to women."

Her mouth tugged down. "Words every woman wants to hear from her future husband."

Thomas laughed. They might not see eye to eye on everything, but at least her sense of humor was better than her sense of fashion. "Come on. Live a little. You might like it."

Her eyes softened then, so subtly that he may have missed it if he wasn't constantly enchanted with them. "Fine. I'll be right back."

She had just barely stepped foot into the store when she stopped and turned to face him. "Would you…would you like to come in? See how it looks? Only if you want."

Thomas was next to her in a heartbeat. Sure as hell beat standing outside.

He waited near the dressing rooms, surrounded by the shopping bags. His stomach let out a growl. Thomas was almost always in the mood for a nice meal, but the fresh sea air and marathon shopping had made him ravenous. Maybe he'd get one of those giant pretzels once they were done here. After all, not every meal had to be gourmet. Sometimes the simple things were best.

A door squeaked. "Thomas?"

He turned around, and his jaw dropped. Vivian looked incredible. At least he *thought* it was Vivian. In front of him stood a goddess in the burgundy wrap-around dress. Was it possible her eyes looked even more green?

She bit her lip. "Do you like it?"

Thomas nodded. He liked it a whole damn lot. What an unfortunate time to forget how to talk.

"I don't know." She smoothed the skirt, which drew his gaze to her legs. He gulped. Her very shapely legs.

Thomas finally remembered how to form words. "You need to get it. It's perfect for tonight."

Vivian frowned. "Tonight?"

"I'm taking you out to dinner."

After all, what was the point of having a hot fiancée if he couldn't show her off?

# CHAPTER ELEVEN

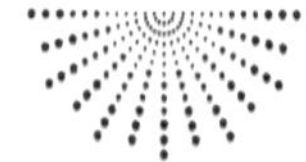

THOMAS

Even though it had only been a little more than two weeks, Thomas realized he had been in Alaska for way too long.

His first thought when he saw downtown Juneau was how big it was.

Big compared to what? Darling, of course. By New York standards, this town was nothing.

He shook his head. Clearly, it was well past time to leave.

They drove to the hotel, parking on the street and heading inside. Thomas had booked the nicest place in Juneau, but even then, it was far from five stars. Luckily, he had spotted more than one bar on the way there.

Thomas unlocked the door to his room. As promised, he had booked two rooms: one for Vivian and one for himself. Thank goodness, because otherwise, he wouldn't get much sleep lying in the bed next to her and thinking about that damn dress.

He swallowed. Another sign he'd been in the middle of

nowhere too long. Thomas was not attracted to Vivian. No way. She was a skinny, annoying prairie girl who was possibly as ruthless as his dad. Didn't women dream their entire lives of getting married? Not Vivian. She leveraged it to get what she wanted.

Thomas unzipped his suitcase. Beautiful. Determined. Smart. He better watch out. She was just his type.

He freshened up, changing into a button-up and slacks. Thomas shrugged on his coat again, instantly hiding his fresh outfit. The rain hadn't let up since they had gotten there. He was beginning to understand why fashion wasn't a priority in southeast Alaska.

Thomas walked to the lobby to meet up with Vivian. When they checked in, he had enlisted the help of the front desk to set up a dinner reservation. The young man told Thomas he was glad to do it but that a reservation really wasn't necessary.

Shocker. Even in Alaska's capital, there probably weren't enough people to fill a restaurant. But Thomas insisted all the same. It might be the only time in Vivian's life she ate at a place that required reservations and actually charged for the food. And while Thomas wasn't interested in marriage as a rule, he at least wanted to treat his future wife well.

Thomas rolled back on his heels, waiting for Vivian to come downstairs. He didn't realize he was holding his breath until he saw her.

He grinned. She had worn the dress. "Hello, gorgeous. Hungry?"

Vivian shrugged on her jacket. "Starving. Shall we go see what this village offers?"

With a chuckle, Thomas opened the door for her. They headed up the street, following the concierge's directions.

Thomas pretended to be looking at the town when, in

actuality, he was sneaking glances at Vivian. He had known she was pretty, but who had any idea there was a total knockout under that prairie girl package?

She shot him a look. "You're so obvious."

Thomas almost tripped over his own feet. Had she caught him staring? "What do you mean?"

Vivian pointed across the street. "You're eyeing every bar we pass."

Thomas blinked. Actually, he hadn't thought about booze at all. A first for his time in Alaska. "Oh, that. I can wait until we get to the restaurant."

"Did you know there used to be a law here that there had to be a church for every bar built?"

"No way."

"Why do you think there are so many churches?"

Thomas laughed. "What about you? No coffee, no alcohol. Do you have any vices?"

Her lips curved up in a smile. "Wouldn't you like to know?"

He lifted an eyebrow. Was she actually flirting with him?

As soon as they arrived at the restaurant, Thomas was certain the concierge hadn't let them down. The place had an incredible view of the channel. Cruise ships, small boats, and float planes dotted the water, surrounded by forest and buildings that looked more like they belonged in the gold rush era than modern times.

He turned to Vivian. "Mind if we sit inside? I had envisioned a very nice dinner on the patio, but I think our food might get soggy."

"Good idea. Your whiskey would get watered down outside, and I know you prefer it straight."

Thomas laughed again, holding the door open for her.

After they ordered, Thomas leaned back in the chair and

took a sip of his drink. "God, that's delicious. It feels good to relax for a change."

"For a change? What exactly have you been doing in Darling?"

"I mean relax from this." He gestured between them. "This whole act."

Vivian fixed him with a look. "I've got bad news for you. We still have a long way to go. And there will be no relaxing. Not here."

"Do you see anyone?" He looked from side to side in exaggerated seriousness. "No one here cares, Vivian. Let your hair down for once."

But she wasn't laughing. "You don't get it, do you? Alaska might be a big state, but things don't go unnoticed here. I'm shocked we haven't seen someone we know yet. I promise you, even if we didn't tell anyone we were going to Juneau, someone in Darling would know."

Thomas studied her. What the hell had happened to this woman? It was more than just the possibility of losing her family's store. People weren't born that careful, so fastidious that they ran their lives like a German train table. "Do you want to talk about it?"

"About what?"

"What made you so afraid of life?"

Her eyes shifted to a darker green, and she glanced away. "You don't know anything about my life."

The server came by, delivering their meal.

Thomas picked up his fork and took a deep breath. He wasn't going to let a little tension ruin one of the only things he actually enjoyed. He took a bite of his halibut, savoring the delicate fish and bright lemon sauce. "I don't think I've ever had halibut this fresh."

"Probably caught it here. Or nearby. They do a lot of

halibut fishing around Ketchikan." She twirled her pasta around her fork

"When I made the reservation, the concierge told me that we have to order the chocolate cake. I think I'm tempted to believe him." Thomas took another bite of food.

A faint smile played at her lips. "I'll be sure to save room for dessert."

He puffed his chest out. Her smile, the thought that he had something to do with it, made him feel something almost forgotten. Pride. "Seriously. This place is giving my restaurant a run for its money. I'm impressed."

Her eyes widened. "You have a restaurant?"

"Does it count if I'm financing it? I'm not in the kitchen, so I can't take credit for the food. I'm more behind the scenes."

She pushed the pasta around her plate. "That explains it."

"Explains what?"

"Why you need that money so bad. I figured you haven't been working for your dad all these years for free. So why not take your savings and run?" Vivian studied him. "But you don't have any savings, do you? You have a restaurant instead."

Thomas bristled. He wasn't done with his whiskey yet, but already, he needed another. "And let me guess. You think that's stupid."

She looked him in the eye. "Not at all. Two careers? I think it's impressive. You're a hard worker."

"Thanks." His throat tightened. It was more of a compliment than his father had ever given him. Heck, even though they hadn't spent much time together, Vivian seemed to see a side of him that no one else ever did. The fact that Thomas might be more than just a trust fund.

"It's kind of funny, actually. Not that you'd believe it, but that used to be what I wanted to do."

Thomas blinked. At least he couldn't say she never surprised him. "You were going to open a restaurant?"

Vivian placed her silverware on the plate and leaned back in the booth. "Not just mine. My boyfriend and me. He was going to be the chef. And I was going to be the pastry chef."

"That explains the pie. Which I still dream about, by the way." He smiled. "So what happened?"

She lifted a creamy shoulder. "Things changed."

Thomas set down his fork. He lost his hunger for food and his thirst for drink. There was only one thing he craved, and that was to know more about Vivian. But she couldn't have sent a clearer message if she had *Case Closed* written across her forehead. "Now that I know that, I insist we try the cake. I'd love to hear your expert opinion."

Vivian shot him a cheeky smile. "You know I never miss a chance to give you my opinion."

They finished dinner and, over a slice of exceptionally good chocolate cake, discussed their favorite meals. Vivian loved good food as much as he did. Even though they were only getting married for money, it was a pleasant surprise to discover they had more than desperation in common. He couldn't remember the last time he had talked to someone like this.

Thomas felt his shoulders relaxing, an unfamiliar feeling coming over him. He was actually happy.

Once every crumb of cake was gone, they headed back to the hotel, full and exhausted from their day. Thomas hadn't even finished his drink. All he wanted was to fall into a deep, dreamless sleep.

As they plodded out of the restaurant, a whimper caught his ear.

Vivian looked at Thomas, her eyebrows pulled together. She must have heard it too.

They followed the sound around the other side of the

building. The area was lined with giant dumpsters that stank like rotten fish.

A man in a grease-stained uniform was holding massive garbage bags. A small dog nipped at his heels, and the man kicked at the dog.

His foot caught the dog in its head, and the poor mutt let out another whimper.

"Hey! What the hell?" Thomas ran up to the man. He might not be citizen of the year, but he drew the line at mistreating animals.

The man scowled at Thomas, not looking the least bit sorry. "Ain't my dog. The stupid thing comes around every night and tries to get scraps. Makes a damn mess. One of these days, he'll learn not to."

He tossed the trash in the dumpster and went back inside.

Thomas squatted down and reached out his hand, whistling. The dog hesitated before taking tentative steps towards him.

Vivian walked up to Thomas. "Is it okay?"

"I think so." Thomas scooped up the dog, holding the small canine to his chest. A Chihuahua was the last kind of stray Thomas expected to see in Alaska. How the hell had the little thing survived? The dog looked like it might be a light color, but Thomas wasn't sure. Its coat was filthy, and it didn't smell much better than the dumpsters.

"He's shaking. Poor little thing." Vivian rested a hand on the dog's apple-shaped head.

Thomas couldn't help but compare Vivian to Celeste. Not that there was any comparison to begin with. But his ex-fiancée would never have touched the filthy dog. Vivian didn't hesitate to comfort the small animal, no matter how dirty it was. She might not have a private education or a trust fund, but she had something most people in his world didn't. A heart.

Vivian scratched the dog's ears, and it licked her hand. "So what now?"

The dog leaned into Thomas, rubbing its head against his chest and ensuring that his jacket got as dirty as possible. Thomas sighed. "I think we just got a dog."

# CHAPTER TWELVE

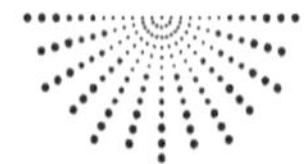

VIVIAN

Vivian had always wanted a dog. Not that she had ever imagined picking up a stray in Juneau with her fake fiancé. She certainly hadn't envisioned a grungy Chihuahua who was so skinny that every bone in the poor thing's body showed through its short fur.

But life was like that, wasn't it? There was no point in guessing how things might happen. Because even when Vivian thought she knew, life just proved her wrong again.

It turned out the dog was a blessing. Once back from Juneau, Vivian had fielded a million questions about her time with Thomas from her parents. Their interest was understandable. After all, Vivian had gone from her first date in seven years to an overnight trip in just one day. She knew her parents were happy for her, but their apparent relief at her newfound relationship status only made her feel like more of a loser than usual. Had she really seemed that hopeless?

But thanks to the Chihuahua, not every single question

was focused on Thomas and Vivian's budding relationship. Just most of them.

After several baths, it turned out the dog was a soft butter yellow. Vivian selected a pink collar from the store, having also determined the dog was a girl. Her parents had accepted having the dog at home more easily than Vivian's new relationship. They were probably just excited for Vivian's social circle to be expanding. But she still hadn't decided whether or not to keep the dog. Alaska wasn't a great environment for a Chihuahua, although she was the perfect size to keep indoors during cold days. But after a few cans of dog food, it was clear the dog had decided to keep Vivian.

Naturally, Thomas didn't help with any of this. He claimed Vivian had the better living situation for the dog right now. While that might be true, she suspected his specialty was creating problems, not solving them. He was great at taking action. But Vivian had yet to see him follow through on anything to completion. It wasn't a comforting thought, considering how much she was depending on him. Including dinner tonight with her family.

The dog hopped on the bed, climbing into Vivian's lap. She sighed and scratched the dog's ears. "You're impossible to say no to, Trixie."

Vivian smiled to herself. That was probably another reason Thomas didn't want to be the dog's main caretaker. He had made it clear he wasn't a fan of the name Vivian had chosen for her.

A knock came from the door, followed by her mom's muffled voice. "Sweetheart? Uncle Robert will be here soon. Should I set the table?"

Vivian's shoulders pinched together. She had been dreading this all day. Uncle Robert could eat with his bare hands for all she cared. Or better yet, Trixie could eat at the table, and Uncle Robert could eat from the dog bowl. "Be out in a minute, Mom."

Closing her eyes, Vivian took a deep breath. She needed to pull herself together, and keep herself together, for the rest of the night. A tall order for dinner with both her uncle and Thomas.

By some miracle, Uncle Robert had agreed not to tell her parents about Vivian buying the store. The last thing she wanted to do was keep track of yet another lie, but it was a necessary one. She would be able to explain everything once Thomas had access to his trust and Vivian officially owned the store. Not that she had told her uncle the truth about where the money was from. Vivian let him think it was from savings. She had been selling baked goods for years, and there was little to spend money on in Darling, so it wasn't completely unbelievable. Vivian hadn't told her uncle about dating Thomas either. Her dad had broken the news when he spoke to his brother a few days ago, after Vivian and Thomas had gotten back from Juneau.

Vivian couldn't shake the feeling that she knew why Uncle Robert had agreed not to tell her parents about selling the store to her. He never did anything unless it worked best for him. And even though he agreed to sell to her, he had left the store in escrow. Either way, he was going to make a sale.

It only took her uncle a few days to show up in Darling after her dad had told him that Vivian was dating Thomas Becker. Vivian half expected him to bring an autograph book for Thomas to sign. Her uncle was obsessed with the Becker family and, more importantly, their money.

She pushed herself up from the bed, and Trixie hopped down to follow. It seemed Vivian couldn't go anywhere without the small dog trailing after her.

Earlier that day, Vivian had prepped homemade lasagna and baked a flourless chocolate cake. The lasagna was warming in the oven now, and the cake was chilling in the fridge. She whipped up heavy cream, adding in a sprinkle of powdered sugar and a dash of vanilla extract. Vivian stuck the bowl in the fridge next to the cake, grabbing the lettuce for the salad.

She tore up the leaves before tossing together a simple vinegar and olive oil dressing. The last thing to prep was mixing up the garlic butter to spread over slices of sourdough toast. Vivian would wait to put that in the oven until everyone was here.

Her shoulders relaxed. There was something wonderful that happened when she was in the kitchen. All the problems of real life melted away so that she was no longer the shy, scared person she was so used to being. Things made sense in the kitchen. They were tidy and organized.

That's why she loved baking most of all. It wasn't just an art. It was science. Neat measurements, exact amounts, and voilà! Something that made people happy. Something that she had created. Something that she could count on every time.

Philippe had always teased her about her fastidious nature. He was more adventurous. More comfortable with risk. That was what made him such a genius in the kitchen. It was what had made her fall for him. And later, it was what broke her heart.

Her hands shook as she set the table with three extra places. This would be the first time her family would spend real time with Thomas. Thank God Marina was coming too. Hopefully, that would take some of the attention off Vivian and Thomas.

What if her parents caught on to the whole scheme? They were her *parents,* after all. No one knew Vivian better. They had found it hard to believe that Vivian had gone on a date in the first place. How could she expect them to really believe that she had a boyfriend already? And soon enough, a fiancé and then a husband.

Though Vivian didn't plan on breaking that news to her parents until *after* she and Thomas were officially married. She would tell her parents the truth, the whole truth, and nothing but the truth. But not until she held the deed to the store.

Vivian stood back to inspect the table. There was one good thing about all this. Either she and Thomas would fail and Uncle Robert would sell the store to a complete stranger, or they would be successful. Either way, Vivian didn't foresee very many more dinners with her uncle.

Her mom came into the kitchen. "The store is officially closed for the day." She glanced at the dinner table. "Oh, honey, it looks great. I could smell the lasagna from downstairs. Uncle Robert will love it."

Vivian smiled, briefly debating swapping out a plate for a dog bowl. "Thanks."

A commotion came from the living room, followed by familiar voices. Uncle Robert and her dad were there. Vivian's stomach tightened into a knot. Showtime.

But where the heck were Thomas and Marina? They were supposed to get here *before* her uncle. Had Thomas chickened out on dinner with her family?

Uncle Robert walked into the kitchen. "Vivian, dear. You look lovely. So nice to see you wear something that actually fits for a change. Those baggy clothes were just awful."

Her smile froze on her face. *Those baggy clothes* were still in her closet. Suddenly, the blouse she wore felt too tight. Vivian tugged at the collar, wishing she had worn something different. Something familiar. Especially if Thomas wasn't going to bother to show up. "Nice to see you too."

"You got a dog?" Uncle Robert and Trixie eyed each other.

Trixie stayed put on the dog bed in the corner, not bothering to greet him.

Vivian lifted an eyebrow. So far, she had never seen Trixie be anything but friendly. Apparently, the dog was a great judge of character.

"Actually, she's our dog." Vivian turned at the sound of Thomas's voice and saw him standing in the doorway, holding a bottle of wine.

Her dad stood next to Thomas, beaming. "Your boyfriend got here right after us."

Thomas walked up to her, pressing a kiss to her cheek. It was simple. Innocent. Fake. No reason to feel a zing all the way down to her toes. "Isn't that right, sweetheart?"

"Thomas *Becker*. So nice to finally meet you." Uncle Robert stretched out his hand.

Thomas gave him a short handshake. "Likewise. Vivian mentioned we're in the same industry."

Vivian could practically see the pupils in Uncle Robert's eyes morph into dollar signs. How the heck could she even be related to this guy? She could never understand people who cared about money that much. Another reason she and Thomas could never date for real, not that she wanted to. "I can't say my operation compares to your dad's. But they're the same species of business. Is he here, by the way? Your dad?"

Thomas shook his head. "Nah, dear old dad doesn't heed the call of the wild. My sister and I are the only ones who visit Darling."

"Speaking of Marina, is she on her way?" Vivian gave Thomas a pointed look.

"She decided to sit this one out. Didn't want to crash my first family dinner." Thomas gave Vivian an apologetic smile as he bent down to scratch Trixie on the head with his free hand.

"That was thoughtful of her," Vivian muttered as she cleared the extra place setting. Great. Just great.

"Anyone in the mood for a glass of wine?" Thomas straightened and held up the bottle. "When Vivian told me she was making lasagna, I knew the perfect pairing. Almost as perfect as us together, of course." He wrapped his arm around her and drew her close. Vivian stiffened. She hated PDA, even if her skin did tingle at Thomas's touch.

Her parents and uncle stared at them as if they couldn't believe what they were seeing. Vivian had never been a touchy-feely person, not even as a kid. If this had happened after dinner, they would probably wonder if they had accidentally ingested hallucinogenic drugs. Vivian had made a mushroom lasagna, after all.

A timer dinged, and Vivian wiggled away. Saved by the bell. She pulled the lasagna out of the oven and slid in the garlic bread. "Dinner will be ready in about ten minutes."

"And drinks are ready now." Thomas opened the wine, pouring everyone a glass.

Her dad cleared his throat. "What do you say we sit in the living room and give these kids some privacy to say hello?"

Vivian bit back a laugh as they walked away. She wasn't sure who was more reluctant to leave for the very few minutes until dinner was ready: her parents, curious about their daughter's dating life, or her uncle, fangirling over Thomas.

Thomas smiled at her, still holding the wine bottle. "How about you? Care for a splash?"

Vivian held up a hand. "None for me, thanks."

"Have a little fun, sweetheart."

Vivian stepped closer, dropping her voice to a whisper. Through the doorway, she could see her parents from their seat on the couch. But if she spoke quietly enough, they wouldn't hear her and Thomas. "Don't you think you're laying it on a little thick?"

He matched her whisper. "We have less than two months to make this believable. Thick is the only option. Unless you want to tell them the truth now?"

Vivian squirmed. She hated this. She hated being the center of attention. She didn't even like to tell people when it was her birthday. "You've done enough. Everyone is already staring at us."

"Perfect." Thomas flashed that blindingly handsome smile that belonged on billboards. He leaned forward and kissed her right on the lips.

Her head spun, but before she could figure out which way was up, Thomas pulled away.

"Our first kiss." He winked. "Now, let me see if anyone needs a refill."

Vivian nodded and checked the garlic bread. Her face was warm, and it wasn't from the heat of the oven. She felt stupid. Stupid that her stomach turned to mush when he kissed her. And even more stupid to think she mattered to him at all. Clearly, she didn't. Because Thomas didn't even remember their *actual* first kiss that night at the Buck.

She slid the garlic bread out from the oven. If Vivian had any doubt Thomas would look back after this was all over and want more, well, she could rest easy. To Thomas, she could be anyone. All that mattered to him was his money.

Vivian tried to shake it off. And what was so wrong with that? It was the same reason she was with him too.

She glanced at Trixie sitting in the corner. The dog lifted her head, giving her a sympathetic look. Vivian took a deep breath, feeling a smidge better.

She fixed a smile on her face before stepping into the living room. The show must go on. "Dinner is ready."

As everyone came into the kitchen and took a seat around

the dinner table, Vivian poured herself just a tiny bit of wine. Maybe she could use a drink after all.

Everyone dug in, complimenting Vivian on the lasagna, but her mind was a million miles away as she chewed each tasteless bite. It was ridiculous, but of all the things that were wrong right now, the one that bothered her the most was Thomas completely forgetting about that night. He had practically begged her to stay. But maybe she was the problem. Maybe all first kisses were unremarkable.

Vivian reached for her glass, preferring the wine to lasagna tonight. But it was empty.

"More wine, darling?" Thomas grabbed the bottle, adding another splash to her glass.

Her uncle scooped up a bite of lasagna. "So, how did you two meet anyway?"

Vivian gulped. Even though she had expected it, the question still put her on edge. When her parents had asked her specifics about her relationship with Thomas, Vivian had promised they would get to ask all their questions at this dinner. Hopefully, Thomas would keep the details vague like he and Vivian had discussed.

Thomas took a sip of wine. "I noticed Vivian the very first time I visited Darling. It's such a cliché, but for me, it really was love at first sight." He looked at her adoringly. "What can I say? When you know, you know. Just took me a few visits to work up the courage to ask her out."

Vivian resisted the urge to gag. To think she had thought he was laying it on thick earlier. Her appetite completely disappeared. At this rate, Trixie would get most of her lasagna.

Her dad looked at Thomas. "And do you foresee many more visits to Darling?"

Vivian shifted in her seat at the obvious implication in

her dad's question. She was almost thirty, not fifteen. Was there really a need to nail down Thomas's intentions?

"As often as I can get here. Maybe one of these days, I'll stay forever." Thomas took Vivian's hand and gave it a squeeze. He looked at her with such sincere warmth that Vivian was thankful she knew this was all fake. Otherwise, she might actually believe it.

The rest of the dinner passed in a blur. Thankfully, Uncle Robert kept a good portion of the conversation on business, even though Vivian was certain her parents would rather hear more about their daughter's new boyfriend than his dad's company.

Her mom helped Vivian clear the table for dessert. As she set a stack of plates by the sink, her mom leaned in to whisper in Vivian's ear. "He's so nice. And so handsome!"

Vivian nodded, her stomach churning. If only she had fallen for something as simple as Thomas's looks. She hated keeping this secret from her parents. And here Vivian had been silly enough to think the store only cost money. She didn't realize it would take her peace of mind too.

She plated the cake and topped it with whipped cream, serving everyone a slice.

Her dad turned to Thomas. "So how long are you planning on staying in town this time around?"

"As long as Vivian will put up with me." Thomas smiled.

Uncle Robert chuckled and shook his head. "But you can't stay here forever. You have a life in New York. A career. Darling isn't the best place to begin with, and definitely not for a man like you."

Vivian clenched her fist beneath the table. Could her uncle get through one dinner without insulting her family's entire life?

"I like Darling. And luckily, time off at work is flexible. I know the owner." Thomas took a bite of cake, scooping up a generous amount of whipped cream with it. "Holy cow. This is incredible. I had no idea you could bake like *this*."

"Didn't you?" Vivian shot him a look. She didn't think that he had forgotten their conversation at the restaurant in Juneau. And now he didn't even remember the pie from that night at the Buck anymore either? Hopefully, he wouldn't forget about their deal once he got his trust. His memory seemed to have more holes than swiss cheese.

Unlike Thomas, her uncle wasn't interested in chocolate cake. Not when there was money to think about. "Maybe Vivian would consider going to New York. You'd like it there, Viv. So much more to do. More shopping, for one."

"You know me so well," Vivian said dryly. Apparently Thomas wasn't the only one with a memory problem tonight. Had her uncle really forgotten that Vivian had already lived in New York? Or was he just that starstruck by Thomas's presence?

Vivian forced herself to eat one more bite before she set her fork down. She hated wasting food, but there was no way she could eat anymore. Her stomach was in knots. In fact, the only thing that sounded good was more wine.

She stood to get the bottle from the kitchen counter and held it over her glass. Only three pathetic drops came out before the bottle gasped its dying breath. "Is there any more wine?"

Thomas shook his head. "Not unless you have some. I only brought that one."

"Sit down, Vivian. Forget the wine." Her uncle gestured to her seat. "We're in the middle of a conversation."

She winced. Her parents always said Uncle Robert was too busy with work to have a family. Vivian doubted that. Her theory had always been that his personality was the problem. She felt Thomas watching her as she sat back down. Vivian kept her focus on the table in front of her, too embarrassed at being scolded like a child to meet his gaze.

"So, are you two thinking of having kids?" her uncle asked.

Vivian gritted her teeth. Why had she ever agreed to this family dinner? It was only digging her into a deeper hole. "We just started dating."

"Never too early. Especially not at your age." Uncle Robert finally took a bite of his cake.

"At my age?" Vivian gasped. "I'm not even thirty."

He sighed. "It's different for women, you know that. You don't have time to waste. Look how long it took to find someone interested in you since your last relationship."

Vivian's stomach twisted up even tighter. She was furious at her uncle and ashamed Thomas was hearing any of this. And why weren't her parents saying anything? It was one thing to be berated behind closed doors. She didn't need her fake fiancé to know what a loser she was on top of it.

Thomas's hand covered hers, and she looked up to see him smiling at her. "Vivian is perfect just the way she is. It's a good thing we didn't meet sooner because I'm not sure I would've been good enough to deserve her. Heck, I'm not sure I'm good enough now. Anyone who doesn't see that is a fool."

Her throat closed up.

*It's all fake.*

But that didn't mean she wasn't allowed to feel good. Feelings were real, weren't they?

Thomas looked at Uncle Robert, his dark eyes steely. "Wouldn't you agree?"

"Of course." Uncle Robert nodded. "I'm just worried about her well-being, is all. Didn't mean for it to come out the wrong way."

It took everything Vivian had not to gape at her uncle.

This man who had criticized her all her life, who thought himself above everyone, cowered in Thomas's presence. It seemed the only languages Uncle Robert understood were money and power. When Vivian thought about how much those two things would change her life if she had them, it made her a little nauseated.

"Of course not," Thomas agreed in a tone of voice that said he had taken it exactly the wrong way.

"I'm going to get started on the dishes." Vivian stood, gathering up the dirty plates and taking them to the sink. Let the rest of them sit there all night. She was done with dinner. She left Uncle Robert's plate behind, the cake not yet gone. Hopefully, he enjoyed it. Because as soon as the store was hers, she was done with her uncle too.

Her dad suggested enjoying a glass of whiskey in the living room, and Uncle Robert took him up on it. After making sure Vivian didn't need help, her mom joined the men in the living room. Vivian suspected her family was giving her and Thomas privacy again. But all Vivian wanted was to be alone.

Her shoulders pinched together as she scrubbed a plate silently. Hopefully, Thomas would get the hint and go home. The night was over.

Thomas came up next to her, grabbing a dish towel from the hook by the sink. "Mind if I dry?"

Vivian clenched her jaw. "You don't have to help me. With anything."

"Nonsense. That's what boyfriends are for." He took the clean plate from her. "Besides, the sooner we're done here, the sooner we can go."

"Go where?"

He smiled. "To the Buck. You need a drink."

# CHAPTER THIRTEEN

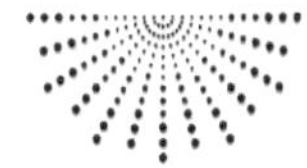

THOMAS

Thomas wasn't doing Vivian any favors. The truth was he couldn't stand to be at that dinner for another minute.

Thomas and Vivian crossed the street to the Buck. Traffic on Main Street was nonexistent, as usual. As the early spring day turned to dusk, the windows of the restaurant glowed, a beacon of hope and, more importantly, beer.

Thomas cleared his throat. "Your parents are really nice. And your uncle seems…interesting." *He's a piece of work* was what he really wanted to say.

Vivian snorted. "That's the most hilarious thing you've said since I met you. It's okay. I know the kind of guy Uncle Robert is. You don't have to lie to me."

His throat tightened. No, they didn't have to lie to each other. Just the rest of the world.

He opened the door for Vivian, following her inside the restaurant. "Booth or bar?"

She shrugged. "You're the drinker here. You pick."

"There's nothing to do in Darling but drink, okay? Give

me a break." Thomas glanced around the dining room. The booths along the windows were full, but the center tables and bar were practically empty. That's what they needed. Privacy. "Bar it is. And for the record, I don't know how the hell *you* don't drink more with that guy around."

"Because it wouldn't do anything to fix the problem." Vivian pressed her lips into a thin line as she perched on the stool next to him.

Thomas had to give her credit. Her resolve to take the high road was as impressive as her stick-straight posture on that barstool.

"This is a nice surprise." Wolfie smiled as he walked up to them. "What can I get you?"

"I'll take a beer." Thomas pointed at the tap before turning to Vivian. "And for the lady?"

"I don't usually drink." Her nose was stuck in the air. Literally.

Thomas sighed. This from the woman who just asked him if there was more wine. "So you've said. But we're at a bar. Drink water for all I care. But drink *something*."

She frowned slightly, looking a little less snooty and a little less certain than she had a few seconds ago. Interesting. Her self-confidence seemed as fragile as his own sometimes. "I guess I'll have a glass of white wine."

Wolfie pulled a bottle from the fridge. "I'll be drinking the same thing in another month or so when summer hits. I always had white wine on hot days at the biergarten. Even if all my friends hassled me for not drinking beer."

After he served their drinks, a bell dinged, and Wolfie excused himself to the kitchen to pick up an order.

Thomas lifted his glass. "Cheers."

Vivian's frown deepened. "And what exactly are we cele-brating?"

"Surviving that dinner."

"Now *that*, I'll drink to." Vivian clinked her glass to his.

As Vivian sipped her wine, Thomas couldn't help but notice her full mouth. Again.

Thomas took a gulp of his own drink. He had kissed Vivian to sell their story. Nothing more. There was no reason why he should be thinking about it two hours later. Especially when he wasn't, and never would be, interested in a real relationship.

Vivian set her glass down. "So when do I get to meet *your* parents?"

His shoulders tightened. The best-case scenario would be never, but he knew that was wishful thinking. "You already met Marina. Isn't that enough?"

"Nope. I've been counting on meeting your parents. You gave me a big speech about what they would think of me. Remember?"

Thomas cracked his neck. Oh, he remembered. But that was a week ago when life was a lot easier and he didn't know what it was like to kiss her. "Well, considering I've been working remotely for almost three weeks and am about to announce I'm engaged on top of it, I'm guessing sooner rather than later. There's no way my dad is going to let this slide. He never lets anything slide."

Vivian's mouth turned down. "Maybe that's something that wealthy people have in common. Your dad. My uncle. They're just not *nice*."

"And me? Do you think I'm that way too?" He shifted on the barstool.

She studied him for a moment. "I don't know what to think of you."

Thomas swallowed. It was perhaps the most honest thing she had said to him yet. Maybe that anyone ever had said to him. He was used to people making their judgments before they knew anything at all. But Vivian wasn't like anyone else. Something Thomas wouldn't forget.

Despite the sticky bar top and the fluorescent lights, something about being at the Buck with Vivian felt strangely intimate. Did she feel it too? Was it even worth mentioning? Or would it only add more complications to an already complicated situation? But then a dish broke, the restaurant cheered, and the moment disappeared like a doe into the woods.

Thomas sipped his beer, almost thankful for the interruption. He wasn't interested in anything more than a fake relationship. So why tempt real feelings with the woman who would be his wife in less than two months? Vivian had said it best. It was a business deal. Nothing more. "Then you might hold the highest opinion of me yet. According to my dad, I'm a disappointment at best."

Her eyes rounded, and she looked at him with so much compassion that Thomas almost felt embarrassed. He liked it better when she was annoyed with him. Thomas knew how to handle conflict. Compassion was another story. "Doesn't it bother you? Dealing with someone like that all the time? I can barely stand when my uncle visits, and that's not very often."

Thomas clenched his jaw. If only she knew how much he hated it. People only saw the money. The privilege. The advantage of being part of the Becker family. They didn't see what it cost. What's more, no one really cared. "I've spent a lifetime wishing things were different, sweetheart. I've come to accept that the only person who can change my fate is me."

Her eyebrows rose slightly, and she took another sip of wine. "I guess it'll be worth it when this is all said and done. You'll have everything you've ever wanted. Do you have any plans besides the restaurant?"

He shrugged. If only money was all that he wanted. But

like he had told her, wishing hadn't done jack shit for him over the years. Money might not buy happiness, but at least he wouldn't be miserable anymore. That was the extent of his dreaming. "I'm just focused on that right now. The restaurant is the most important thing in my life. I really think it could be something."

"That might offend a normal girlfriend, but lucky for you, nothing about this is normal." Vivian gave him a small smile. "And you're talking to someone who is very interested in restaurants in general."

He chuckled. "Why don't you tell me about *your* restaurant? The one you want to open?"

"*Wanted* to open." Her eyes dimmed, and Thomas was almost sorry he asked. Not because he expected her to be happy all the time but because she had been happy, and he'd made her sad. If he could count on one thing in life, it was screwing up. "It was a long time ago. Doesn't matter anymore."

Before he could stop himself, Thomas reached out and placed a hand on her arm. "You aren't going to tell me what happened? You can't even talk to your future husband?"

She looked down at her hands and sighed. "My dad cheated on my mom. It was stupid, and he was sorry. But my mom was devastated." Vivian took a shaky breath. "I came back to Darling to be with her for a while, and I couldn't bring myself to leave. If you had been in my shoes, you would've made the same choice."

Thomas blinked as the puzzle piece fell into place. "When we were in Juneau. That's what you meant when you said things don't go unnoticed in Alaska."

Vivian nodded. "The other woman was in Juneau. And people found out."

Thomas wrinkled his forehead. There was one thing that still didn't make sense. Where was the firecracker that he knew? This version of Vivian sounded resolved to her fate. And ironically, Thomas had spent his entire life fighting against his. "I understand that things were hard for a while. But what about the rest of your life? Your career? It's not like you need a boyfriend to open a restaurant."

"You don't understand." Her shoulders sagged. "I tried, and I failed, Thomas. My parents sold their shares in the store to my uncle so that they could invest in my restaurant. If they hadn't done that, if I had just stayed in Darling, we wouldn't be in this position right now. And I've given up on trying to get my money back from my ex."

Thomas rubbed the side of his face. "Please don't tell me this is the same asshole that cheated on you."

Vivian took a healthy gulp of wine. "The one and the same. The man was a genius in the kitchen, but his true talent is being a jerk. He was cheating on me while I came here to be with my mom after she had been cheated on. How's that for irony? And he must have a type because his new girlfriend ended up replacing me as the pastry chef too.
"

Thomas's jaw dropped. And he had thought he had it bad. This was outrageous. "I don't even know what to say."

"I don't think there's much to say to that." She let out a bitter laugh, and Thomas winced at the hopeless sound. "God, he put on such a good show. Acting so upset when I left. I bet he and that other woman popped the champagne the minute I checked in for my flight to Alaska."

Thomas felt sick to his stomach. No one deserved that kind of treatment. Definitely not someone as incredible as Vivian. "I'm so sorry. I wish there was something I could say."

"You don't have to say anything. I know you understand what it's like. Your fiancée cheated on you too, right?"

He worked his jaw. He hadn't loved Celeste that much, though. Heck, he might not have loved her at all. Their parents had set them up, and he had gone along with it. But Thomas understood what it was like not to feel like enough. Vivian had been betrayed by someone she had loved and trusted. Not feeling like enough must be all she had been left with. "Screw them. The best revenge is living well, right? Let's get another drink, and you can tell me your plans for once you buy the store."

She shook her head. "My plans? Staying right here. I thought that was obvious."

"That's what you *really* want?"

"Yes. Of course."

He searched her face for doubt. But there was none. Just a dogged determination to hold on to her life with both hands.

With a sigh, Thomas caught Wolfie's eye and signaled for another round. The barkeep had been keeping his distance, Thomas guessed to give them privacy. His cousin-in-law had been a psychologist before he stepped behind the bar, and he probably sensed that Thomas and Vivian wanted to talk alone. "Good for you."

She tilted her head. "You don't think it's a good idea?"

Thomas shrugged. Just because she wanted something that he couldn't understand didn't mean a damn thing. They might be getting married, but it wasn't like they were planning a future together. "Sweetheart, it's your life. The only opinion that matters is yours."

"So? I'm asking for your opinion."

He swallowed. Just like that, her words opened a tiny little crack in his world. No one ever cared about Thomas's opinion. That's how he found it so easy to not care about them. But Vivian cared. If not, she was doing a damn good job of pretending. "How about I ask *you* something? Do you really love sitting in that dusty old store, day after day? Same people? Same routine? No one is going to come in there and sweep you off your feet, you know."

"It's not dusty," she mumbled.

Thomas threw his hands up in the air. "Fine. You get my drift."

"Love isn't everything, you know." Her green eyes turned stormy, a steel edge to her voice. "You said no one is going to rescue me. Guess what, Thomas? Not everyone wants to be rescued. Not everyone dreams about happily ever after. I don't. Not anymore."

Thomas raised an eyebrow. "I stand corrected."

Wolfie came over briefly, pouring them another round before making himself scarce again.

Vivian picked up her wineglass, and without taking a drink, she set it back on the cardboard coaster. "I shouldn't. One glass is already a party for me."

Thomas leaned in. She smelled like sugar cookies. "Can I tell you a secret?"

"What's that?" Vivian moved closer to meet him halfway, so close he could see her individual eyelashes.

"Doing what you should never makes you very happy. Take it from someone with a lifetime of experience."

"Is that so?" She sat up again and reached for her glass, shooting him a warning look. "This is it. Just one more glass."

"Deal. I'll even walk you home."

She rolled her eyes. "It's just across the street."

Thomas nudged her shoulder, his skin tingling where it brushed hers. "Hey, you're my future wife. Let me take care of you."

Vivian let out a laugh, a bright, happy sound that beat back the shadows in his heart. "You're impossible."

He gulped. Shit. He was not falling for her. Getting married was complicated enough without real feelings. Vivian just brought the fun side out of him, that was all. And maybe he did the same for her.

And anyway, even if he was catching feelings, that didn't

change anything. She wasn't going to come to New York with him. Thomas wasn't going to stay in Darling. Even if in some crazy alternate universe he was interested, it could never work out.

His heart sagged. It was the story of his life. Everything Thomas wanted was just out of reach.

But that didn't mean he couldn't enjoy the time they had.

Thomas cleared his throat. "So, what do you want to do next in the Great Marriage Scheme? Should we take the dog out for a walk tomorrow? A small but mighty display of our couple status?"

Vivian giggled, and Thomas's heart skipped a beat. She really was quite pretty. "I think Trixie would like that."

He groaned. "Did you really have to name her Trixie? I don't want to chase after a dog and call out a name like that."

"Hey, be nice." Vivian stuck out her tongue. "The poor thing is probably being lectured by Uncle Robert about being a childless disappointment as we speak."

Thomas couldn't help it. He laughed. "You know, you're pretty funny."

"Oh yeah? Well, I think I finally know what to think of you."

"Something good, I hope. But I don't think I'm that lucky."

Vivian looked him in the eye. "I think you're a pretty nice guy. You rescue dogs. Help women buy their family stores. I mean, you can't be too bad."

Thomas held up his hands. "Hey, I'm not doing any of it from the goodness of my heart, you know."

"But you also don't need to do any of it. And that's what matters."

Her words melted a little of the ice around his heart. She didn't have to say anything nice just for the sake of it. They both knew where they stood with each other. But the thing was that when Vivian said something, he could believe it.

His gaze dropped to her mouth. Thomas could hear his own heart beating in his ears, drowning out the hum of conversation in the restaurant, the clinking of forks against plates, and the ever-playing jukebox. "You know, I think it would do a lot for our public image if I kiss you right now."

The corners of her mouth turned up. "Thanks for the warning this time."

Thomas swallowed, lifting his hand to cradle the back of her neck. Slowly, they moved closer to each other until his lips were pressed against hers.

He could taste the wine, feel the warmth of her mouth. She tasted like everything missing in his life. Goodness and honesty and conviction. She tasted the way water tastes to a man dying of thirst.

Thomas felt light-headed as he pulled back. What the hell was in that beer? Because there was no way he was actually falling for his future wife. That was not part of the plan. "Not too shabby for a second kiss."

Vivian gave him a look. "I hate to break it to you, but that was the third kiss."

He blinked. "What are you talking about?"

"You really don't remember." She sighed. "That night here, outside? Or maybe you don't. You were eating an entire pie. You must've been drunk as a skunk."

He shook his head. "I remember the pie. I don't remember kissing."

Vivian traced her finger along the bar top. "That's too bad. "

Thomas ran his hand over his face. "Vivian, I'm sorry. I don't remember at all. I shouldn't have—"

"If you're worried about hurting my feelings, don't be." She gave him a half-smile that he doubted she meant any more than he bought it. "Like I said before, I'm not looking for love. I just want my life back. I want something no one can take away from me."

Thomas rubbed the back of his neck. He *had* been drunk that night. And for most of his time in Darling. He had almost no alcohol tolerance when he arrived in Alaska, which was dangerous when combined with Wolfie's potent home brew.

But Thomas could also understand exactly what Vivian meant. So for this moment, he chose to focus on what they had in common. "I get that. Really. That's why I love the restaurant so much. It's mine. Not my dad's. Not my family's. Just mine."

"I want to know more about it. Your restaurant."

"Change of topic. One of my favorite techniques." He dipped his chin. "It's a French restaurant. Modeled after a brasserie."

"I love that." Her face softened. "We were going to open a French restaurant too. The plan was to go to Europe, eat everything, and then come back and create the place of our dreams."

Thomas couldn't help but smile. Vivian was pretty under the worst of circumstances, prairie girl clothes and all. But when she talked about what she loved? She was radiant. "Well, if you ever change your mind about growing old in Darling, I'm sure I could scrounge up a pastry chef job for you."

"How generous of you to scrounge up a job for your wife." She flashed him a teasing smile. "I'll keep that in mind."

"Just give me a heads-up. I might technically own the place, but the chef thinks he does. This is the first restaurant where he is a minority owner, and he's not adjusting well."

Vivian laughed. "If he's as good as you say, I'm not

surprised. Geniuses in the kitchen usually have big egos. I know firsthand."

"Then this guy must be the best chef to have ever lived because he is temperamental as hell. I knew Philippe was good—the best, really—but I didn't realize I was signing up for a weekly temper tantrum. Hopefully, that translates to the most incredible restaurant the East Village has ever seen, even though I know that's a tall order."

Her face paled slightly. "You don't mean Philippe Martin, do you?"

"You know him?" Thomas's eyebrows shot up his forehead. Then again, he shouldn't be surprised. She might be in the middle of nowhere now, but if Vivian had been in the cooking world, she would know who Philippe Martin was. Everyone knew who he was, even people whose only involvement with restaurants was eating at them.

Vivian looked caught somewhere between spitting mad and completely sick. "Know him? I dated him."

Thomas' eyes widened. His future wife used to date his restaurant's chef? The odds were next to impossible. It was just his luck. "No way. My Philippe is your piece-of-shit ex?"

She nodded, her face strained. "I know he's a good—great—chef. But I'm telling you, you can't count on him." Vivian looked Thomas in the eye. "Do you trust me?"

"Don't I kind of have to trust you?"

"Then get rid of him. Find a new chef."

Thomas's jaw dropped. Did she realize what she was asking? Why did it even matter to her so much? She and Philippe were ancient history. Ancient history who lived thousands of miles apart. It wasn't like he had anything to do with her anymore. "You can't be serious. Vivian, he's incredible. Having Philippe in the kitchen is the closest thing to guaranteed success I could hope for."

"You said he's an asshole."

"A *genius* asshole."

Vivian glared at him. "And how am I supposed to marry someone who is partners with my ex? How am I supposed to *trust* you now?"

Thomas's head spun. He understood that Philippe had hurt Vivian. But this was the definition of overreacting. If Thomas cut ties with everyone who had ever wronged him, he'd have to move to a deserted island to get away from them all. "Honestly? Because you have no other choice. The same way I don't."

She drained her glass of wine and stood. "I'm going home."

"I'll walk with you." Thomas placed a few bills on the counter. He'd probably find the money tucked under his pillow later. Wolfie and Charlotte wouldn't accept a dime if they could help it, family or not.

"It's fine, really."

"I promised." Thomas stood and scooted his stool back under the bar.

Vivian threw her hands in the air, turning on her heel. Thomas caught up with her in a few steps, and they walked back across the street in silence.

Once they stood in front of the store, he turned to face her. "I'll see you tomorrow, then?"

"I guess so. If we want to keep doing this."

He shook his head. "This? What do you mean?"

"This whole thing. This whole plan."

Thomas rested his hands on her arms gently, looking her in the eye. "I'm a man who keeps my promises, Vivian. One disagreement isn't going to change that."

She shrugged off his touch, and it was impossible not to take it personally. Because that was exactly the way she meant it. "I keep my promises too. I'll see you tomorrow."

Vivian opened the door and stepped inside, slamming the

door in his face. Thomas winced. Whether or not he had feelings for her, Thomas didn't think he had to worry about her catching feelings for him anytime soon. Or ever.

Thomas rubbed the back of his neck. God, he really couldn't win. First, he was too drunk to remember their kiss; now that thing with Philippe? But how the hell was Thomas supposed to know that was her ex-boyfriend? He didn't know that when he hired the guy. It wasn't like Thomas had done it on purpose.

But then again, he didn't have to do it on purpose. He just had a knack for screwing stuff up. Thomas had thought that getting the money from his trust would be the answer to all his problems. But it seemed his losing streak would follow him no matter what his bank account said.

Regardless, he couldn't fire Philippe. Even though Thomas understood Vivian's anger, it was an unreasonable request. She would realize that on her own soon enough, once the shock wore off. The restaurant meant too much to Thomas. It wasn't just a business. It represented the person he wanted to be. The life he wanted to live.

As he crossed the street, Thomas glanced up at the sky. Didn't sailors used to use the stars to navigate? Maybe there was a clue up there about what the hell Thomas should do. But the constant cloud cover hid even that from him.

Thomas didn't need to see the stars to know what he had to do. He wouldn't break his promise to Vivian. But the sooner they got this over with, the better. Vivian might be good for Thomas, but he was no good for her.

# CHAPTER FOURTEEN

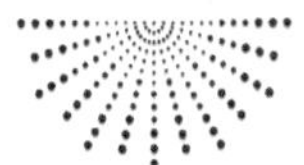

THOMAS

Whoever was calling him must have a death wish. Thomas had only gotten to bed a few hours ago, courtesy of one more detour to the bar after he'd walked Vivian home. He had needed another drink after their evening ended with a bang, and *not* the good kind.

The phone rang again, and Thomas let out a groan. There was no goddamn reason, good or bad, why anyone should need to talk to him right now. Couldn't it wait until a more civilized hour?

Thomas pulled the homemade quilt over his head, but the butter-soft fabric did absolutely nothing to drown out the obnoxious trill. It was his fault for not putting his phone on silent, but he hadn't needed to in Darling so far. Even given the time difference from New York, people rarely called him this time of day. The restaurant manager usually just emailed Thomas, and most of the work he did for his dad was via email as well.

After the third call, Thomas gave up and grabbed his

phone from the nightstand. Whoever it was clearly wasn't going to give up. Maybe if he yelled at the offender, Thomas could fall back asleep. But that plan vanished from his mind when he saw who was calling. "Vivian? What's going on? You should be asleep right now." He flopped back on his pillow. "*I* should be asleep right now."

Even though they had only spent a little less than two weeks together, Thomas knew one thing about Vivian already. She never minced words, at least not with him. And that was on a good day. After the way things ended last night, Thomas braced himself for no mercy. He was shocked she had called him at all, especially since they already had a plan to meet up later that required no talking.

Vivian sniffled. "It's Trixie. She ate chocolate. I don't know—"

Thomas sat up in bed, his annoyance replaced with worry. Vivian was *crying*? This was bad. The woman was usually tough as nails. "How did she get chocolate?"

Vivian hiccupped. "My room. I have this stash of chocolate. I know it's stupid. But I woke up, and she was finishing off an open package. I don't know...I don't know what to do. What if she's not okay? She's so small."

He took a deep breath. One of them had to be calm. "Where is the nearest vet?"

"Ketchikan, probably."

Thomas stood, pulling on yesterday's jeans with his free hand. "I'm going to see if Mac can fly us there ASAP."

"Thomas, I can't afford that. He's probably already booked today, anyway." She took a shaky breath. "We just have to wait for the ferry and hope for the best."

"Screw that. I'll take care of it. Just get ready to go."

How was he going to get in touch with Mac? Charlotte always arranged Marina and Thomas's connecting flight between Ketchikan and Darling.

After a moment's hesitation, he went and knocked on Charlotte and Wolfie's bedroom door. He felt awful for waking them up at this hour, but Thomas didn't have any time to waste right now. At least it wasn't too much earlier than they would've been up for breakfast service at the Buck anyway.

Wolfie opened the door, dressed in a bathrobe that had seen better days. His mustache stuck up at one end and down at the other. The older barkeep didn't look any more prepared for an emergency at this hour than Thomas was. But Wolfie sprung into action, giving Thomas the phone number for Mac and asking if there was anything else he could do.

Thomas saved the number to his phone. "So Mac. How much money do you think it would take for him to clear his schedule today?"

Wolfie's cockeyed mustache twitched. "Just say it's for a dog."

Thomas nodded and called Mac. Hopefully, he answered. But it seemed to be a morning of surprises because it only took two rings for Mac to grumble into the phone. Hadn't these people ever heard of airplane mode?

Thomas shot off a quick text to Vivian to update her and got ready to leave.

He didn't bother styling his hair or shaving. Who even cared? His mom wasn't there to lecture him on making a good impression. Not that there was anyone around to make a good impression on at this time of day.

Next, Thomas threw a change of clothes into a backpack, along with a toothbrush and his phone charger. That would have to be good enough. It wasn't like he was packing to go to the Maldives.

He hurried downstairs and across the street. Vivian

waited for him in front of the store, holding Trixie. "You got a bag packed?"

"Yep." She turned to show him the eggplant-purple backpack.

"Good. I don't know if we have to spend the night yet, but just in case. I've never had a dog before."

"Me neither."

He swallowed. Fine job they were doing of it.

Thomas peered at Trixie. Her beady black eyes watched him, but she didn't react. Didn't get excited or try to lick his face off. Shit. Now, he was worried about the damn dog.

"Okay, you." He lifted Trixie from Vivian's arms. "Let's take a trip."

The three of them headed up the road to Mac's dock. They were a long way from sunrise, but dawn peeked out and lit their way. Even though it was the middle of April, it felt more like winter. The morning was more than brisk, and Thomas could see his breath.

Mac waited for them next to his plane. "You ready?"

Vivian twisted her hands. "Mac, you don't have to do this. I know you're busy. And the money—"

"Don't worry about the money," Mac grunted. "You know I don't give a damn about that shit. Besides, your boyfriend here already promised to pay me a fortune."

Vivian paled. "He didn't."

"Yep." Mac bared his teeth in what might be a smile, but his bushy beard made it hard to tell. "Gotta tell Elle she can get that special fridge that she wants. Costs more than any fridge has a right to. Makes special ice or some stupid shit. Now, come on. Less talk, more go."

Mac helped Vivian into the plane first. Then, he took Trixie from Thomas and passed the dog to Vivian. The dog looked impossibly small and helpless in the man's giant arms.

Without offering Thomas so much as a hand up, Mac stomped around to the other side of the plane.

With a sigh, Thomas climbed into the plane. Nice to know what a fortune could buy a man around here. He secured his seat belt and put on the headset.

Mac came back around one more time, wordlessly slamming the door shut. Then he climbed into the cockpit and turned to face Thomas and Vivian. "You've both heard my safety speech before, right?" His voice crackled through the headset.

Thomas and Vivian nodded in unison.

"Good. Then we don't need to waste time on that today." Mac faced forward, the engine roaring to life. With an adjustment of the numerous knobs and dials in front of him, he guided them away from the dock. The plane glided across the water before a surge of power lifted it into the air.

Thomas looked out the window as Darling faded from his view, growing smaller and smaller until it disappeared behind them. The town blended in quickly, one of hundreds of islands that dotted the dark sea.

Thomas glanced at Vivian. Her face was strained as she lightly stroked Trixie's small head.

His throat grew thick, their argument last night suddenly so pointless. Instead, he was overwhelmed by how much he cared about the small dog and the woman who held her. Less than two weeks ago, the only thing that mattered was getting his trust fund and his restaurant succeeding. Now, all of that seemed as distant as the hundreds of islands that dotted the sea below the plane.

Thomas took a deep breath. It had been so much easier when he had less to love. How the hell had he gotten here?

If only they'd picked a different restaurant that night and never met that dog.

If only he'd never agreed to marry Vivian.

If only.

# CHAPTER FIFTEEN

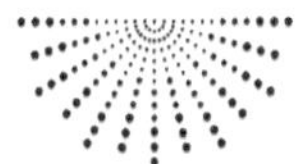

THOMAS

Even though Thomas didn't know Alaska well, he was fairly certain that Mac didn't take the long way to Ketchikan. But damn if that flight didn't feel like it lasted forever and a half. Stress, exhaustion, and worry pecked away at Thomas, making the flight pass painfully slow. A few times, he stared at his phone until the clock changed, wondering if maybe time had stopped altogether.

But they had gotten there eventually. Thanks to the early morning flight, Vivian and Thomas stood outside the door to the vet before it even opened. He may have screwed up countless times in his life, but he didn't want taking care of Trixie to be one of those times.

A car pulled into the parking lot, and a woman stepped out, eyeing them. Thomas guessed they looked a little disheveled from their early morning panic. "Can I help you?" she called out.

Vivian held up Trixie. "It's this dog. We just got her. She

ate chocolate. We live in Darling. I don't have a vet. We just got her—"

"So you said." The woman walked over, peering down at Trixie. "I'm Dr. Schafer, the vet on duty today. Let me go inside and get everything opened up, and I'll let you in. It'll just be a few minutes."

Vivian's brows squished together. "We don't have an appointment."

Dr. Schafer smiled. "No one ever does."

She unlocked the front door and stepped into the building. The windows lit up one by one, and Dr. Shafer ushered them inside only a few minutes later, as promised.

They gathered in an exam room, and the vet asked a few questions as she looked Trixie over. "You'll have to excuse me. My vet tech isn't in yet, and this is going to take a minute. Do you mind stepping into the waiting room?"

"Of course." Vivian nodded, but she didn't move. Clearly, she was still rattled. Thomas put his arm around her, guiding her back down the hall.

Unfortunately, there was nothing to distract them in the waiting room. There wasn't even a magazine to pretend to read. Only a few chairs decorated the space, not a single frill to be seen. If that didn't describe Alaska in a nutshell, Thomas didn't know what did.

Vivian wrapped her arms around herself, looking impossibly small and pathetic. She wore a plain rain jacket and a faded pair of jeans. Her face was bare, of course. Panicked or not, she never wore makeup. Even then, she was still pretty. Thomas felt bad for pointing out her lack of makeup before. She definitely didn't need it, and it was her prerogative if she wanted to wear it or not. But despite her good looks, her character was the most attractive thing about her. Maybe prairie girls *were* his type.

Once again, Thomas couldn't help but compare the woman in front of him to the woman he had almost married before. He remembered surprising Celeste with brunch one time. He had been excited about the food. She had been excited about being seen. Celeste took so long doing her makeup, hair, and whatever the hell she had to do that they missed the reservation. Maybe he should tell that little story to his dad the next time he brought up Thomas's failed engagement. One of the million reasons Thomas wouldn't have been happy with Celeste, not that his dad cared about that.

Thomas cleared his throat. "Trixie is going to be okay."

Vivian tipped her head back, gazing up at the ceiling. "How do you know? You're not a vet. You've never had dogs."

"The vet didn't seem too worried, for one. For two, that dog was living off garbage before we got her. She probably has the digestive system of a goat."

Vivian's lips twitched. "I suppose those are good points."

"What a momentous day. The day Vivian thought *maybe* I could be right. I'll never forget this."

She sighed and slumped into a chair. "I feel like such an idiot. I'm the one who did this to her."

Thomas sat next to Vivian. He understood how she was feeling. After all, he had a lifetime of experience screwing stuff up. On purpose or not, it made it hard to have compassion for oneself. "Stuff like this happens. Besides, it wasn't all bad."

Vivian looked at him. "How was it not all bad?"

He gave her a small smile. "I finally found out you do have a vice. Chocolate."

Vivian let out a laugh before her mouth turned down again. "I'm not sure I can even eat chocolate anymore. It'll just remind me what a horrible person I am."

"So horrible that you tried to find a solution right away and asked someone I am pretty sure you're mad at for help." He patted her back lightly. "Cut yourself some slack. Do you always hold yourself accountable for things out of your control?"

She picked at her jeans. "I've never thought about it like that."

Thomas rested his hands on his knees and stood. "Well, think about it. Otherwise, life is going to be rough, sweetheart."

Dr. Schafer stepped into the waiting room. "So far, so good. I would like to keep her for observation. Are you able to come get her in the morning?"

"No problem. We will be back tomorrow. Thank you so much for your help." He offered his hand to Vivian. "Come on, sweetheart."

Vivian bit her lip, looking between the vet and Thomas. Making her decision, she grabbed her backpack and took his hand. Which was almost nice, if she hadn't immediately dropped it once they were outside.

Thomas clapped his hands together. No bother. He finally had a problem he knew how to solve. One that involved money. "First things first. Breakfast and then a hotel. Separate rooms, of course. The usual."

"Are you sure?" Vivian glanced back at the vet's office one more time.

"Totally sure."

They found a restaurant on the water. Thomas was lured in by the seductive scent of freshly brewed coffee. He needed a good dose of caffeine.

Thomas and Vivian took a seat by the window, reminiscent of their dinner in Juneau. He ordered an omelet, and Vivian got chocolate chip pancakes.

"Careful." He flashed her a teasing smile. "Last time you ordered those, you ended up with a fiancé."

She giggled. "Thanks for the warning."

After he finished his breakfast, Thomas felt wide-awake despite almost no sleep. The three cups of coffee may have helped too.

Vivian didn't set down her fork until there were no pancakes left behind. It appeared chocolate wasn't ruined for her after all. "Almost as good as the Buck. And look, no extra fiancés."

Thomas chuckled. "What next? Do you want to get a hotel room and rest a bit?"

She lifted a shoulder. "I'm not really tired."

"Me neither. You know what I'm thinking?" Thomas smiled. "Let's be tourists for a day."

"Not exactly in the mood." Vivian played with her napkin.

"Being miserable all day isn't going to make Trixie better. Let's just enjoy it while we can."

She lifted her gaze. "I had no idea you were such an optimist."

"Don't you know me by now? I'm an *opportunist*." Thomas asked the server for the check.

Vivian eyed Thomas. "I thought all your money was tied up in the restaurant? How are you affording this?"

"Another gift from your father-in-law." Thomas held up his credit card. "Trust me, my dad treats family like a business anyway. He won't blink at this."

After they left the restaurant, they strolled down the street in the direction of the souvenir shops and did some window shopping.

"You weren't joking about this when we were in Juneau, were you?" Thomas flicked through a rack of T-shirts. Every single one of them had the word *Alaska* on it. "I think the true miracle is that your entire wardrobe doesn't have your state's name on it."

Vivian laughed. "You should get something for your dad."

"Oh, trust me, he doesn't need any reminders that I'm in Alaska."

She bit her lip. "Is he mad at you still? About the wedding?"

Thomas shrugged. When was his dad not mad at him? "I'm sure he is, but he hasn't said anything to my face. Beckers won't ever turn down the chance to fight, but they prefer to do it dirty."

She shuddered. "So you're just going to stay up here for the whole two months? No explanation? I couldn't stand to have my parents upset with me. And what about your job? And the restaurant?"

"The restaurant manager emails me regular reports. As far as working for my dad, he knows I'm here. I've wrapped up most of my projects anyway, and those left are close to completion. I usually like to be on-site as a project manager, but at this point, it can all be done by email." He tried on a baseball hat and peeked in the mirror. "And yeah, my parents probably aren't thrilled with me right now, but that's nothing new. Regardless, I'm sure they'll want to meet you soon enough. Just enjoy the peace while it lasts."

Vivian nodded. "Fair enough."

Thomas took her hand. He didn't want to think about all the problems waiting for him outside Alaska. He'd rather enjoy the day with Vivian. "Let's go. I think there is some jade jewelry we haven't seen yet."

They made their way down the street, stopping at every store. Thomas bought her a jade bracelet Vivian swore she would never wear. He insisted she needed a memory of her day in the big city, to which she rolled her eyes. Towards the end of the afternoon, the vet called them with an update.

Trixie was fine, but it would still be best to keep her overnight.

After hours of walking and getting the good news about Trixie, their appetites returned with a vengeance. They ate fish and chips by the water, throwing the occasional fry to the ravens. Boats floated by, and a single ray of sunshine peeked out from the clouds. It was almost kind of nice, at least for Alaska. But Thomas's favorite part of the day was spending it with Vivian.

As they cleaned up their picnic table, Thomas realized he wasn't just satisfied from the delicious lunch. He had a sense of emotional satisfaction too. He couldn't remember the last time he felt this way. Had he ever?

On their way back to the hotel, Thomas spotted a bright pink shop that promised cupcakes. "Room for dessert?"

Vivian rested her hand on her stomach. "No way. I'm stuffed."

"You're as skinny as a stick. No. A twig of a stick." He peered in the window. "They have three kinds of chocolate. Come on. Consider it industry research."

"You're impossible," she muttered, following him into the shop.

Thomas bought one of every kind of chocolate and a carrot cake cupcake for himself. Vivian swore she couldn't possibly eat another bite at that moment, so they took their bounty back to the hotel. It only took the short walk for Vivian to decide she did have an appetite for dessert after all.

Maybe it was the exhaustion—delirium, really—mixed with the adrenaline of the day and the relief of knowing Trixie was okay. But as they sat on the bed and talked about nothing in particular, Thomas couldn't get over how happy he felt.

Under any other circumstance, Thomas would've been anything but content. Not only was he exhausted from no sleep and worrying about the dog all morning, but the hotel was far from pleasant. The room was god-awful. The bed creaked, the carpet was permanently smashed flat, and the entire place smelled like mildew. It had been the best he could find at a moment's notice.

Not that Vivian noticed. She was more excited about the little soaps in the bathroom and the hot tea available in the lobby. Thomas was beginning to think it wasn't the worst thing that she had wasted years on that little island. At least she could still enjoy life.

The interesting thing was that Thomas was enjoying life more lately too. Not that he wanted to make a habit of only sleeping two hours before diving headfirst into an emergency. But he thought less and less about what his dad thought or Celeste's face when he told her he couldn't marry her.

In fact, there was only one face he thought about. A face that currently had a smear of chocolate buttercream next to full lips. He reached out with a napkin, gently wiping away the frosting. "You got a little something right there."

Her cheeks turned pink, and dammit if she wasn't the prettiest thing he had ever seen. He gulped. When did she go from prairie girl to perfect? "I probably look disgusting, sitting here stuffing myself with cupcakes."

He gave her a reassuring smile, remembering that her self-confidence was more delicate than the cupcake she held. "You look like you're enjoying yourself. It's a good look. You should do it more often."

"Maybe." She lifted the corner of her mouth. "Things just seem like more fun with you."

His heart skipped a beat. Finally, something they could agree on. In fact, suddenly, he couldn't remember anything he didn't like about her.

The sugar high and tiredness and relief swirled

together, pushing Thomas towards her. "Speaking of fun, I think we need to redo that first kiss. Since I botched the first one."

She smiled. "I suppose one more kiss wouldn't hurt."

Before he could talk himself out of it, his lips found hers. They were warm and soft and tasted like chocolate. Vivian pressed into him, and Thomas's body turned hot enough to melt a glacier. He finally pulled away with a gasp. "Damn you."

"Damn me?" she whispered, her eyes half-closed. "Why?"

"You're irresistible. That's why." Thomas stood, gathering the trash from the bed and tossing it in the garbage can. He paced the room, running a hand through his hair. "Is it hot in here? I think it's hot in here."

Vivian's gaze followed him. "Thomas? What's wrong?"

He swallowed. Good question. What the hell *was* wrong with him? He shouldn't want this. Shouldn't do it. They both knew how this ended, and it wasn't with them together. Not that he even wanted a real relationship, right? Or at least he hadn't until Vivian had walked up to him one day and suggested they get married. Thomas would've been content with someone he could at least respect. But not only could he respect Vivian, he wasn't even sure he deserved a woman like her. "I'm leaving. You're staying. This is a business deal, remember? Not a relationship."

"Exactly. We know what to expect from each other. No one is going to end up with a broken heart." She patted the bed, and Thomas bit back a groan. This wasn't happening. And yet, he'd never wanted anything more. "Now, if you don't get over here, I'm going to think there's something wrong with me."

Before another second passed, Thomas pounced on her with a growl. It might not be the smartest move. But he couldn't very well let her think there was something wrong with her, could he? Nothing was wrong with Vivian Locke. In fact, everything was very, very right.

It was a thought that scared him to death. Thomas had first partnered with Vivian so that he wouldn't lose everything. It never occurred until now to him how much he had to gain.

# CHAPTER SIXTEEN

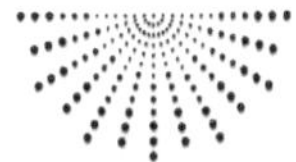

VIVIAN

Vivian had no idea where she was. She was walking somewhere. She thought it might be a house, but nothing made sense. A door opened up to another door. When Vivian walked downstairs, she somehow went up. Walls faded away and then reappeared in front of her. She tried to run, to get out, but all the doors disappeared. Then a wall vanished, she tripped, and suddenly, she was falling through the air, down, down, down...

She shook awake, and her body sagged with relief. It was just a dream. She was in her hotel room in Ketchikan. Everything was fine. Trixie was fine.

A man groaned next to her, and the bed shifted. Her eyes grew wide as last night came back to her. Everything was *not* fine.

This was a hotel room in Ketchikan, alright, but it wasn't *her* hotel room. Her room had a bed that hadn't yet been slept in and a bar of soap that had been used only once.

It was *his* room. Thomas's room. Where she had spent the night.

Vivian squeezed her eyes shut. What had she been thinking? Had she been drunk on cupcakes?

But she knew the answer, and it had nothing to do with buttercream. Vivian could see the Wheel of Fortune card clear as day in her mind's eye.

*You make your own luck.*

Vivian gulped. Oh, she had done that and more. She had been exhausted yesterday, true. But she couldn't blame delirium.

She was fed up with reacting to life. Just for once, Vivian had wanted to do something on purpose. And if that something had been sleeping with Thomas this one time, what was so wrong with that?

Nothing, as far as she could tell. They were getting married, after all. Ketchikan at least offered an iota more privacy than Darling. And, most importantly, Thomas was the safe choice. She already knew exactly where this relationship was heading: nowhere.

Vivian had never had a one-night stand in her life, and there was no way she would ever do it with an actual stranger. While she had only spent the last two weeks with Thomas, Vivian knew enough about him to not completely despise him anymore. In fact, she kind of liked him.

Thomas was a hard worker. And more than that, he didn't give up easily. From what she had seen, he didn't give up at all. Not even when so many other people would have. Thomas had spent years working under stressful circumstances to achieve his dream, and now he was working two jobs at once. He was nice to Trixie, despite grumbling about her name. And it didn't hurt that Thomas was relatively good-looking.

Her body warmed at the memory of last night. Okay, *fine.* Maybe more than relatively.

But did she *really* know Thomas? Was he actually different from any other rich guy? Philippe had his good points too, or she never would've been interested in him in the first place. Look how that had ended. And now Philippe worked with Thomas, the thought of which irked her all over again.

Vivian shook it off. She was getting ahead of herself. That was the thing about a one-night stand: it only happened once. After today, this whole thing would be a distant memory. Besides, did she really think a guy like Thomas, a guy who had *everything,* would really be interested in a girl like her for more than a short fling?

But one last peek couldn't hurt.

She rolled over slowly, inch by inch, turning to face Thomas. His dark lashes fanned out against his golden skin, his face perfectly framed by a strong brow and distinct cheekbones. A lock of hair flopped over his forehead while another curled around his ear.

Her pulse quickened. He was definitely more than relatively good-looking.

She smiled to herself, a smidge less regretful about waking up in his bed this morning. When in Rome and all that. Or when in Ketchikan, at the very least.

Vivian's gaze traveled just over his shoulder to the clock on the nightstand. According to the glowing red numbers, they had to get up in forty-five minutes.

The plan was to pick up Trixie when the vet first opened. Mac would be back an hour after that. It was early, but that way, Mac wouldn't have to cancel the flight he had booked for later the same day.

Vivian leaned back against the bed and stared up at the ceiling, feeling surprisingly well rested.

She had thought she wouldn't sleep at all. Thomas had offered to walk her back to her room or even swap with her if she preferred, always the gentleman. But Vivian had refused both offers, cuddling up next to him instead. If she was going to have the guilt, then she wanted the pleasure that went with it.

"Good morning, beautiful." Thomas's voice was husky. He draped an arm across her midsection and cozied up closer.

Vivian all but held her breath, trying to make herself as small as possible. She didn't know what to do with her hands. Clearly, Thomas had experienced more of these kinds of mornings than Vivian.

She stiffened. Was that really a surprise? A handsome, rich man had different expectations in life. He might be nice, but that didn't mean he was different from any other rich guy. All the more reason sleeping together could only happen once. Anything else would be setting herself up for heartbreak. "Morning."

Thomas blinked one eye open. "You okay?"

She gave him a small smile. "Fine."

"Oh, that's convincing." He gave her a squeeze. "Just relax."

Vivian let out a huff. *Just relax.* Easy for him to say. If she relaxed, she'd have to admit how much she enjoyed being with him. How it was both the strangest and most wonderful feeling. If she let herself relax, she would have to face him leaving one day. It seemed the brave woman last night had disappeared into her dream, leaving only plain old Vivian.

Thomas opened his other eye and glanced over his shoulder at the time. "It is way too early to be awake."

"We have to get the dog—"

"I know, I know. But can you blame me for wanting to lie in bed all morning with a beautiful woman?"

Her face warmed, and she commanded her body to get a hold of itself. It was just a line.

"Do you want to tell me what you're thinking? Or just lay there, all tensed up?" Thomas played with a strand of her hair. "Good thing Trixie isn't with us now. You're anxious enough to make her howl."

She scooted away. "Don't."

"Don't what? Because it's too late for some things." Thomas smiled wryly.

"Not that." Vivian huffed. "Don't be nice. Don't say all the right things. Because we both know how it ends. I don't want either of us to have false expectations."

"False expectations?" He propped himself up on an elbow. "What are you talking about?"

Vivian sat up, holding the sheet to her chest, even though Thomas was right. It was too late for some things. "We both know this was a onetime thing, Thomas. You don't have to be, you know, all touchy-feely."

She twisted as she stepped out of bed, wrapping the sheet around herself. Vivian had to get out of here. How could she have possibly thought this was a good idea? All she had done was complicate an already complicated situation. With only a little more than six weeks until escrow closed, that was the last thing she needed.

Vivian picked her clothes out of the heap on the floor with one hand as she held up her makeshift toga with the other. All the while, Thomas lay in bed and watched her silently. She glared at him. "What are you looking at?"

"I think I'm finally figuring you out."

Vivian barked a laugh. "Oh? Please enlighten me. I'm curious about what you've discovered in a couple weeks that I haven't figured out in almost three decades."

"The minute you get something good, you're already preparing yourself for it to disappear. It's like you'd rather have nothing at all than care too much and be disappointed. No wonder you're so desperate to hold on to your store—"

"Desperate!" she shrieked.

"That was a poor choice of words. Sorry." Thomas held up a hand. "What I'm saying is, I don't know what made you so scared to be happy, but there is nothing wrong with enjoying this moment, Vivian."

She clutched her clothes to her chest, her stomach twisted in a knot that would confuse a sailor. "That's exactly what I said. This was just a *moment*. So why are we even still talking about it?"

Thomas sat up in bed, looking at her as if she were some kind of wild animal that didn't realize he was trying to help her, not hurt her. "Is that what you're worried about? For God's sake, Vivian. I am going to buy the store for you. I flew the damn dog here at a moment's notice. And, oh yeah, we're going to get *married* regardless of sleeping together or not."

He ran a hand through his hair. "I'll let you in on a little secret. One-night stands aren't nearly that much work. I hope it's obvious I actually care about you. That I'm not the total piece of garbage you are making me out to be. I wasn't even sure we should do this, remember? I never want you to feel pressured to do anything you don't want to. If you want this to be a onetime thing, fine. I'll never bring it up again."

Vivian swallowed. He had a point. But that didn't do anything to quiet the fear in her heart. "What do *you* want?"

He held her gaze. "That's easy. What I want is for you to not hold yourself back from life. To not torture yourself when you do live a little. Vivian, you're incredible. You deserve a life to match."

Thomas stood from the bed and reached for his shirt on the floor, the muscles of his back rippling with the movement.

Her stomach flip-flopped and not just from his good looks. Thomas was right, of course. That only made her more upset. Maybe Vivian wasn't confused. Maybe she was just incapable of being honest with herself. But didn't Thomas deserve honesty in between all the lies? Didn't she? "Thomas. Wait."

He pulled on his shirt and looked at her. "What is it?"

She gulped; the olive branch was in her hands, apparently. But would he take it? "You said it yourself last night. This is going to end sooner rather than later. You'll leave Darling, and I'll stay here."

"And *you* said no one is going to end up brokenhearted."

She nodded, her throat tight. Apparently, her lying streak was going hot. Because at this point, she didn't see herself escaping with her heart intact.

Vivian had seen what had happened with her parents. She had lived through it herself. She knew what heartbreak could do to a person. Her mom wasn't the only reason that Vivian had hidden herself away in Alaska. It was safe there. In Darling, she knew what to expect, even if it wasn't what she truly wanted. "I have too much to lose, Thomas."

He crossed the room, his dark hair gleaming in the morning light that skirted around the dicey blinds. Thomas pulled her close, his sandalwood scent instantly causing her brain cells to abandon her. "Some things are worth the risk, sweetheart. Being happy is one of them."

Her heart squeezed, and Vivian fought to keep her feet on the ground. "You don't know what you are talking about. You were just engaged, for God's sake."

"To someone I didn't love. Didn't even like."

"You hate it here," she mumbled into his shoulder. "You'll get your money and leave."

"Or maybe we'll just take lots of vacations."

"You told me I look like a prairie girl."

"Did I? Then let me be the first to say prairie girls are my type."

Vivian stepped back, resting her hands on his chest and looking up at him. "What are we doing here?"

He smiled. "Getting married, last I heard."

Vivian shook her head. "It didn't seem this complicated when we first made the plan."

"How about a new plan? One just for this morning? I promise it's *very* simple."

"And what exactly would that be?"

Thomas took her hand, guiding her back in the direction of the bed. "We have just enough time to get a little more money's worth out of the room before we need to be at the vet."

Her pulse fluttered. "Forget it." But it sounded like a bluff even to her own ears.

"Not even a quick cuddle?" He gave her a mischievous smile. "Come on, sweetheart. If you're going to do the time, at least do the crime."

Despite her best intentions, Vivian couldn't stop herself from mirroring his smile. It was Thomas's fault. He always found a way to make her feel better.

But all the unknowns still hung over her head. They hadn't solved anything, not really. Thomas hadn't promised to stick around forever, and Vivian hadn't exactly asked him to. How could she when she wasn't even sure that was what she wanted?

Still, he had a good point. They were already in this deep. Why not enjoy it, no matter how long things lasted?

She took a deep breath, squaring her shoulders. Screw it. A few more minutes were not going to make or break her.

Vivian dropped the sheet, and Thomas swooped her up. She giggled as he carried her across the room.

Her heart squeezed as he gently placed her on the soft

bed. Their kiss at the Buck was supposed to be a onetime thing. So was sleeping with him last night. It was quickly becoming apparent to her that once was never enough when it came to Thomas. Suddenly, her strange dream from last night made a lot more sense.

Vivian was falling, alright. Falling in love, fool that she was. To think she had thought Thomas was the safe choice.

# CHAPTER SEVENTEEN

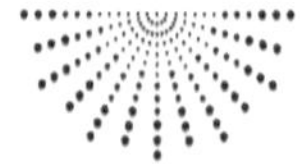

THOMAS

"So, how is it going? And tell me the truth. Save the BS for everyone else." Marina leaned against the doorway of his bedroom.

Thomas pulled off his shoes and tossed them aside. The last thing he wanted to do after getting back from Ketchikan was discuss his personal life with his sister. He was exhausted and off his game. Which was exactly what made it the perfect time for her to ask whatever questions she wanted. Had Marina been taking evil genius lessons from their father? "It's going fine. Better than fine, actually."

Marina narrowed her eyes. "Do you mean what I think you mean?"

He cracked his knuckles. Marina might be a pain in his neck sometimes, but he could trust her. Maybe she could help him sort out his own confused thoughts. "So what if I do? We're getting married, after all."

"So what?" Marina gaped at him. "Let me count the ways. This family is a tar pit. You just broke off an engagement. You're planning on getting divorced in six months." She spread her hand wide, all five fingers extended in the air.

"I think your counting is off."

Marina barked a laugh. "I should hold up all ten fingers and ten toes too." She shook her head. "I can't believe you're actually falling for her. I knew this was going to bite you in the ass."

Thomas rubbed the side of his face. Sleeping with Vivian had definitely been a mistake, not that his sister knew that little detail. Before he and Vivian had spent the night together, Thomas had actually believed they could both pull off this scheme without getting emotionally involved. Now, *complicated* didn't even begin to describe it. "Well, you were right. Does that make you happy?"

Marina sighed. "I knew you were doomed when I saw you two at the Buck that night."

Thomas frowned. Just like he had told Vivian, he didn't remember much from that night. Definitely not his finest moment. This was why he rarely drank back home. "I don't remember seeing you when I was with Vivian."

"Shocker." Marina rolled her eyes. "You were in your own little love bubble."

His chest felt tight, and he stood from the bed. "Marina, I swear. It's not love, and you know it."

"Then why are you getting all worked up?"

He ran a hand through his hair. Good question. But it definitely wasn't love. It was too soon for that. Right? Thomas had enough to deal with before adding love to the mix. "Shit, I don't know."

"Thomas." Marina's voice was quiet, the scolding tone replaced with concern. "I know things aren't going exactly according to plan, but you can't chicken out now. It's going to suck whether you end things now or later, so you might as well have a stack of money to show for your trouble. Plus, you don't want to let Vivian down."

He sank back down on the bed. The springs squeaked, sounding as tired as he felt. Marina was right about following through. But there was one point he didn't agree with: why did he have to end things with Vivian at all?

Thomas knew the answer to that already. Because it was crazy. Vivian never wanted to leave Darling. Thomas never wanted to stay here. It was simple math. Even an idiot like him could figure it out.

But she had left before, hadn't she? Was it too crazy to think she might take a chance on him? Thomas might not be the most desirable man on earth, but he certainly wasn't the least either.

The two of them wouldn't be the worst pairing in the world. Maybe he could make Vivian happy. She was an incredible baker and at one point was interested in the restaurant business herself. Thomas already had a restaurant, and he could open the next one with her in mind. Then, they could both do what they loved. It was almost perfect.

His shoulders sagged. But there was his family to consider. *Tar pit* wasn't too far from the truth. It was one thing for Vivian to marry into the Becker family when she was three thousand miles away. It was another thing to be part of it if she and Thomas tried for a real relationship. Did he really want to subject her to his miserable family dynamics?

The alarm on his phone blared, and Thomas switched it off. This wasn't the day to figure this out. Besides the fact that he was exhausted, Vivian's parents had been so grateful that he had helped save Trixie that they invited him over for a special dinner. The invitation extended to Marina too. "We gotta go."

"Ready when you are." Marina gave him a pointed look.

"But we need to finish this conversation later. You can't avoid real life, Thomas."

With a grumble, he slipped his shoes back on, and they headed out. Even though Vivian's parents were nice, a family meal was the last thing he was in the mood for right now. But it at least gave Thomas the opportunity to avoid his sister's questions until he had a good night's sleep. Maybe everything would make more sense tomorrow.

His shoulders relaxed as he walked downstairs. He was getting himself worked up for nothing. It was going to be fine. Just a nice, quiet dinner. Not to mention delicious if Vivian had helped prepare it. Then he'd come home and sleep like a rock.

No sooner had Thomas stepped foot outside on the worn wooden walkway than he heard a sound that chilled his spine to Arctic temperatures.

"Thomas, Marina! Perfect timing!" a familiar voice called out.

Marina glanced at Thomas, her face a shade paler. "You don't think…"

"That's exactly what I think." Bracing himself, Thomas looked to the left to see his worst nightmare stepping out of Mac's truck.

Thomas wasn't sure which was more shocking. That his parents were in Alaska or that the Darling gossip mill hadn't warned him ahead of time. Then again, Mac was a man of few words, and none of them were ever gossip. If he was the only person who knew they were coming, then no one else probably did. And Mac likely assumed that Marina and Thomas already knew about the visit, the way a family that wasn't completely dysfunctional might.

Panic flooded Thomas's body as he walked up to his parents. This was the last thing he needed right now. "You didn't mention that you were coming."

Mac shot Thomas a funny look but said nothing. Yep. The pilot clearly had no idea that this visit was a surprise for the Becker children.

"Hopefully, you aren't too busy." It was his dad's version of a joke, as if someone could fill a calendar in this place. That's how it always was with him. It was what his dad didn't say that said everything.

"We actually have plans," Marina piped up. "We're going to dinner at Thomas's girlfriend's house."

His dad lifted a dark brow. "I'm sure they can set the table for a couple more."

"You really want to have dinner with my girlfriend right now? You just got here." Thomas glanced back at the restaurant. "I'm sure Charlotte is excited to see you."

His mom waved her hand. "She doesn't even know we're coming. It would've ruined the surprise!"

Mac coughed, lifting two small suitcases from the back of the truck and setting them down. "I'll bring the rest tomorrow." He climbed back into the truck and drove off down Main Street.

Thomas's mouth went dry while his brain grasped at words. The rest? He turned to his parents. "And, uh, how long are you staying?

His father lifted a shoulder. "That remains to be seen. We're playing this trip by ear."

The gears in Thomas's mind ground to a halt. As if his dad ever did anything without a plan. And Thomas would bet that the plan for this trip centered around his new relationship.

He had mentioned it to his mom the same day Vivian had promised her uncle that she would be able to buy the store. Thomas had known it was only a matter of time before his parents butted in. He just hadn't planned on a complete ambush.

"Then it's settled. We'll join you." His mom smiled, her brown eyes warm. She must be where Marina got her peace-keeping gene from. Thomas and his dad preferred to keep the boxing gloves on full-time.

"We're *so* looking forward to meeting your new girl-friend." His father looked like the cat who ate the canary.

Thomas worked his jaw. Oh, who was he kidding? No gloves needed.

"I'll help you upstairs, and then we can walk over together once you're settled in." Marina picked up one of the suitcases. "Thomas, you should go to Vivian's and see if she needs help with anything."

Thomas nodded. He definitely owed Marina one. She had bought Thomas something he desperately needed: time. "Sounds like a plan. See you all there. And no rush—I'm sure you're tired from the trip."

"Tired? Not at all." His dad smirked as he picked up the other suitcase and followed the women inside.

Thomas glared, his body hot. To think he had thought things were complicated before his parents showed up.

He charged across the street, the chill of the ever-present mist doing nothing to cool him down.

Change of plans. Thomas had to do something big and soon. With only two and a half months until his thirtieth birthday, the time for playing it safe had come and gone.

# CHAPTER EIGHTEEN

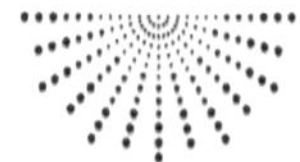

THOMAS

So much for a quiet family meal.

The seven of them squeezed in around the Lockes' dinner table, which comfortably fit four. Vivian's parents hadn't blinked an eye at the extra guests. In fact, they were more excited to spend time with his parents than Thomas or Marina were. If that didn't sum up the Becker family dynamics, Thomas didn't know what did.

His mom flaked off a delicate bite of grilled salmon. "This is delicious, Vivian. You're a wonderful cook."

"Thank you." Vivian smiled, seeming to have recovered from her initial shock at his parents' impromptu visit. He understood the feeling, and they were his own family. There was a reason Thomas had warned her against meeting them when she had asked about it a few days ago.

Marina must've given his parents some kind of pep talk because so far, his dad had actually been polite. Thomas didn't worry about his mom. She always had impeccable manners, no matter the situation. Simone Becker could be dropped onto a battlefield and not have one feather ruffled.

But his dad excelled at being a perfect ass, and while Thomas sometimes struggled to stand up for himself, he wouldn't tolerate his dad being rude to Vivian or her family. They deserved to be treated with respect.

Thomas helped himself to salad, trying not to bump Vivian or Marina on either side of him in the process. The cozy dinner table was a far cry from his parents' huge dining room back in New York. But Thomas felt more at home in Darling than he ever had in his parents' house. He couldn't help but think Vivian had something to do with that. "If you think dinner is good, just wait until you try dessert. Vivian is a talented pastry chef. Went to cooking school and everything."

"What an interesting coincidence." His dad took a sip of wine, his dark gaze trained on Vivian. "You must know that Thomas has a restaurant?"

Thomas tensed. Vivian hadn't asked him about firing Philippe again, but he figured that had more to do with Trixie's emergency than anything. Hopefully, the mention of the restaurant wouldn't remind Vivian of their argument and upset her all over again. This family dinner was stressful enough as it was.

But Vivian just nodded. "Funny enough, I almost opened a restaurant myself."

His dad lifted an eyebrow. "Seems like you two have a lot in common."

Vivian's mom helped herself to another sourdough roll, adding a generous pat of butter. "They sure do. These kids are too cute together. And the way Thomas took care of that little dog? It still melts my heart."

His mom smiled and glanced at Trixie, who sat on her dog bed in the corner. Pets weren't part of the Becker household and definitely not inside animals. But again, his mom's feathers were perfectly smooth. "She is a *very* cute dog. I'm glad she's okay."

When Thomas had first introduced everyone, Vivian's parents had explained the reason for the special dinner. He had braced himself for some smart-ass comment from his dad, but Stefan Becker only smiled and nodded. Thomas didn't know whether to be thankful for his dad's good behavior or suspicious. But if life had taught Thomas anything, it was that suspicion was the safer bet.

His dad reached for his wine. "So, Vivian. Do you still have plans to open that restaurant someday?"

She shook her head. "Darling is too small."

"Outside of Darling, then?" His dad tilted his head.

Vivian gave him a small smile. "I don't see myself leaving. Besides, I enjoy cooking at home. It's a much less critical audience than fine dining."

Thomas's mom dabbed at her mouth with a napkin. "I'm stuffed, but I already can't wait to try dessert. Dinner was incredible, and that isn't even your specialty, Vivian. I can't imagine how good your baking must be."

"It'll be even better," Thomas promised. That's how it was with Vivian. Things always got better. Unlike everything else in his life, which always seemed to get more difficult.

Vivian blushed. "If you like carrot cake, that is."

His mom's face lit up. "That's Thomas's favorite. He always has it on his birthday." She smiled at him. "Lucky you, you don't have to wait until July."

Vivian's mom looked at Thomas. "Your birthday is in July? That's so funny. So is Vivian's. What day?"

Thomas nearly choked on his salmon and took a gulp of water. He pounded his fist against his chest as he coughed. "Sorry. Went down the wrong way."

Hopefully, no one deduced the *real* reason he was flustered. Thomas had been so focused on his upcoming birthday, and the ticking clock that went with it, that he had never thought to ask when his future wife's birthday was. Apparently, Thomas was giving his dad a run for his money for being the biggest ass in the Becker family. "It's July first."

Vivian made a little sound, reaching for her own water.

Her mom's jaw dropped. "Incredible. You two have the same birthday!"

Goose bumps rose on Thomas's arm, luckily hidden beneath long sleeves. If he needed a sign that he was doing the right thing tonight, he had it. "That *is* incredible."

Vivian's mom nodded. "Same birthday. Same age. And you both lived in New York!"

Thomas almost lost his composure again, but Marina saved his bacon with her own shock. She gaped at Vivian. "You did? I didn't know that."

Vivian gave a small nod, a shade paler. "Yes. That's where I studied pastry arts. Then I stayed to work for a few years. It's a wonderful city."

Thomas felt like an idiot. Of course. The other restaurants Philippe had ownership in were in New York too, one of which was presumably the place he had wrangled away from Vivian. Thomas had no idea what to say.

But luckily, that wasn't a problem just then. With more common ground between them, conversation between their parents picked up, and Marina joined in too. Their dad even managed to keep his polite demeanor for the rest of the dinner. It was a damn miracle.

Thomas, however, stayed quiet when at all possible. He still felt dumb for not knowing these things about Vivian. He noticed that she didn't say much either. Did she have the same questions running through her head? How was it possible they hadn't known these things about each other? Shouldn't people know each other better before they get married? At the same time, wasn't having so much in common a good thing?

The more Thomas got to know Vivian, the more he admired her as a person. After their time in Ketchikan, it was clear that they had chemistry. Then came the revelations tonight. Everything seemed to point to the same conclusion: this could be so much more than a fake relationship.

After they had dessert, Thomas's parents, Marina, and Vivian's dad went to the living room to enjoy a glass of port. That left Vivian, her mom, and Thomas.

Vivian shooed him away, gathering up the empty bowls. "Go relax. Catch up with your family. I've got this."

"I want to help you." Thomas picked up the silverware and napkins.

She set the bowls in the sink. "It's fine. My mom is helping me."

"Please. Don't make me go sit in that living room. I can't take it anymore."

Her lips twitched. "Fine. You can dry."

She threw a dish towel at him, and Thomas caught it easily, taking his spot next to her at the kitchen sink. Had it really only been two days since he had been standing right here? Yet it felt like a lifetime had happened since then.

While they started on the dishes, Vivian's mom wiped down the counters and the table. Once finished, she joined everyone else in the living room, leaving them alone.

Thomas stepped closer to Vivian, lowering his voice. "That wasn't so bad."

She nodded. "I'm glad I finally met them. Your dad is nicer than I thought."

Thomas bit back a laugh. She could say that again. He had never seen his dad act so nice. If only Thomas could shake the feeling that it meant something was wrong. "I can't believe I didn't realize you lived in New York before. And how funny is it that we have the same birthday? Although I guess it's even funnier that our parents figured it out at the same time we did."

Her face strained. "Yeah. Hilarious."

Thomas frowned as he dried a plate. "Is something wrong?"

Vivian scrubbed the pan a little more vigorously than necessary, fine wisps of dark hair escaping from her ponytail. "Don't you think that's problematic? I mean, shouldn't we get to know each other *before* we get married? *Really* get to know each other?"

Thomas dried a wineglass. He had the same doubts as her, but none of them outweighed everything they had to gain by going through with their plan. He would get his trust fund, and Vivian would get her store. But it was more than that. Going through with the plan would also give them a chance to discover if there was more than a mutually beneficial relationship between the two of them. Something they didn't have the time to do before they got married if they wanted a chance at getting the trust. "Where were these morals when we first made the deal, huh?"

"That's before I knew you." Vivian dried her hands, turning to lean against the sink. "Back when I thought you were just rich and spoiled, and there wasn't much else to know."

"Oh, yeah?" Thomas moved closer to Vivian, resting his hands on the counter on either side of her. "And what do you think now?"

She bit her lip, that full, perfect lip, and his stomach jerked with lust. "I still think you're rich and spoiled. But now I like you."

"Like me, huh?" He gave her a quick kiss. Thomas's feelings were a lot stronger than *like*, but he'd take what he could get from Vivian. After everything he'd learned about her tonight, he was even more certain about marrying her. Even if it never amounted to more than a friendly arrangement, at least it was an arrangement with someone he respected. "Then you're going to really love tonight's second act."

Her forehead wrinkled. "Huh? What are you talking about?"

Thomas took her hand. He couldn't tell her. Surprise was a critical component. "You'll see."

He led them to the living room, Trixie trotting at their heels. Thomas could hear his own heartbeat pounding in his ears. He knew he had to do this. But that didn't mean he wasn't terrified.

Thomas cleared his throat. "I'd like to say something."

The room grew quiet as everyone turned to look at Vivian and Thomas. She shot him a panicked look, and he forced a small smile, even though he felt just as scared. But with only six weeks until escrow closed and his parents in Darling, there wasn't a better time than this.

Thomas reached into his pocket and got down on one knee, holding the ring between his thumb and pointer finger. Vivian let out a gasp and took a step back, but he kept her hand firmly in his. "Vivian Locke, will you marry me?"

When Thomas had proposed to Celeste, there had been no surprises. She had even picked out her own ring. Celeste saved the shock value for cheating on him.

So with that as his only point of reference, Thomas didn't know if it was normal for the future bride to look like she was about to barf. It wasn't like getting married was a surprise to her. But maybe the public proposal hadn't been a great idea. "Vivian?"

"Yes, of course. Yes." She gave him the world's smallest smile.

Thomas slipped the ring on her finger. He was proud of himself for thinking of purchasing the fake diamond when he spotted it at a tourist shop in Ketchikan. He had bought it just in case. Tonight was the perfect time to deploy it.

Vivian's mom leapt from the couch and wrapped her daughter in a hug. "Sweetheart, I'm so happy for you."

Vivian's dad came up to Thomas, shaking his hand. "I'm happy too, even if it *is* a bit soon."

Thomas smiled. "When you know, you know."

Trixie barked and spun in a circle at the hullabaloo.

"Congratulations, big brother." Marina patted Thomas's shoulder, seeming almost resigned. He didn't see any point in finishing their conversation from earlier today as promised. He might not have made it to the altar before, but there was no backing out now. He wouldn't let Vivian, or himself, down.

His mom's good manners didn't fail her as she hugged Thomas. "Oh, honey. I'm so glad we were here for this."

His father stood silently at the side of the room, which was a small blessing. Thomas knew his dad. He wasn't just upset. He was formulating a counterattack. Hopefully, it wouldn't be a public one.

Vivian's dad clapped his hands together. "What do you say, everyone? Shall we go across the street to the Buck to celebrate with a glass of champagne?"

Marina looped her arm through Vivian's. "I'd love to celebrate finally having a sister. I've always wanted one."

"Me too." Vivian smiled, seeming happier about the idea of having a sister than she had about accepting Thomas's proposal. Kind of hard not to take that personally, but it didn't change his mind about anything. As overwhelming as the situation was for him, he could understand it must be even worse for her.

"My treat." Vivian's dad ushered everyone out the door.

Thomas's dad cleared his throat. "If you don't mind, I

would just like a moment with Thomas. It's not every day that one's son gets engaged."

"Of course." Vivian's dad nodded. "Take as much time as you like. Our house is your house. We're going to be family, after all."

Guilt twisted in Thomas's stomach. Vivian's parents were incredibly kind to him and his family despite just getting to know each other. He hated deceiving them but reminded himself they'd be better off in the end for it. He and Vivian had nothing to lose by getting married. Just, perhaps, his heart.

Vivian paused in the doorway and looked back at him. "Do you want me to wait for you downstairs?"

Thomas smiled. "I'll meet you there, sweetheart."

She hesitated for a moment before disappearing out the door with everyone else.

Once the door had closed, Thomas braced himself. He knew his dad wasn't happy, but the man had the self-control of a monk. Now that they were alone, that self-control was out the window. "What is it, Dad?"

His dad looked down his nose at Thomas. "I played along tonight, but the game is over. There is no way you can marry that girl."

# CHAPTER NINETEEN

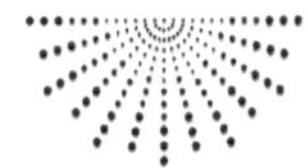

THOMAS

Thomas sure as heck didn't need any champagne. The room was already spinning. Just like he had suspected, his dad's good behavior was an act. What else was new?

His dad had never been violent. He had never raised a hand to his children. Hell, Thomas didn't even get a spanking growing up. But that didn't mean his dad didn't attack. No, he was just much more subtle, much more calculating, than that.

Thomas swallowed. Marina had been right. Was this the kind of family he wanted to drag Vivian into? For her sake, maybe it would be best to live their married lives separately.

His dad's face hardened. "You better tell me what the hell is going on."

Thomas worked his jaw. He had placated his dad time and time again. But this wasn't just about Thomas anymore. It was about Vivian too, and Thomas refused to back down. "It's pretty simple, actually. Boy meets girl. Boy marries girl. Dad writes check."

His dad's eyes lit up. "And here I thought I was going to have to pry the truth out of you."

"Sorry to disappoint you. You're the one who plays games here, not me."

"No one is playing a game, Thomas. And thanks to your selfishness, our family is involved in this mess. As is hers."

Thomas felt his blood pressure rising. The last thing he needed was a morality lesson from the least moral person on the planet. "Nothing you can say will change anything. Believe it or not, I care about Vivian. We're getting married."

"You're so damn stubborn. Can't you see the problems this will create? How are you supposed to manage projects from here? And what about your restaurant? Not exactly easy to run from three thousand miles away." His dad let out a huff. "Or do you just want the money that badly? If you're marrying Vivian only to get your trust fund, that's pathetic. But if you actually care about her and go through with it, that's even worse."

Thomas's body turned hot as anger coursed through him. His dad's words hit a little too close to home, echoing the same worries that had been going around his own mind. That Vivian did deserve better. That Thomas could never be who she needed. "Isn't that what you did?"

His dad clenched his jaw. It wasn't a secret that Thomas's mom had brought the wealth into his parents' relationship. Whether or not that's why his parents actually married, Thomas didn't know. But based on his dad's character, Thomas wouldn't be surprised if that was the truth. "God, you're impossible. You're so stubborn that you'd rather ruin your life and Vivian's than admit defeat. She's a nice girl, Thomas, but this has to stop. If you don't get your trust, it won't be the end of the world. You'll always have a job with me."

Thomas's vision wavered for a moment, and he thought he might be sick. He had waited for decades for his first chance at independence, and he wasn't going to let his only way out slip through his fingers. It was the same reason he and Vivian had joined forces in the beginning. With just six weeks until escrow closed on her store, going through with the scheme was more critical than ever. "The trust doesn't say a thing about *who* I marry, and that thing is ironclad. If it weren't, I wouldn't be in this situation in the first place."

"I know what you think."

Thomas barked a laugh, and Trixie whimpered and slinked out of the room. He understood the feeling. But this was one time that Thomas wouldn't back down from his dad. "You know what *I* think? Do tell."

His dad held his gaze, and Thomas's body turned cold when he saw the honesty reflected in his father's brown eyes. It was the last thing Thomas expected, and nothing could've unnerved him more. "You think that I don't care about you. That I'm too hard on you."

Thomas looked away, his eyes burning. He didn't think that. He *knew* it. And nothing his dad said now would change that. "Don't try to guilt me out of this. I know you, remember? I've known you my entire life. You've always cared more about the family legacy than your actual kids."

"I do actually care, Thomas. Whether or not you believe it." His dad sighed. "You're the one who waited until the last minute to get married. And you could've had Celeste..."

Just the mention of the woman's name made Thomas's mouth sour. He had been stupid not to see Celeste for who she was. Even if he told his parents the truth about her, if he hadn't already promised Celeste what happened would stay between them, Thomas would only feel worse. Everyone, including Thomas, knew he was an idiot. The world didn't need more proof of that. "No, I couldn't have. It was a mistake to even get engaged to Celeste. Going through with the wedding would've been worse. End of discussion."

He walked to the door, the room shrinking around him. Thomas couldn't stay in this room with his father for another minute. "I'm going to celebrate with my fiancée and our families. You can choose to come with me or not. I don't really care."

"Thomas, wait. Please."

His shoulders sagged, and he slowly turned around. His dad had never once asked politely for anything. The change in tone was almost more terrifying than him being pissed. "What, Dad? What more could there be to say? That the marriage won't work out? That she could take half of my money and run? I've already thought about all of it, and it doesn't change a thing. This is happening whether you like it or not."

"I know. But think about this: you come from two completely different worlds. Pull your head out of your ass for five seconds and stop thinking about the money. Do you realize what you're asking of her? You think this is going to change her life in a good way. But what if the opposite happens?"

Thomas took a deep breath. Even though it wasn't a secret that marrying Vivian was the key to gaining access to the trust, Thomas didn't feel the need to fill his dad in on the exact details of their arrangement.

Especially when the irony was that his dad was right. Thomas and Vivian came from two different worlds. But with each day he spent with Vivian, he was less worried about her cramping his style and more worried about the fact that they *would* go their separate ways. That he didn't want to leave her in Darling. But he couldn't stay either. And that if he told her how he was really feeling, it could ruin everything.

"I'll see you at the Buck. Or not. Whatever."

Thomas pounded down the stairs and hurried across Main Street. He couldn't get away from the conversation with his dad fast enough.

As Thomas walked up to the Buck, he spotted Vivian through the window. Marina stood in front of her, his sister's back turned to him. Vivian smiled prettily, her cheeks turning pink as she laughed at something Marina must've said.

His heart squeezed. Maybe Thomas was wrong. Maybe Vivian wasn't curious about life outside of Darling anymore. After all, at this moment, she looked so happy. So at home. And did he really want to take that from her?

As much as Thomas wanted to ask Vivian if she wanted more from their relationship, the truth was that would be stupid. It was better to leave things as they were than risk ruining them altogether. If he really cared about Vivian, he would give her what she wanted and not ask for anything else.

Thomas passed the door to the Buck, walking up to the next building. He would join everyone at the bar eventually, but he just needed a minute to calm down. Between his conflicting feelings and the conversation with his dad, Thomas's mind was a mess. He didn't trust himself around other people in this state.

He turned around the corner of the building, stepping into the shaded alleyway between the two faded wooden structures. Thomas hung his head, kicking at the ground and leaving scuff marks in the dirt.

As much as it pained Thomas to admit it, what if his dad was right? Vivian did seem bound and determined to continue life in Darling, or at least she had when they first made their deal. Thomas could respect that kind of grit. And to be fair, Thomas had felt the same way in the beginning. This was a relationship of convenience. Nothing else. But that was all *before*.

Before he discovered they both loved good food. Before they found Trixie and fell in love with the little dog, despite her cringeworthy name. And before that night in Ketchikan that made Thomas wonder about having more than he had ever dared dream. If things had changed for him, perhaps it wasn't too crazy to think they had changed for Vivian too.

"Oof!" Thomas stumbled as he crashed into something, or rather, someone. More surprised than hurt, he reached out to steady the petite older woman in front of him. Under her jacket sleeves, her arms felt as fragile as toothpicks. "I'm so sorry. Are you okay?"

But the woman wasn't frazzled in the least. Her blue eyes crinkled at the corners as she smiled up at him. "There's nothing to be sorry about. I was distracted. Thinking about you, actually." She giggled. "Perfect timing."

Darling was small. Even if he hadn't met everyone, he felt like he knew who they were. Thomas hadn't met this woman, or he would've remembered, especially with her faint but distinctive Russian accent. So why was she acting like she knew him? "Have we...have we met?"

She shook her head, a few wisps of blonde hair mixed with gray escaping from her hood. "I live outside of town. I'm Natasha."

Thomas gulped. That's how she knew who he was. Based on the brief snippets he had heard about Natasha and her psychic abilities, Thomas had expected someone a little more kooky-looking. This woman appeared more like a nice grandma. Then again, he had never met a psychic before. Maybe they all looked like nice grandmas. "Nice to meet you. But I actually have to be somewhere..."

She clasped her hands together. "I know that you don't really want to spend time chatting with me. Not when you have a celebration to get to. And celebrate you should. I can't imagine a better match. You both deserve to be happy."

Thomas shifted to his other foot. Maybe the psychic part was more than a rumor. "Uh…thank you?"

Natasha peered up at him, the humor gone from her expression. "Did you hear what I said? You *both* deserve to be happy." Her smile reappeared. "I think it's time to get going. Vivian is waiting for you."

"Uh, yeah. I better get going." He took a step back, as eager to see Vivian as he was to get away from this weird conversation. Between the argument with his dad and his detour on the way to the Buck, Vivian probably thought Thomas had ditched her at their own impromptu engagement party. Little did she know Thomas would do anything not to let her down.

Natasha smiled and gave a little wave. "Congratulations, Thomas. See you around."

He nodded and turned on his heel, hurrying back to the Buck. Forget champagne. He needed the hard stuff.

With a deep breath, he pulled open the door to the Buck, spotting Vivian right away. She smiled, waving him over.

As he crossed the room, Thomas's heart beat faster, his confusion vanishing quicker than the Alaskan summer as soon as he saw her. When it came to marriage, Thomas had never hoped for romance. He didn't waste time worrying about love. Until Vivian.

He might not know how she felt, but Thomas was suddenly certain where he stood. His argument with his dad and the strange conversation with Natasha both pointed to the same thing. Everything Thomas fought against, everything he feared, underlined the truth he could no longer ignore.

When it came to their fake relationship, his feelings had become very real. If there was any chance Vivian felt the same way, Thomas might have something he had never dreamed of. Not just the trust. Not just a partner that he respected. But someone he truly cared about to experience life with.

# CHAPTER TWENTY

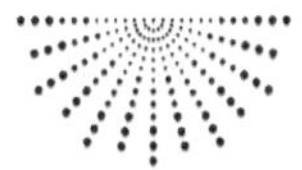

VIVIAN

"You know, baking pies is definitely *not* as much fun as eating them."

Vivian glanced at Thomas, biting her lip as she fought a laugh. For a guy who normally was so put together, there was something oddly endearing about the sight of him covered in flour and flecks of egg white. Something endearing *and* hilarious. He seemed like an altogether different species than the man she had grudgingly made this bargain with a little less than a month ago. "You didn't have to help me, you know."

"But I want to." He flashed her that gorgeous smile that always sent a shiver to her toes. "And like I just said, eating the pies is the fun part."

Vivian shook her head as she wiped down the counters. The two of them had been baking all morning while her parents worked at the store. The kitchen was warm from the oven and the rare late April sun beating down on Darling.

Her shirt was stuck to her back with sweat. Still, it was an oasis compared to the places she had worked in New York. But just a taste of her old life energized her, making her feel like the version of herself that she so desperately missed. "You literally live in the restaurant that sells these pies. You don't have to earn them. But if it helps, you're doing a great job."

Thomas waved around a spoon. "Don't lie to me, woman. You made this look a lot easier than it is." He squished his brows together, focusing as he plopped meringue on top of the lemon curd. "My peaks look more like valleys. And not a majestic valley. A sad, fruitless valley."

This time, Vivian didn't succeed in holding back the laugh. "It'll taste the same no matter how it looks."

Thomas gave her a mock pout. "I think when it comes to food, we can agree I'm better at eating it than making it."

Trixie let out an eager whine, angling for a scrap. Thomas pointed the spoon at the small dog. "See? Even Trixie agrees. My poor culinary skills are upsetting her."

"You and I both know she's just begging for food, not judging you." Vivian plucked the last pie from the table, sliding it into the oven. "Is this the part where I remind you that you didn't have to help me?"

"I like hanging out with you." He lifted a shoulder. "Though I don't know why you're still selling pies. The store will be paid in full soon. You don't need the extra money."

Her back still to him, Vivian chewed on her bottom lip. It wasn't that she didn't trust Thomas. She did. It was herself that she didn't trust.

Everything was right on track. They had plane tickets to go to New York in three weeks, which would give them both a chance to get married and for him to sign the trust documents in person. Then, Thomas would transfer the money for the store to Uncle Robert a little more than two weeks before escrow closed, and Uncle Robert would give Vivian the deed. After that, she could finally tell her parents the truth about her relationship with Thomas.

The other miracle was that she and Thomas were actually getting along. Oh sure, he still made her roll her eyes on a daily basis. But despite making a focused effort to put on appearances when they had first made this plan, it seemed more and more natural to spend time with Thomas. In fact, it was something that she looked forward to. Since Marina had gone home three days ago with her parents, it seemed like Thomas had been by Vivian's side nonstop, and she was quickly getting used to him being around.

She already missed Marina's sunny personality, but Vivian wasn't terribly upset to see Thomas's parents leave town. His mom seemed nice enough. But while Thomas's dad had been perfectly polite to Vivian, she could tell his presence put Thomas on edge. That was reason enough for her not to like Stefan Becker. Sometime in the last several weeks, Vivian had become protective of Thomas's feelings.

She faced him, smiling. "I have good news for you."

His eyes lit up. "It's time for the taste test?"

Vivian laughed and shook her head. "I was going to say we're done after that one comes out of the oven. But yes, you can have a slice. Just as soon as you help me clean up the kitchen."

"I have a new appreciation for the back-of-house staff," Thomas grumbled. But he pitched in, working just as hard as she did, and they had the kitchen cleaned up lickety-split.

Vivian selected one of the first pies they had baked, trusting it would have cooled enough. "How much would you like?"

"Just a small slice."

She made the first cut, and then before she eased the knife into the pie again, Thomas cleared his throat. Vivian glanced at him. "Yes?"

"Just a *little* bigger, please."

Vivian inched the knife over a smidge. "This much?"

He studied the pie. "Maybe a bit more."

She moved the knife over again. "*This* much?"

The game continued until Thomas ended up with a comically large slice.

"This is really cutting into my profits." She handed him the plate. "Next time, I'm going to allot you an entire pie. It would be more accurate."

He nodded. "That's the necessary amount, in my opinion." Thomas took a bite, his eyes rolling back in his head. "Oh my God. This might be my second-favorite pie I've ever had."

Vivian narrowed her eyes. "*Second*-favorite? Those are fighting words."

Thomas shot her a teasing smile. "The first is, and always will be, your banana cream. It's the pie that brought us together, after all."

Vivian giggled, serving herself a slice, though much smaller than Thomas's. She grabbed a fork and scooped up a bite, letting out a moan at the perfect balance of the tart lemon curd and sweet, fluffy meringue. "Nothing against our relationship, but this is giving banana cream a run for its money."

Smiling, Thomas reached out and ran his finger alongside her mouth. "You got a little something right here."

Heat shot through her body, and Vivian all but held her breath. Instantly, she was back in the hotel room in Ketchikan. And she had thought the kitchen was hot before. "Thanks."

His eyes crinkled at the corners as he looked down at her, and Vivian's mouth went dry. He looked so good close up.

But that was how it was with Thomas. The more she got to know him, the more she liked him.

Vivian cleared her throat, setting her plate down and getting a glass of water. As she filled the glass, the ring winked at her from the windowsill over the sink. Vivian had set it there when she took it off to roll out the dough.

The worst thing wasn't the shock of Thomas proposing. It wasn't lying to her family, albeit just for a little while longer. It was that for a nanosecond, when Thomas had been down on one knee, Vivian had wished it was real. Which was silly. Normal people didn't get engaged after less than a month.

Then again, nothing about this was normal.

After their impromptu engagement celebration at the Buck, Thomas had let her know that the ring was from one of the tourist shops they had visited in Ketchikan. Vivian had almost been relieved. A real diamond would've made her feel even more awkward. She wasn't used to nice things.

The ring was no more special than the jade bracelet he had bought her. That's what made everything so simple about their original arrangement. There was nothing to risk and everything to gain.

If only Thomas weren't so dang easy to like. If only he really had been the spoiled brat she thought he was. Then it wouldn't kill Vivian to wonder about something more. To wonder if maybe he wanted more too.

Her stomach tightened. The morning after Thomas had proposed, her mom had tossed around ideas for the wedding between bites of scrambled eggs and whole wheat toast.

Vivian had mentioned more than once that they were going to keep it small, and that was an understatement. She had never loved the idea of a big wedding, fake relationship or not, and there was really no reason to go all out in this case. She and Thomas only needed the bare minimum to get legally married, not that Vivian told her mom those particular details.

But her mom hadn't listened, and by the end of it, Vivian was caught up in the excitement of the moment. Every time she remembered it wasn't real, it was as if someone held a needle to a balloon. *Pop!* All the good feelings would drain away.

Vivian forced a deep breath. She was securing her family's future in Darling, something much more important than flower arrangements and a wedding dress and being happy.

She picked up her plate again, leaning back against the kitchen counter as she faced Thomas. "Have you heard from Marina at all?"

He shrugged. "Only that she misses Darling. She's like the town's number one fan."

"Maybe she should move here."

Thomas barked a laugh. "My parents would just *love* that. Then both of their children would be disappointments." He frowned. "Actually, they would probably never let Marina move here. She's the favorite. They don't care where I live. But maybe that's a good thing."

Vivian's heart squeezed. Despite accusing Thomas of having a major ego when she had first met him, she had learned nothing could be further from the truth. And as someone who suffered from low self-esteem, she could easily recognize it in another. "You're not a disappointment, Thomas. You have a restaurant. You're going to be a success. You're better off than most."

He nodded, his gaze not quite meeting her own. "Yeah. I guess so."

"And I can't imagine a better husband."

He searched her face, and Vivian almost winced at the hopelessness she saw reflected in his dark eyes. The easy-going guy from a few minutes ago had vanished. "Except you'll leave me too, won't you?"

Vivian drew her eyebrows together. Why did he sound so upset? She had been trying to make him feel better, not worse. "That was the deal, wasn't it? And strictly speaking, you'll leave *me*."

"Of course." He turned his back to her, clearly upset. Thomas set his plate in the sink and grabbed his jacket from the back of a chair. "If you're all good here, I think I'm going to take Trixie out. I need some fresh air."

*Tell him*, her brain begged her. *Tell him now.*

Her heart pounded, and the words tumbled out before she realized what she was saying. "I don't know what you want me to say, Thomas. I wasn't expecting any of this. I thought it was going to be so easy, not loving you."

He turned and stared at her, unblinking. "What did you say?"

"Forget it." She took her dish to the sink, turning on the water and scrubbing it vigorously. Her body turned hot with embarrassment. Why had she said anything? Why ruin things between them when they were only weeks away from everything they ever wanted?

Thomas's arm reached around her, shutting off the water. "You…you love me?" he asked, his voice a whisper.

Her heart slammed into her ribs, and she felt the strangest urge to cry. Vivian turned to face him. "I don't know. I barely know you. This wasn't the plan—"

His mouth pressed against hers, and she melted instantly into the kiss. Melted into his sandalwood scent and his warm touch. Melted into his soul, a dangerous and delicious place where she might not find herself again.

It was crazy, of course. Even crazier than getting married to a guy she didn't know and, at least in the beginning, didn't like. And things were going so well. Why complicate them

with feelings? Vivian's track record with relationships definitely advised otherwise.

Then there was the ticking clock, the date on the calendar
that would whisk Thomas away. All she had to do was make
it that long with her heart intact, and she could return to life
as normal. It should be easy.

If only her heart would listen.

He pulled away and looked down at her with those dark
eyes. "I love you too."

Her nose burned, and Vivian glanced away. Trixie circled
their feet, whining. "What the hell are we going to do?" Her
voice shook. "Are we crazy?"

"Not exactly the reaction to a declaration of love that I
had hoped for."

Vivian let out a strangled laugh. "I'm trying to be realistic.
You have a restaurant in New York City. My family is here.
This would be a horrible idea."

Thomas tucked a strand of hair behind her ear, her body
tingling at his touch. "All I am suggesting is we *try*. That we
try this relationship thing for real." His mouth quirked up.
"After all, we're already getting married. So what if we're
doing things a little out of order?"

Vivian swallowed. "And let's say, theoretically, I go along
with this insane idea. How would we…where do we start?"

"The only place to go for a date in Darling." Thomas
smiled. "The Buck, of course."

She shook her head. Now, that was *really* crazy. "I'd feel
way too awkward. It was one thing to pretend. I can't
imagine going on a real date around here."

His lips twitched. "You lived in New York, sweetheart.
Darling is a pretty low-stakes environment by comparison."

Vivian shifted her feet as the memory of her life on the
East Coast tugged on her heartstrings. "I don't know. In New
York, I felt like a different person."

Thomas held her gaze, and Vivian shivered. He seemed to see right through her. "You can be whoever you want to be, Vivian. I'll love you no matter who you are."

His words draped over her heart like a warm blanket, both comforting and tempting her. Vivian wanted to. She really did. But it had been so long since she had tried for anything at all. And she doubted she had outgrown her bad luck.

*You make your own luck.*

Vivian took a shaky breath. Then again, if she was going to make her own luck, there was no one she would rather do it with than Thomas. "Okay, fine. Let's go on a date."

Before he could answer, Trixie whined, and they both looked down at her.

Thomas cleared his throat. "Is something…is something burning?"

Vivian sniffed the air, her eyes growing wide. "The pie!"

She ran to the oven, smoke billowing out and choking her as soon as she opened the door.

With a cough, Vivian managed to pull out the pie. Thomas opened a window, and they used dish towels to coax the smoke out of the kitchen. The last thing she needed was to summon the local volunteer fire brigade. That would be ten times more embarrassing than a date at the Buck.

Vivian and Thomas looked at each other at the same time, his face flushed and eyes wide. She probably looked just as frantic as he did. A giggle bubbled up inside her, and soon, they were both doubled over in laughter.

She finally pulled herself together, wiping a tear from her eye. "That's one way to get done with baking early."

Thomas sighed. "What a waste of a pie. Sorry, sweetheart."

She shook her head, still buzzing from the cathartic relief

of her laughing fit. The way she looked at it, the moment hadn't been wasted at all. "Nothing to be sorry about."

After a lifetime of feeling like a loser, Vivian was thankful for the first time that everything in her life had happened the way it had. Because if it hadn't, she wouldn't be here with Thomas right now.

She wouldn't be this happy.

# CHAPTER TWENTY-ONE

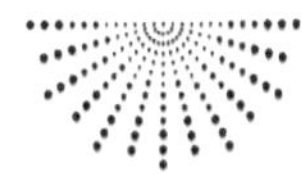

VIVIAN

Vivian stepped carefully around a large fireweed plant, not yet in bloom, that spilled over onto the faded forest trail. "Are you excited to go back?"

"To Darling? Sweetheart, we might have reached a turning point in our relationship, but my feelings on the town are still neutral at best." Thomas shot her a teasing smile.

"You know what I mean." She let out a huff and stomped a little harder than necessary on the spongy forest floor. Even if they had reached a turning point in their relationship, Thomas still had a particular talent for annoying her. When she had dropped off the most recent batch of baked goods at the coffee shop, Vivian had mentioned this to Grace. Her friend had smiled knowingly and mentioned something about love. That had only annoyed Vivian more.

Thomas shifted Trixie to his other arm. There was no way they could've left the dog behind for the day. Neither of them had the strength to resist Trixie's pleading gaze. But the dog's small legs had tired quickly, and Thomas had spent more than half of the hike carrying her. "It's kind of a complicated question. I love New York. I can't wait to be back at the restaurant, of course. Even though the manager sends me updates every day, it's not the same as being there myself. But at the same time, things aren't as black-and-white as they used to be."

Vivian nodded. She felt the same way. When they had first made this deal, it had never occurred to her that she'd miss Thomas's presence in Darling. Then again, they hadn't planned on seeing each other again once he had the trust and she had the store. In fact, the plan had been to *not* see each other. Once he left, Vivian used to think the next time she and Thomas were in the same room would be when they signed divorce papers. "Have you talked to your parents recently? Or Marina?"

"Just my mom. My dad is still in denial. But that's his style. He still hasn't seen the restaurant yet either. Maybe he thinks if he doesn't acknowledge it, it doesn't exist. Apparently, I've been doing a good enough job keeping up with work that he doesn't feel the need to ride my ass too much about that either."

Vivian's heart squeezed. She had thought her family situation was complicated, and even though she hadn't completely forgiven her dad for cheating on her mom, Vivian didn't doubt her father loved her. But after meeting Thomas's dad, and the more she heard about him, she was starting to think Thomas had it a lot worse. "If it makes you feel better, my mom and dad want to visit your restaurant. They never came to see me in New York."

Thomas laughed. "I'd love that. Your parents are great. I'll make sure they get the VIP treatment. Just like you will when we go to New York this month."

Vivian's chest grew tight. Her parents had never met

Philippe. Vivian had begged him to visit Alaska with her, but he'd always come up with an excuse. It took her until after they broke up for Vivian to realize she hadn't been a priority to him. But Thomas always made her feel like a priority. More than that, he made her family feel special too.

"My parents will probably like you better than me after that." She shook her head dramatically, the droplets of moisture that had gathered on her hood from the constant mist flying in all directions.

"Yeah, right. As if I could compete for their love. We both know they like Trixie best." Thomas stopped walking. "Whoa."

Vivian followed his gaze, nodding. "It's something, isn't it?"

A massive house stood in front of them, out of place in the thick forest. *House* didn't do it justice. It was probably the closest thing Darling had to a mansion. Even though Vivian had seen it a hundred times growing up, it never failed to impress her.

She knew Thomas had seen much more magnificent homes in New York. Heck, this place was probably nothing compared to the house he grew up in. But it was definitely unexpected on the edge of the world.

Vivian pointed to the left of the huge building. "If we follow the trail that way, it leads down to a little beach."

Thomas glanced around. "But isn't that kind of like...trespassing?"

"It's exactly like trespassing *if* anyone lived here. Which no one has for as long as I can remember." Vivian lifted a shoulder, her rain jacket crinkling. "But even if they did, we'd probably all be on a first-name basis. You know how Darling is."

They plodded down the trail to the beach. Or at least what Vivian thought was the trail. The constant rain made for a lush landscape. If a trail wasn't used, it didn't take long to be reclaimed by the ever-expanding forest. Luckily, there were only so many places to go on an island before a person hit water. Between that and having cell phones, Vivian didn't worry too much about getting lost.

She adjusted her backpack, remembering when Elle, Mac's wife, had first come to Darling two years ago. Elle had traveled to Alaska from LA with her fiancé at the time, but he had promptly run off to live in the woods. As if the news of a famous influencer visiting Darling wasn't exciting enough, Elle's kooky fiancé kept the gossip mill fueled for weeks with his disappearance. But even for a guy with almost no wilderness survival experience, he hadn't actually gotten lost. He had just wanted a break from the modern world. Eventually, he had come out of the woods.

Vivian smiled. Just when everyone had thought that batch of gossip would be impossible to top, Elle and Mac had fallen for each other, and Elle had moved to Darling. It turned out she and her former fiancé were more like friends than lovers. And Mac? It turned out he wasn't as completely antisocial as he'd led people to believe.

Vivian's shoulders sagged. Elle was also known for her incredible recipes, yet another reason why Vivian would never open a restaurant or bakery in Darling. One celebrity chef was enough for the island. Which was fine. Because if Vivian did open up her place one day, and that was a big *if*, she had a different location in mind. The same city where Thomas had his restaurant. Vivian loved New York, and it helped that her very handsome future husband happened to live there too.

They rounded the back of the house, the small beach stretching out in front of them. It was rocky but peaceful, the surrounding islands protecting it from the wind. Even the waves were polite, lapping softly against the shore. A bench overlooked the water, and a rope swing hung from a tree.

She turned to face Thomas, gesturing to the swing. "What do you think? Want to go for a swim?"

Thomas gaped at her. "Do I want to go for a swim in the *Alaskan* ocean? Let me think about that. No."

Vivian laughed. "It's not that bad. I did it a lot as a kid. We all did."

He nudged his shoulder in the direction of the bench, keeping a firm hold on Trixie. "How about we sit there instead, and you can tell me all about it? Then I can take a break from carrying the four-legged princess."

They made the short walk to the bench, taking a seat. Thomas set Trixie down, and after a brief sniff around, she settled back at his feet.

He sighed. "At least we don't have to worry about her running away. I don't think we could get rid of her if we tried."

Vivian pulled her water bottle from her backpack. "Actually, that's a good question. Which one of us keeps Trixie?"

"I hadn't thought about that." Thomas wrinkled his forehead. "I guess it makes more sense for you to keep her in Darling. You have an entire island for her to run around. My place is small and on the fifteenth floor. Besides, your parents can dog-sit when you visit me in New York."

"I suppose." Vivian shifted in her seat. It should be comforting to know that Thomas wanted to see her again. That whatever this was between them wasn't quite over yet. But even though they had admitted that they loved each other, so many unknowns still hung between them. Even if they got their happily ever after, how would that work with long distance? What if once Thomas was back in New York, he realized he could do so much better than her? What if this marriage was over before it began? "How is it going to work—"

"Don't."

She frowned. "Don't what?"

"Don't try to solve problems that don't exist yet." Thomas held her gaze. "There's nothing to worry about, not right now. It'll be okay, Vivian. I promise."

She swallowed. Maybe he had a point. After all, she had been through so much worse. As much as Vivian still resented what happened with Philippe, it had a silver lining: things between her and Thomas could never get *that* bad.

Thomas glanced over his shoulder. "So what is the deal with this house? Is it haunted or something?"

"We definitely thought so when we were kids. We always wanted to sneak in and check it out, but our parents wouldn't let us. Said it was an invasion of privacy, though we weren't sure whose privacy we were invading. After all, no one lived there." She lifted the corner of her mouth. "But our parents didn't have quite the same moral boundaries with the rope swing. Probably because the kids slept like rocks after a day of jumping into the ocean and swimming back to do it over and over again."

Thomas chuckled, reaching down to give Trixie a reassuring scratch while she snoozed next to him. "I just imagine the owner showing up one day and seeing the unofficial Darling summer camp on his front lawn, or whatever you call a private beach."

"Funny enough, I don't think that's completely improbable. One day, when I was a teenager, some other kids and I came down here for a beach day without our parents. Which meant no one was keeping us from checking out the house."

Thomas lifted a dark brow. "And was it haunted?"

She shook her head. "Even creepier. We tried the front door first since most people here don't lock their doors anyway. It was unlocked, and we walked right in. It looked just like a normal house. I mean, as if the people had just walked out one day and never came back. Like they might be home at any minute."

Vivian shivered, and it had nothing to do with the cool sea mist that fell from the sky and settled on their plastic coats. "It was like…I don't know. Like the house was waiting."

She set her water bottle aside and shoved her hands in her pockets. Vivian hadn't thought about that day in a long time. But looking back, that's exactly how she felt. Like she was just sitting there in Darling for the past seven years, waiting for life to start. Only she hadn't realized it until Thomas came around and reminded her of all the things she had wanted.

Thomas tilted his head. "So did you like the house?"

"What?" She laughed. "What does that have to do with anything?"

"Like, is it your style? What would be your dream house?"

Vivian chewed the inside of her cheek. She hadn't given serious thought to life outside of Darling in so long. Keeping her family, keeping their lives together, was as close to a dream as she had. But since Thomas had crashed into her life, or more accurately perhaps, she had crashed into his, Vivian had been thinking about what she truly wanted more and more. "I don't know. I don't have a dream house, I guess. How about you?"

"I like those loft-style places with exposed brick. My current apartment is super modern, and it looks kind of like a hospital." He chuckled. "I bought the first place I saw just to move out of my parents' as fast as possible. But I want to find something that's a little closer to my style. Still in New York, of course."

"That would be cool." She nodded. "I think my dream house would definitely be somewhere like New York too."

Thomas splayed a hand against his chest. "*Not* Darling? Well, I never."

Vivian nudged him with her shoulder. "Give me a break. I loved New York, minus getting cheated on and dumped."

"Definitely not a great impression." Thomas shook his head. "What else? What else do you like? Where do you want to travel? Dream car? Anything."

She studied the dark islands on the horizon. Despite her massive failure before, Vivian still had a crystal-clear vision for her restaurant. She even had her dessert menu memorized. But it would never be more than that. A dream. "Does it matter? It doesn't change anything."

"Why not?"

"Because I already know exactly what my life is going to look like." Her throat grew tight. With a little less than thirty days until escrow closed, and less time than that until the store was hers, that reality drew closer every day. "Dreaming is a waste of time. Not to mention *embarrassing*. I still feel so stupid about losing all that money in the restaurant. Didn't even get to see it open for a day." She slumped on the bench. "Totally sucks."

"That sucks *a lot*." Thomas reached out, giving her arm a reassuring squeeze through her rain jacket. "But you're about to be in a completely different financial situation. Don't you think that might open up some new possibilities?"

Vivian lifted an eyebrow. "You know, my parents always said that if a problem could be solved with money, it wasn't a real problem."

"That's true. But it does make things a lot easier."

She blew air through her lips. "Don't I know it."

If she had money, she wouldn't have let Philippe's infidelity stop her from opening a restaurant. Maybe she would have nursed her heartbreak for a while, but not for the rest of her life. If she had money, Vivian would've bought the store from her uncle years ago. But then she wouldn't have struck the deal with Thomas. She wouldn't be here right now, happier than she'd been in a long, long time.

*You make your own luck.*

Maybe that didn't just mean changing a person's fate. Maybe it meant seeing the fate she had been given in a different light. After all, did Vivian truly have bad luck? Or was she just too hard on herself? Because looking back, some of her worst moments now seemed like a blessing in disguise.

"Please. There's no one here but us." Thomas gave her a reassuring smile. "I want to know everything."

Vivian held his warm gaze. Talking about it wouldn't change a damn thing. But there was no one she trusted with her dreams more. Even if her dreams only existed in this bubble with Thomas, it was more than she'd had in a long time. Even if Thomas was the only one who truly knew her heart, maybe that was enough. More than enough. "Fine. But you have to tell me yours too."

"That sounds fair. After all, my dreams include you."

# CHAPTER TWENTY-TWO

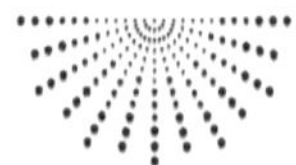

THOMAS

After years of biding his time, everything was finally coming together. With less than two months until his thirtieth birthday, Thomas was going to be able to live the life he wanted, not the life he was allowed.

The restaurant was doing well. According to the updates from the manager and the email reports that Thomas received on a regular basis, the place was already establishing a good reputation.

Less than a month ago, Thomas had thought he had blown his last chance at receiving his trust fund when he walked away from his own wedding. Now, he had a fiancée. Better than that, a fiancée with a future.

Still, none of those things could compare to the fact that Vivian loved him. She really, truly *loved* him. She wasn't pretending just for the sake of their bargain anymore, and neither was Thomas. For a guy who never imagined he'd be in a loving marriage, that meant more to him than any amount of money.

Thomas hummed as he tidied up his room. The place was looking lived-in after being in Darling a little more than a month, and he might as well get organized. He and Vivian were leaving for New York in just two weeks. Not to mention, it was easier to clean without a hangover. After a couple of rough mornings in Alaska, Thomas hadn't overindulged in Wolfie's beer in over two weeks. Something that had more to do with Vivian's good influence than Thomas's willpower.

Glancing around the room, he had an odd thought. He'd almost kind of miss this place when he left this time. He was always glad to see Charlotte and Wolfie, but Darling itself didn't hold much appeal. Until now. Although that might have less to do with the actual town and more with Vivian and being happy.

A shiver ran down his back. It felt unreal to admit to himself that he was actually *happy*. To admit something, some part of all the lies, was totally and completely real. Thomas was so used to faking everything. He had barely been able to stand his own life. If that wasn't sad, he didn't know what was.

A month ago, Thomas wasn't sure he and Vivian would be able to pull this off. Would she chicken out? Would he? Everything hung on their ability to see the marriage through, no matter how they actually felt about each other. But in the end, it had been harder to pretend Thomas hadn't cared about her. Not just harder. Impossible.

Thomas folded a pair of jeans, chuckling to himself. The irony was that he had his dad to thank. If he hadn't pushed Thomas so hard all these years, he might've never ended up with Vivian. If that's what it had taken to end up with her, to *deserve* her, then it was worth it, dammit. Life with Vivian didn't just justify the hard times Thomas had been through. It gave those hard times meaning.

Now, he wanted to do the same for her. Vivian had made it clear that she intended to run the store with her parents for the rest of time. But Thomas wasn't as convinced. When she talked about New York, he could tell she loved it just as much as he did. In fact, the only thing he was convinced of was that Vivian was too damn talented to *not* see her restaurant dreams become a reality.

The way he saw it, there were two options. If he had it his way, Vivian would agree to come with him to New York and run the pastry program at Thomas's second restaurant. Not that he had a second restaurant yet, but as soon as he had access to the trust money, which wasn't too far away, he could easily acquire another place. Of course, he wanted her help picking it out. He wanted to make sure she got exactly what she desired.

Vivian was more than welcome to work at the restaurant he had now, but Thomas didn't need to ask to know there was no way she would work with Philippe, not that Thomas blamed her. And Thomas still wasn't willing to fire the talented chef.

But maybe if Vivian got to help pick out the next restaurant, if she felt more like a partner than an employee, she wouldn't be so bothered by the fact that Philippe still worked for Thomas. That was fair. After all, she was going to be Thomas's partner in so much more than just business, a thought that still made his heart skip a beat.

Thomas hoped that offer would entice Vivian to consider living in New York again, especially since she liked it so much the first time around. After all, with her parents' future guaranteed, did she really need to stay with them in Darling? Thomas could fly them first-class to New York to visit anytime they wanted. He and Vivian could regularly visit Alaska too.

But Vivian was loyal to a fault, one of the first things that

Thomas had admired about her. And if she wasn't willing to come to the restaurant, then Thomas would bring the restaurant to her. She hadn't asked for it. She hadn't asked for anything other than her parents' business, even though she was helping Thomas secure millions of dollars. Vivian saw Thomas as a person, not just a bank account. It was yet another reason that he had fallen for her. Another reason why he wanted to give her the world.

Vivian had said over and over again that there wasn't room for another business in Darling. But Thomas saw the potential. The town was hungry for things to do. Vivian was already supplying the Buck and the Driftwood Coffee Company with baked goods. It would be much easier to do that with a commercial kitchen. That wasn't even considering the potential for resale.

Tucking a stack of folded clothes into a dresser drawer, Thomas hooked his finger around the curtain over the window and pulled it back. Surveying Main Street, he rubbed his chin with his free hand. The old pizza place looked promising. Even if it needed to be completely renovated, it had to be cheaper than putting together a restaurant in New York.

Thomas hated the idea of living a continent away from Vivian, but he'd do it if that's what she wanted. Maybe he could work out some kind of frequent flier deal with Mac. The giant grump would never win any customer service awards, but Thomas wouldn't let that stand between him spending as much time as he could with Vivian. As far as what to do with the dog, they'd figure out that detail later. As much as Thomas didn't want to say goodbye to Trixie, he figured Vivian didn't either. In that case, he would understand the dog staying in Darling, and he had said as much.

His phone buzzed, and Thomas pulled it from his back

pocket. With a sigh, he slid his thumb across the screen to answer his sister's phone call. "Miss me already?"

Marina let out a laugh that sounded more like an air horn, and Thomas briefly held the phone away from his ear. Their poor mother. Marina's etiquette classes had never taken hold, and thank God for that. There had been many days growing up when his sister was the single ray of sunshine in his otherwise cloudy life. "Do I miss you? No. Charlotte, Trixie, and Vivian? Yes."

"So everyone but me. Got it," Thomas said dryly. "In that case, why don't you call someone you actually care about? Just 'cause we're related doesn't mean we have to talk."

Marina snorted. "Speaking of *related*, our father has been in a snit since we got back from Alaska. He's so touchy I'm beginning to wonder if someone didn't stuff pine needles into his undies. Not even Mom can soothe his feathers for once. Want to take a wild guess why he's so pissed?"

Thomas ran a hand through his hair. It was one thing for him to be three thousand miles away from his father's high standards. But his mom and sister weren't so lucky. "I've answered every single email. Taken video meetings. Nothing has slipped through the cracks."

It helped that Thomas had wrapped up most of his projects well before he took off to Alaska. He had thought he was clearing up time to go on a luxury honeymoon with Celeste, a thought that now made him ill. And he hadn't taken on anything new since he'd been in Darling either. It had been tricky enough to balance his remaining workload and manage the restaurant from afar.

Marina blew air into the phone. "Yeah, well, it doesn't change the fact that when we took off to Alaska, you told him it would be a week or two. It's been more than a month, Thomas. And you're coming home with quite the souvenir: a wife."

He massaged his forehead. Everything made sense now. His dad wasn't upset because Thomas was doing a poor job, which he wasn't. His dad was upset because soon Thomas would be completely independent. When he had first headed to Alaska, a jilted bride in his wake, his dad had probably thought Thomas would be working for Becker Commercial Properties for the rest of his life. After all, it wasn't like his dad ever had much faith in Thomas's restaurant being successful.

But with Vivian in the picture, the tides had turned. And if there was one thing his dad hated more than anything else, it was not being in control.

Thomas took a deep breath, clarity settling over him. He wasn't subject to his dad's whims anymore. Thomas could do what he wanted. And more than that, he knew *exactly* what he wanted to do. And who he wanted to do it with. "Dad shouldn't be annoyed by that much longer. Because I'm quitting."

Silence came over the line, and Thomas glanced at the phone screen to make sure the call hadn't been disconnected. He didn't have much confidence in the reception on the island. It probably only took a raven flying in the wrong direction to completely lose service. "Marina? Are you there?"

"Sorry. Just trying to figure out if I heard you right. You're *quitting?*"

Thomas paced the room, careful to step lightly. While the Buck was far from quiet, he also didn't want the patrons below to think an Irish step dancer was holding rehearsal upstairs. "You heard me right."

"And you're going to tell Dad when exactly?"

Thomas swallowed. As happy as he was to be done with the Becker family business, he knew his dad was not going to share the feeling. Thomas hated to think that his sister and mom had to deal with his dad's bad mood at home. But unlike Thomas, neither his mother nor Marina worked with his dad, so they could more easily avoid him if needed. "I'm going to tell him today."

"Don't you think that's a bit…premature? You don't want to wait until *after* you have the money?"

He rubbed the back of his neck with his free hand. Under any normal circumstances, Thomas would've agreed with his sister. Heck, he would've agreed with her even as recently as last week. Back when his feelings about Vivian had a question mark hanging at the end of them.

But now they were trying for something more than a business deal. Not just trying. Succeeding. And suddenly, Thomas didn't understand why he hadn't seen Vivian for the incredible woman she was from day one.

Yes, she was gorgeous. But it was more than that. Thomas had been underestimated his entire life. Written off. Worse, he had written himself off. But he was guilty of doing the same thing to Vivian because underneath that prairie girl package, the woman was a firecracker.

She was strong and loyal and persevered when others would've laid down and given up. And if Thomas was going to go through life with anyone, he couldn't imagine someone better than her. When they first joined forces, they had agreed to get divorced after six months. Now, Thomas realized he wanted to give Vivian every reason to stay married forever.

But that meant proving he had skin in the game. He had to go all in on them. Something to show he had complete faith in their ability to create a life they loved together. Quitting the job at his dad's company seemed like a good place to start, followed by offering her a restaurant of her own.

"Vivian and I are engaged. It's not like Dad will be completely surprised when I turn in my two weeks' notice. I already have the restaurant, and he knows how much the trust is worth. He had to have seen this coming."

"I know, I know. But aren't you worried about the other shoe?"

Thomas's back tensed. He'd been worried about the other shoe his whole life. And there was *always* another shoe. Just when he thought it would be okay, *bam*, the shoe would fall to the ground and stomp all over everything he had going for him.

But that was before Vivian. Before Thomas realized that some things were worth the risk. By quitting his job, he wasn't giving up everything. Instead, he was gaining a life better than he had ever dreamed.

"I'm telling you, Marina. It's going to be fine. To be honest, it's kind of unnerving to hear these doubts from Vivian's maid of honor."

"It's not you I doubt. It's life." Marina let out a huff. "And you know I'm going to be there, rain or shine."

"You better. We'll all go out to the restaurant to eat after that. Maybe Mom and Dad will join us."

"Now, that would be a real wedding-day miracle."

Thomas could hear the smile in her voice. They might not see eye to eye all the time, but he never doubted that Marina had his best interest at heart, just like he did for her. "Thanks, kiddo. So how about you tell me what's new with you?"

"Nothing. You're the one with the exciting life."

Thomas laughed. "That's bleak. The person who is in Darling should definitely not be the one with the exciting life."

"I'm happy for you, Thomas. Really. You deserve this. You deserve someone as wonderful as you."

His throat tightened. "You do too, you know."

Marina tsked. "Well, that goes against my policy of relationships being a waste of time, doesn't it?"

Thomas sighed. Even though she annoyed the heck out of him sometimes, his sister was one of the best people he knew. Unfortunately, that seemed to make it hard for her to find someone who was her equal, especially when she didn't care about being in a relationship at all. Thomas might be new to this whole love thing, but it definitely agreed with him. Why didn't Marina want to find someone who made her feel the same way? "I just want you to be happy."

"I am happy." She cleared her throat. "So what are you doing today?"

Thomas didn't miss the change in topic, but he understood not being in the mood to discuss certain things. Besides, he really did need to get going. "Actually, I have big plans."

"Oh yeah? Big plans in the most *boring* place on earth?" Marina teased.

He smiled. After a lifetime of not feeling like he was good enough, Thomas had finally found his purpose. It was so much more than just living the life he wanted. It was living the life that Vivian wanted too. Because Vivian being happy made him happy. "I'm going to make some dreams come true."

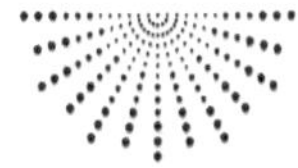

THOMAS

Thomas had never thought the day would come where he was more excited about making someone else's dreams come true than his own. But when that person was Vivian, nothing could make him happier than helping turn her dream into a reality.

He opened the door to Locke Grocery, smiling at Vivian. The minute he saw her, he knew without a shadow of a doubt that he was doing the right thing. "Fancy meeting you here."

"Ha, ha." She stuck out her tongue. "What's going on? I thought I told you that I was working today."

"You did. Although I'm still not sure why." Her parents had mentioned a similar thought the last time Thomas joined the Lockes for dinner. But no matter what he or her parents said, Vivian insisted on working as many days as possible before she and Thomas left for New York. She worried about her parents having to run the store by themselves while she was away. One thing was for sure. Vivian definitely wasn't a gold digger, not that Thomas had ever truly thought she was. Gold diggers didn't work that hard.

"I don't mind." She lifted her shoulder. "If you came to see Trixie, my parents took her for a walk."

He shook his head. "I just needed to grab a few things for our trip."

"Let me know if you need help finding anything. I basically have this place memorized," she said dryly.

"I think I've got it. Thanks." Thomas wove around the short aisles, filling his arms with five different magazines, a large bar of Vivian's favorite chocolate, and a beanie.

He was relieved to notice that he was the only customer there. This was nerve-racking enough without an audience. Not because Thomas doubted Vivian. No, it was himself he was worried about. If he would be enough. If she would say yes.

Thomas set everything on the counter, and Vivian peered down at the collection. She picked up the hat, giving him a funny look. "I know I haven't been to New York in a while, but I don't remember it being that cold in May."

Before Thomas could answer, a nervous laugh escaped, and Vivian went from looking confused to genuinely concerned for him.

He gulped. How was it possible that he had agreed to marry her on the spot, but he was nervous now?

Because this wasn't just about getting married. It was about building a life together.

"Right, the hat." He rubbed the back of his neck. "I just thought you might need it, you know, once the weather changes."

"We're only going to be there for one week. I know global warming is a problem, but I didn't realize it had gotten *that* bad." Her mouth quirked up. "And what are the chocolate and magazines for? To shut me up when I annoy you?"

He chuckled. "It's to keep you entertained on the flight."

"I think I can survive a few hours."

"Actually, our plane tickets had a schedule change. It's going to be a bit longer than a few hours."

She wrinkled her forehead. "What kind of change? Did you let Mac know?"

"I don't think Mac will be able to do much, unless he is operating transatlantic flights now."

Vivian blinked. "Huh?"

Thomas reached across the counter, taking her hands in his. Her hands were delicate but rough. The hands of a hard worker. The hands of someone who had been through challenging times and deserved good ones. And Thomas wanted to be the man to give those to her. "Look, we both know I wasn't going to work for my dad forever. Once I have the trust, I'm going to focus on the restaurant. But that also means I set my own work schedule."

"Okay. What does that have to do with going to the lower forty-eight for a week?"

He swallowed, his mouth dry. When was the last time he had put his heart on the line? Never?

*You both deserve to be happy.*

A sense of calm came over Thomas, and the tension drained from his shoulders. He loved Vivian, and she loved him. It was going to be fine. More than fine. Spectacular. "I was thinking once we leave New York, after we're married, we could finally take that trip to Europe. After all this trouble, don't you think we deserve a honeymoon?"

Vivian bit her lip, her eyebrows squished even tighter together. Not quite the reaction Thomas had been hoping for, but he tried to reason with himself. He had been thinking about the idea since his phone call with Marina two days ago. Maybe Vivian just needed a minute to wrap her head around it. "I don't know. That's a lot of time to be away from the store."

"I'm sure your parents would be thrilled to know you're enjoying yourself. And they ran the store by themselves before, right?" Thomas squeezed her hands. "Besides, you're going to need inspiration for my next restaurant. Because I want you to run the pastry program."

Thomas all but held his breath. He couldn't wait to see her reaction. Would she scream? Cry? Thinking he was messing with her? But Vivian's gaze searched his face, and she wasn't smiling. She looked anything but happy. "What are you talking about? A second restaurant where?"

"In New York, of course." He offered a cautious smile. "It was your only requirement for a dream house, so it seemed like a good start."

"New York. As in, I'd have to live in New York."

"With me, yes." Now, Thomas was the one who was confused. This was supposed to be good news. So why was Vivian acting like Thomas had just ruined her day? "I mean, that's what I'd prefer. But if you don't want to move yet, I understand. I can also buy you a place in Darling. That old pizza parlor probably has a good setup. We could easily get it remodeled into a commercial kitchen for your baking."

"Oh, Thomas." Her voice was quiet. "That's very nice. Really. But I just don't know."

His stomach sank, his underarms prickling with sweat. Suddenly, the store seemed too warm, too stuffy. He might be in the Last Frontier, but Thomas felt he didn't have the space to take a breath. "Don't know about what? Me? Or actually following your dream?"

"Please. Try to understand. It's just a really sudden change. I love New York, but you're asking me to leave my family behind. My whole life."

"To start a new life with me. I thought that was the plan?"

Vivian pulled her hands back, her face strained. "Don't pressure me, Thomas."

"Pressure you?" His voice cracked. "Pressure you how exactly? To pursue something you love? Something you wanted more than anything before you got scared and came back to Darling?"

She shot him a look that could caramelize crème brûlée, and Thomas gulped. That was definitely the wrong thing to say. "I wasn't *scared*. I was taking care of my mom."

"I'm sorry. That's not what I meant." He shook his head. Shit. Thomas was thrown off by her reaction, and everything he said only made it worse. She didn't know that he quit his job. That he was already all in on this relationship. Thomas had thought she had been in the same place. "All I am trying to do is give this relationship the best chance I can. You're important to me. And I want you to know that."

She studied him, her expression blank. Was she still angry? Upset? "Fine. If I'm that important to you, you don't have to buy me anything. I already told you what I wanted. For you to fire Philippe."

Thomas's jaw dropped. They hadn't talked about Philippe since that night at the Buck. Thomas thought she had finally realized it was an unreasonable request. "Are you serious? We've been over this. I can't—"

"I don't give a damn about your reasons." Vivian looked at Thomas like he was a stranger, all the familiar warmth in her gaze gone.

His head spun more wildly than the night he had drank Wolfie's schnapps. This wasn't happening. "You don't understand what you're asking. Do you realize everything I'll lose?"

"I think I understand perfectly. You'd rather lose me, then." Her voice quivered. "You're the one who doesn't understand. My life fell apart the last time I tried for more than what I have in Darling. And you want me to do it all again? To risk having to put myself back together again? I'm going to need some reassurance."

Thomas ran his hand through his hair. He understood she had been hurt. But he wasn't Philippe. Even if things didn't work out between them, a scenario Thomas didn't want to see happen but seemed more likely with each word of this conversation, he would make sure she was taken care of. Screw the deal that they made in the beginning. Thomas wouldn't just give her the store and send her on the way. She meant more to him than that. "That's not what I am saying. Vivian, the restaurant is doing well. You know what a miracle that is in the industry. Look, I didn't know you two had history when I hired him. Hell, I didn't even know *you* then. Forget Philippe. I'll buy you a place of your own. You can have your own business. Anything you want. Anywhere you want."

"You think that's what I'm asking? This isn't a problem you can fix with money, Thomas."

Thomas fought the urge to tear his hair out. He had come in here planning on making her dreams come true. Instead, he had created a damn nightmare. "Isn't that the point of this whole thing? To get the money? I thought that was what we were doing here."

Her eyes narrowed. "How silly of me to forget."

Thomas gritted his teeth. God dammit. She was being impossible, but he refused to give in that easily. He wouldn't give up on them. "Vivian, please. I'm sorry about Philippe. Really. But don't let that ruin things between us. Hasn't that bastard hurt you enough in the past? Does he have to take your future too?"

"That bastard still works for you." Her green eyes glistened. "Please. Please fire Philippe. I don't want him to have anything to do with my life. I don't want him to have anything to do with you."

Her voice cracked, and Thomas's heart squeezed. He would do anything, anything, to make Vivian happy. Anything but the one thing she asked. That restaurant was the very first thing Thomas had done for himself, his first grasp at independence. Couldn't Vivian understand better than most just how much a dream realized was worth? "Isn't it enough reassurance that we're getting married? That I want to make your dreams come true just as much as I do mine? If you don't trust me by now, I don't think anything I can do will change your mind. Not even firing Philippe."

Her gaze traveled over his face as if she was seeing him for the first time. "Maybe you're right."

The defeat in her voice was a sucker punch in his stomach. Was she actually writing them off so easily? Was Thomas really worth so little to her? "Vivian. Please just think about it. You're too talented to sit here and live the same exact life as your parents just because it's scary to try something else."

Her face paled, and Thomas wished he could take his words back. "I don't need to think about it. It's not happening."

"What's not happening? Your restaurant? Or us?" Thomas asked, afraid to know the answer but knowing he had to.

"Take a wild guess."

Thomas sucked in his breath. "You don't mean that."

Vivian gestured to the empty space between them. "Whatever this was? A temporary lapse in judgment on my part."

*Was.* The floor fell out from under him. That told him everything he needed to know. She wasn't just having doubts. Vivian had already given up.

"I'll keep my end of the deal if you want. We can still get married. But after that, I need a break from this relationship. From you." Her voice was shaky. "Everything was so simple before you. I need space to get my thoughts together."

Thomas was going to be sick. He had been waiting his whole life for that money. For the chance to be the person he wanted to be, out from under his father's thumb.

But he knew one thing with a calm certainty. As much as he thirsted after a life beyond his family, Thomas wouldn't hold Vivian to their deal. He couldn't. Not only would it be wrong, but he didn't want to marry someone who didn't at least trust him.

Maybe he was the disappointment his dad always called him. After all, Thomas was so close to having it all, and he couldn't bring himself to do it. He was too weak to see this marriage through.

He swallowed, tossing out one final desperate attempt. The same thing that had motivated her to take a chance on him in the first place. "You don't want to get married anymore? What about the store? Escrow closes in just four weeks."

Her shoulders sagged. "My family will figure something else out. Maybe it's time to accept things happen the way they're meant to. Even if we don't like it."

"Vivian, please. You don't want to do that."

"Don't I?" Her green gaze held his, the defeat in her eyes crystal clear. "That was always the plan, wasn't it? To go our separate ways? Nothing has really changed, Thomas. In fact, it's all stayed exactly the same. You're leaving. I'm staying. And I might not keep the store."

His nose burned. He could not, would not cry. Even if his heart was breaking into a million little pieces, each one finer than the mist that fell down over Darling. "So that's it, then? That's the end?"

"Are you getting rid of Philippe?"

"Vivian. Don't be ridiculous." Once the words left his mouth, Thomas flinched at the harsh tone in his own voice.

Her face turned to stone. "The only ridiculous thing was

thinking I could ever go through with this. Don't bother saving me a seat on the plane."

Thomas met her cold gaze. Maybe she didn't love him. But not even this painful argument could change his feelings. "I have to go back to New York, okay? It's been too long. I haven't been at the restaurant for nearly a month. If you change your mind and want to talk…"

"I won't." Vivian turned and went upstairs, leaving him in the store by himself.

Thomas felt all the light leave the room as he watched her grow smaller and smaller until finally, she disappeared, and even her footsteps faded away.

His chest tightened, and he sucked in a ragged breath. Why did she have to ask him to do the impossible? Why had he ever come to Alaska? Why couldn't he have fallen in love with someone else?

Only a few days ago, he thought he would die from being so happy. Now, he had thrown it all away out of what? Pride? The desperation to prove he was capable of being successful? The fear that he loved her more than she loved him?

Not that it made a difference when he was talking about the one person on the planet who didn't care about money. She didn't even get into this for herself. She did it to help her parents.

*You both deserve to be happy.*

Maybe Vivian did. But Thomas surely did not.

No wonder he had never imagined marrying for love. How was that possible for a man who would never be enough?

# CHAPTER TWENTY-FOUR

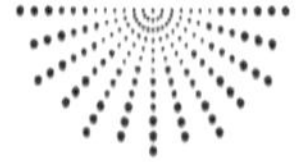



"Do you want to talk about it?" Grace set a cup of hot chocolate in front of Vivian.

"No, I really don't." Vivian wrapped her hands around the warm mug. But it didn't do anything to drive the chill from her body, something she hadn't been able to shake since Thomas left three days ago.

Since he'd been gone, Vivian had replayed their last conversation in her mind about a million times. Why had she insisted Thomas get rid of Philippe? Why hadn't Vivian gone to New York? Why had she told him that she didn't care anymore?

But she knew the answer already. The truth was that when he had offered her everything she had ever wanted, Vivian had been too scared to think straight. Scared it was too perfect. That perfect never lasted.

She had her reasons not to trust men. Philippe had taken their restaurant and her dreams. Uncle Robert controlled the store. Her dad's behavior had left her mom devastated. But for all the reasons Vivian had not to trust men, Thomas had never given her one. That didn't stop her from being terrified, though. From caring too much and worried that made her vulnerable. So she pushed Thomas away. Now, Vivian had no one and nothing. Thomas was gone, and soon, the store would be too.

To think, Vivian had thought nothing could be worse than her breakup with Philippe. Life had proved her wrong once again.

Vivian took a small sip of her hot chocolate. Drat. She had lost her appetite, another result of Thomas's absence. She had hoped her favorite drink would do the trick, but the creamy, rich hot chocolate had as much flavor as tepid tap water. But it had been sweet of Grace to make it, so Vivian forced a second sip.

A particularly loud snort came from the floor. Ruby and Trixie were flopped on the dog bed together, sleeping quietly in the coffee shop. Or at least Ruby was sleeping quietly. Trixie was sprawled out on her back, snoring away.

Grace chuckled as she looked at the dogs. "At least you got one good thing out of it. Even if Trixie snores."

"That's true." Vivian's heart squeezed, remembering the way Thomas had carefully held the scruffy dog in Juneau, even though she'd been filthy. They might not have ended things on the best terms, but Vivian couldn't deny that Thomas was a great person. She was the one who had come up short.

"The good news is that the hot chocolate here is bottom-less." Grace winked.

Vivian lifted the corner of her mouth. She didn't want Grace to think that her lukewarm attitude had anything to do with the quality of the hot chocolate at the Driftwood Coffee Company. No, the problem was Vivian. She had messed something up. Again. "Thanks. I'll try not to drink you out of business."

"Speaking of business, any updates on the store?"

Though it was just the two of them in the coffee shop, there was no need for privacy. Everyone knew that Locke Grocery wouldn't be in the Locke family for very much longer. But few people knew that Vivian and Thomas had almost saved it. Too bad *almost* didn't count for much. It definitely wouldn't count for much if the new owner closed down the store. The locals would be forced to take the ferry to Juneau or Ketchikan to do their shopping.

"Nothing has changed." Vivian ran her finger up the side of the cup, scooping up the melting whipped cream and licking it off her finger. As she suspected. Also tasteless. "Escrow closes in less than four weeks. My uncle is going to sell it."

Grace's eyes rounded in apparent sympathy. "I'm so sorry."

"Like you said before, maybe there is a silver lining to this situation." Vivian forced a small smile, even though her stomach was sinking. The only silver lining she could think of was that at least Thomas wouldn't be around her anymore. She had a talent for messing things up, and Thomas would be better off far away from her.

Grace sighed. "Yeah. But that doesn't mean I won't miss you."

"I'll miss you too." Vivian took another sip of her drink. If she kept talking, she was afraid she was going to cry. The last thing she needed was to sit here blubbering. Grace would probably put her on a hot chocolate IV.

The bell over the door chimed, and Charlotte stepped into the coffee shop, smiling at Grace. Her gaze landed on Vivian, and her smile faltered. "I'll, uh, come back later."

She turned on her heel and hurried out the door.

"Charlotte, wait!" Vivian left her drink on the counter and followed Charlotte outside.

The older woman stopped in front of the coffee shop, turning to face Vivian. Charlotte's usually sweet smile was replaced with worry lines. "I just feel awful. He's my family—"

"Please don't." Vivian squinted into the glare of the cloudy sky. A steady mist drifted down, as fine as sifted flour. It might be on the cusp of summer, but the weather seemed as hopeless as Vivian. "You didn't have a thing to do with it."

Still, Vivian couldn't deny the sight of the woman brought back painful memories of Thomas. Maybe it was good if Uncle Robert sold the store. Maybe leaving Darling would be for the best. Vivian could go somewhere without memories.

Charlotte twisted her hands. "It's just so hard, seeing the two of you like this."

"The two of us?"

"I talked to Thomas on the phone last night." Charlotte lifted the corner of her mouth. "I think every question he asked me had something to do with you. He probably thought he wasn't being obvious, but I saw right through it. The poor kid has it bad. You got him, hook, line, and sinker."

Vivian shook her head, her heart aching. If only that was true. Then Thomas wouldn't have left her. But if she had truly loved him, wouldn't she have gone with him? Wouldn't she have not asked him to choose between her and the restaurant? After all, didn't Vivian know better than most how much a dream was worth? "I don't know about that."

"Then you should ask him yourself. Why don't you give him a call? It might help you both feel better to talk now that you've had some time apart. You never know."

Vivian's nose burned, and she tried to focus on taking deep breaths. It was bad enough to almost cry in the coffee shop. She might actually die of embarrassment if she cried in the middle of Main Street. "I don't think that's a good idea. We didn't end things well. And I…"

She swallowed, not able to bring herself to admit that she was the one who had screwed things up. Thomas had left the door between them open, and Vivian had slammed it in his face. Maybe she deserved to be miserable. If chocolate never tasted good again, it would serve her right.

"My dear girl." Charlotte gave her a reassuring smile. "Sometimes we don't see things as they really are."

"I'd be happy just to see things at all," Vivian admitted. "Between Thomas and the store, life is so confusing right now."

Charlotte snapped her fingers. "That reminds me, I have something for you." She reached into her purse. "Natasha asked me to give it to you when she came into the Buck last week. She likes to come by and have a glass of champagne once in a while."

A shiver ran down Vivian's back when Charlotte handed her the card. The minute Vivian felt the thick paper, even without seeing the picture, she knew what it was.

The Wheel of Fortune.

The last time Vivian had seen that card, she had it. How the heck did Natasha get it back? Was she running around with a pocket full of Wheel of Fortune cards?

"If you ever want to talk, you know where to find me." Charlotte patted Vivian's arm. "Now, if you don't mind, Wolfie is expecting a latte."

Charlotte stepped back inside the Driftwood, leaving Vivian by herself.

She stared down at the card. It seemed a lifetime had passed since Natasha had first handed it to Vivian. Back when Vivian had thought she had known Thomas to his core. Back before she knew how wrong she was.

*You make your own luck.*

Vivian's eyes burned, and she walked around the corner, ducking through the back door and into the storeroom of Locke Grocery. She didn't want to risk walking through the store and running into someone. Vivian wasn't fit to be around people. Luckily, her parents were running the store today.

She gripped the card, her body hot. Stupid, lying card. Vivian should tear it in half and throw it away. It was complete and utter junk. She had tried to make her own luck. Really, *really* tried. And what had that gotten her?

A big, fat nothing.

She had figured out a way to save the store, but then she had ruined it. She had fallen in love, but then she had pushed Thomas away. Just when Vivian had a life better than she had ever dreamed, she was left with almost nothing. And she had done it to herself.

Vivian squeezed her eyes shut, and a few tears escaped. *Almost* nothing. Even if her family wouldn't have the store after a month, they at least had each other. No matter where they lived or what they did, her parents would always be her parents. And isn't that what mattered? That they still had each other?

But after dedicating the last seven years of her life to exactly that, suddenly, it wasn't enough. She wiped at her eyes with her free hand. That was something else that had come out of her time with Thomas. He had stirred something in her soul, reminding her of the person she yearned to be.

Perhaps some things were fated. Because no matter how many times Vivian went over the events from the past months, she kept coming to the same conclusion: this was the only way things could've ended. She would've never gone to New York. Thomas certainly wouldn't stay in Darling. Did Vivian really think her luck could change?

She sighed, tucking the card into her back pocket. Still, Vivian couldn't deny that the past month had been filled with more changes and excitement than the past seven years combined. Uncle Robert was going to sell the store. Her family would leave Darling. A month from now, Vivian's life would look entirely different.

Her heart squeezed. But of all the changes, the hardest one to accept was the absence of Thomas Becker in her life.

# CHAPTER TWENTY-FIVE

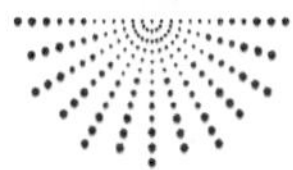

THOMAS

"So this is where you've been hiding."

Thomas snapped his head up to see Marina standing in the doorway of his office at the restaurant. "Who let you in?"

"Nice to see you too." She rolled her eyes. "The bartender. I caught her eye through the window when she was doing prep work. This might shock you, but people know I'm your sister. I've been here about five times before."

He leaned back in his chair, more embarrassed than annoyed. Marina hadn't been by the restaurant since before their most recent trip to Darling. But Thomas had told her what was going on with the place. He had to tell her *something* so she'd finally leave him alone and let him mope about Vivian in peace. But his sister seeing the state of the restaurant in person was a lot different than just chatting about it over the phone. And it made Thomas feel like even more of an idiot than he already did. "And?"

Marina gave him an encouraging smile. "It's not *that* bad."

Thomas stood, gesturing for Marina to step inside the

office and closing the door behind them. "Yes, it is *that* bad. Every time I see the place, I swear it looks worse."

After the longest, most miserable flight of his life, he had arrived back in New York, ready to throw himself into work at the restaurant. Until he had walked into the space and realized that Philippe had taken full advantage of Thomas being gone to implement a flurry of changes.

Thomas's body had gone numb with shock as he went over everything with a fine-tooth comb. The four-top tables had been switched out for two-tops. They had cut lunch service. The menu had been completely worked over. And that was just the tip of the iceberg. This was supposed to be a cozy, welcoming place. Thomas had envisioned something like a little brasserie in Paris. Instead, it had an elite, distant feel that made him feel out of place in his own restaurant.

It seemed Thomas hadn't lost his special talent for screwing up situations. He had stayed away from the restaurant too long. He shouldn't have quit his job at Becker Commercial Properties. And he definitely should've listened to Vivian when she warned him that Philippe didn't play nice. Even if her request to get rid of the talented chef had been extreme, she hadn't been wrong about the guy's morals.

"None of the reviews mentioned anything that would've clued me in about the changes either." Thomas shook his head. "I should've had you coming in here while I was still in Alaska. Not that it would've made a difference. From the paperwork, most of these changes happened when we were both in Darling."

Marina's eyebrows climbed up her forehead. "Damn. It's almost kind of impressive how fast he got everything done."

"If you saw the bills, you'd realize how it got done so fast. The guy paid for a rush order on everything. Or rather, authorized a rush order. The actual bills come back to me." His gaze dropped to the floor. And unfortunately, unlike in his old job, Thomas couldn't just put all the expenses on a company credit card. Everything had to be paid for out of his rapidly shrinking savings account. "I'm such an idiot."

"Dude, you couldn't know that the manager was lying to you."

Thomas clenched his jaw. But he should've known. Or at least been more scrutinizing after Vivian had warned Thomas exactly what kind of person Philippe was. After all, the manager was hired based on the chef's personal recommendation.

But Marina didn't know that little detail. Thomas couldn't bring himself to tell her. Not because he had trouble admitting that Vivian was right about the quality of Philippe's character. Not because Thomas was kicking himself for not listening. But because even thinking about Vivian made Thomas feel a hundred times worse than the situation with the restaurant. Talking about her was unbearable.

His throat closed up. Thomas loved her, and he had believed she felt the same way about him. But the more he thought about it, the more he couldn't help but wonder if their relationship was one-sided.

After all, Thomas hadn't demanded Vivian come to New York. He had also offered to help her start a business in Darling if she preferred. He didn't care where she was. All Thomas wanted was to make her happy and give this relationship a chance. He would've done anything to make her dreams come true, and he had tried to do just that. But if Vivian had loved him as much as he loved her, would she have really asked Thomas to sacrifice his own dream so quickly?

Thomas covered his face with his hands. "What am I going to do?" he mumbled into his palms.

"Sorry, what's that? I can't hear you when you're pouting like a little kid."

He dropped his hands and glared at his sister. "I am *not* pouting."

"Oh, yeah?" Marina cocked an eyebrow. "Then why have you been hiding out in the restaurant since you got home? Any chance it has less to do with the new menu and more to do with Vivian?"

Thomas winced at the mention of Vivian's name out loud, trying to disguise it as a shrug. Based on the amused look on his sister's face, she hadn't bought it. Regardless, the topic of Vivian was off the table. He couldn't handle it right now. Heck, he had seen a random dog on his way to work today that reminded him of Trixie, and it took everything he had not to burst into tears in the middle of the street. "Seriously, Marina. I'm at work. Now is not the time to harass me about my personal life."

"God, Dad really did screw us up, huh?" She shook her head slowly. "I'm not harassing you, Thomas. I *care* about you. And how am I supposed to talk to you about this stuff outside of work when you're at work literally all the time?"

Thomas threw his hands in the air. "I've been busy trying to fix this shit show."

"Are you sure you're not just staying busy to avoid fixing *this* shit show?" She tapped on his chest directly over his heart. "What the heck happened, Thomas? You two seemed so happy together."

"We made a plan. The plan changed. End of story." His stomach twisted. The last thing Thomas wanted was to discuss what happened. He had been thinking about what had happened since he left Darling, and he still couldn't make sense of it. "I am fine. How many times do I have to say it before you believe it?"

She barked a laugh. "I'll believe it when you do."

"Why are you so worried about me, huh? Don't you have, like, the busiest social life on the planet?" Back when Thomas lived with his parents, he remembered Marina going out almost every night. It wasn't uncommon for her not to come back until sometime the next morning. His sister wasn't just the life of the party. She *was* the party.

"I've been keeping it quiet." Marina lifted a shoulder. "So, what are you going to do?"

"No idea. I definitely need to get rid of the manager to start." Thomas massaged his temples. "But it's hard to find good people, and I don't have quite the capital that I thought I would at this point. I'm just thankful that the restaurant is doing well, or I don't know how long I would be able to keep it open. "

Marina's eyebrows knit together. "I'm sorry about the trust, Thomas. If I get mine, which we both know will be a miracle, I'll share, okay?"

His heart squeezed. No matter what happened, Marina would always be there for him. Thomas promised himself he would do the same for her. After all, it's not like they had anyone else. The Becker family may have been blessed in many ways, but lucky in love was not one of them. "You have plenty of time to fall in love."

"Falling in love isn't what I'm worried about. It's staying in it." She cleared her throat. "Speaking of time, Mom asked if you have time to come to dinner one night soon…"

"Nope."

"She promised to make all your favorites." Marina quirked up the corner of her mouth. "Well, have the chef make them."

Thomas spread his arms wide. "I have a restaurant, remember? I eat good food all the time."

Or at least he had, before his heart was broken in half and he completely lost his appetite.

His sister tilted her head. "Seriously, Thomas. You can't avoid them forever."

"Can't I? I don't work for Dad anymore. I have my own place. I'm not getting the trust. Seems pretty cut-and-dry to me."

"Thomas. They might not be perfect, but they're our *parents*. They love you. Or at least Mom does."

He snorted. "You got that part right. Dad probably loves that I'm never around. If they want to see me, they can come to the restaurant." He held up a finger. "Once I fix it."

"There is nothing wrong with it. I get it's not exactly what you wanted, but it's still a really nice place."

"That's the point. I waited years, decades, for this. Why can't it be exactly what I want?" He ran a hand through his hair. "I thought I finally got away from a power-hungry psycho with control issues. Instead, I just traded him out for one in chef's whites."

"So fire him. He sucks."

Thomas's shoulders sagged. That was exactly what he wanted to do every time he walked into the restaurant and felt pissed all over again. This place was supposed to be a dream. Instead, it had quickly turned into a nightmare. But Thomas hardly had any capital left to attract another chef nearly as good as Philippe. Not to mention Philippe had name power, which was definitely contributing to the great sales numbers night after night.

But none of that compared to the fact that Thomas felt sick inside when he realized if he had just fired Philippe in the first place, Vivian would be here with him right now. Her request had shocked him in the moment. But the more time that passed since he had last seen her, the more Thomas doubted he had made the right decision. After all, if he had made the right choice, wouldn't he be feeling better right now? "It's not that simple."

"Whatever, dude. You own the restaurant. You can fire him. You always say you hate all the games and shit that Dad pulls, but you overcomplicate things too." She blew air through her lips. "I swear, you are your own worst enemy."

Thomas scowled at her. "Did you come here to see the restaurant? Or hassle me?"

She gave him a cheeky smile. "Maybe a bit of both." Her expression sobered. "Actually, I really did want to see how you're doing. I thought you worked a lot when you were working with Dad. But this place has taken over your life. I liked it better when we were in Alaska."

Thomas studied her. "You really like Darling, don't you?"

Marina nodded. "One of these days, I just might stay."

"There's no shopping there. Could you even survive?"

She stuck her tongue out at him. "When I'm there, I don't know. It's like everything is so good that other stuff doesn't matter as much." Marina shot him a playful smile. "On that note, I better get going before I lose track of time. I'm meeting up with Mom to go shopping. And report back on you. She's worried."

Thomas barked a laugh. "Enjoy your shopping. And tell Mom she doesn't need to worry about me. She sure didn't worry about us being raised by a total hard-ass."

"Hey, you still turned out alright. You are the most determined, focused person I know. Or at least you used to be." She looked at him with so much pity that Thomas felt like he had food poisoning. "Now you can't even make a decision about a restaurant you *own*."

Thomas's throat tightened, and he glanced away. Great. A single tear would be all it took to convince Marina that Thomas was spinning out, and then she'd definitely tell their mom that he was *not* okay. The last thing he needed was his mother meddling in his life. "Tell Mom I'm fine, okay?"

"Whatever you want, dude."

They said goodbye, and Thomas closed the door behind his sister.

He had no idea what to do, and he wished more than anything he could talk to Vivian about it. That she was here. That he had listened to her. But Vivian had never called him, and with each day, his hopes that she would shrank a little more.

Thomas still couldn't forget the feeling that came over him, the way his stomach had sunk to his knees, when Vivian told him she didn't see a future between them. He didn't regret not holding her to their marriage bargain. That would've been wrong.

But he regretted not fighting for her. Not doing everything he could to earn her trust. Yes, firing Philippe was an outrageous request. But was it more outrageous than getting married to a virtual stranger for a stack of money? Was it more outrageous than tripping over his own pride rather than fighting for the woman he loved?

Thomas tipped his head back, staring at the stark white ceiling. He had screwed up the trust. He had quit his job. He had lost Vivian. Hell, he had lost control of the restaurant.

Natasha had told Thomas that both he and Vivian deserved to be happy. And maybe she was right. But that didn't necessarily mean that Thomas and Vivian would be happy together.

He wanted her to be happy. He wanted so badly to be the one to make Vivian feel that way, and it killed him that he hadn't been able to.

But it was one thing to be heartbroken. It was another to wonder if perhaps he was the only one who felt that way. That perhaps Vivian didn't really love him at all.

And she had made it clear that her love did have a limit. It had conditions. And Thomas had suffered through conditional love his entire life. His dad's expectations were exhausting. He hadn't expected Vivian to make her own demands.

The worst, most pathetic part was that if Vivian walked back into his life, he didn't think he'd be able to stop himself from loving her. Sure, they'd have to rebuild their trust. But the way he felt about her didn't have conditions. It'd be easier if it did.

He took a deep breath. There was no point in wishing for something that would never happen. Maybe Thomas did deserve to be happy. But he hadn't been good enough to deserve Vivian. And unfortunately, he couldn't imagine having one without the other.

# CHAPTER TWENTY-SIX

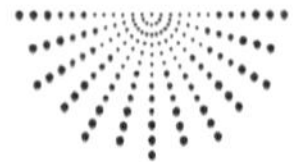

THOMAS

Marina had been right about one thing. Thomas was spending way too much time at the restaurant. Not only was it making him crazy, but he wasn't any closer to figuring out what the heck he should do.

Thomas racked his weights, using his T-shirt to mop up the sweat that poured down his face. He hadn't been to the gym since before he had left for Darling, and Thomas knew there would be hell to pay tomorrow. He already felt sore. But even though he had been working out for two hours, he wasn't any closer to figuring things out.

He had been hoping the hours at the gym would purge the self-doubt from his pores or, at the very least, clear his mind. But so far, it had only made him more tired. Sleep had been nonexistent at best since he came back from Alaska. He spent his nights staring at the ceiling, wondering what to do about the restaurant and what he could've done differently with Vivian.

The irony wasn't lost on Thomas that he'd slept better in some crappy hotel room in Ketchikan than he did on a goose-down mattress with thousand-thread-count sheets.

His throat tightened. Although that had a lot less to do with the quality of the mattress and more to do with the person he had been with. Not just been with. Thomas had liked the person he was with Vivian better too.

But it was becoming clear that she didn't feel the same way because Vivian still hadn't called.

His smartwatch beeped, reminding Thomas that he was meeting with a vendor at the restaurant in two hours. After an ice-cold shower, he changed and threw his gym bag in the trunk of his coupe, driving back to his apartment. Thomas parked in the garage and made his way to the elevator.

Reaching his floor, the elevator doors opened with a ding, and Thomas's shoulder blades instantly pinched together. His mom was standing in front of his apartment door. She had only been here once before when Thomas had first moved in.

His mom gave him a cautious smile. "Thomas. I'm so glad I caught you."

Thomas stepped out of the elevator. "Let me guess. Marina?" He shook his head. "What a tattletale."

"She cares about you. Like I do." His mom twisted her hands. "On that note, I was hoping we could speak for a moment."

Thomas unlocked the door. He didn't have the energy for this right now. "Then you should've come to the restaurant. I'm there all the time. In fact, I'm only stopping by briefly on my way back."

"Marina said something along those lines." His mom nodded. "But this isn't the kind of conversation I want an audience for."

Thomas sighed. He really was in a hurry, but he could at least make a few minutes for his mom. "Okay. Fine. But I need to be out of here in an hour, tops."

His mom flashed him a gracious smile, a childhood of etiquette classes never failing her. "Like I said, it'll just take a moment."

They stepped inside the apartment. Thomas closed the door behind them and tossed the gym bag aside. "Can I get you anything? Water? Water with ice?"

"I see life as a bachelor is treating you well." She chuckled. "And that's what I wanted to talk to you about. What exactly happened in Darling once the rest of us left?"

Thomas stiffened. "Christ, Mom. That's going to take a lot more than a *moment*. And that's if I wanted to talk about it, which I don't." He worked his jaw. "Besides, if you're asking about Vivian, why bother? It's not like you liked her much."

His mother's eyes rounded. "Oh, sweetheart. That's not it at all. I'll admit I was a little surprised that you got in a relationship so soon after Celeste. And of course, I couldn't help but wonder if the trust—"

"Speaking of the trust, I have a question for *you*," Thomas interrupted, his etiquette classes not quite so deeply ingrained. "Why have that stupid rule about getting married at thirty anyway? It's ridiculous."

She lifted her hands. "It's been that way in my family for generations. Back in the day, thirty was practically middle-aged. It's just tradition, Thomas."

"Most people have traditions like eating ham on Christmas Eve," he grumbled. "Not marrying for money."

His mother blinked at him. "Do you think that's what *I* did?"

"Of course not. You were the one with the money. Which makes it even more confusing how you ended up with Dad."

"Because I love him."

Thomas's jaw hit the floor. His mom was patient and gracious and kind, the exact opposite of his dad. Thomas could never figure out what the two of them had in common, and he had definitely never guessed it could be true love. The way he saw things, his parents merely tolerated each other. "You love that asshole?"

"Thomas, please." She gave him a scolding look. "I know he's been hard on you. But he loves you in his own way."

"Whatever. It's not my way."

"So what is your way?" His mom tilted her head. "Is Vivian your way?"

Thomas massaged his temples, the mention of Vivian's name making him hurt worse than his workout at the gym. How long would it take for him to be able to think about Vivian without missing everything about her? How long would it take for him to see a banana cream pie and not think of that night at the Buck? How long until every dog didn't remind him of Trixie and the night he and Vivian had spent in Ketchikan? "Please, Mom. Things between Vivian and me are over."

"But do you *love* her?"

Thomas sucked in a breath. His mom had a talent for getting her way. He might as well just surrender and tell her the truth.

After all, like he had just said, things between Vivian and him were over. This might be Thomas's one chance to tell his side of the story before his memories of their brief relationship mercifully faded away. "Yes, I love her. Happy? You were right." He dropped his gaze to the floor. "You were right about the trust too. That is why Vivian and I got together at first. And then, I don't know. Things happened."

"If you want to talk about it, I would love to listen."

With a huff, Thomas checked the time. That had been

quite enough talking for him, and luckily, he had the perfect excuse to get out of this conversation. He was supposed to meet with the vendor in less than an hour.

Then he looked up at his mom and saw the unconditional love in her eyes. His chest tightened. Suddenly, he wasn't so eager to get away. "Let me make a quick phone call."

He rescheduled the meeting, apologizing for the last-minute change. Then, without pausing once for a breath, Thomas told his mom everything. Well, almost everything. He kept certain details, like the night in Ketchikan, to himself.

Thomas told his mom about Celeste cheating. He told his mom about making a bargain with Vivian so that he could get the trust, and she could keep the store. He told his mom about Philippe, and the restaurant, and Vivian staying in Darling.

And by the end of it, for the first time in almost two weeks, Thomas actually felt a tiny bit better. He wiped at his nose. He hadn't even realized he was crying until he stopped talking.

"Oh, sweetheart." His mom wrapped her slender arms around him in a tight hug. "I am so proud of you."

Thomas stepped back, frowning. "Proud of me? Did you not just hear the story where I got cheated on, broken up with, and tricked?"

She smiled. "Did you not hear the part of the story where you were brave? You chose your morals over money. You risked your heart to help someone. And you chose your own path. Why wouldn't I be proud of you?"

His throat grew tight. Thomas had never thought of it that way. "I guess. Maybe. But I still feel horrible that I let Vivian down. I couldn't save the store. I'd buy it if I could, but all the money is tied up in the restaurant. New York real estate isn't cheap, you know."

"Yes, I'm aware." His mother chuckled. "But there's still enough time."

"Time for what? Even if I could convince Vivian to marry me just so we could get the trust, I don't think we could pull it off before escrow closes in two weeks."

"Oh, that." His mom threw her hand over her shoulder. "I'll buy the store, don't you worry. I'd never want you to marry just for the money. What I meant is you have enough time to find out if Vivian feels the same way you do *and* get your trust. Your thirtieth birthday is still six weeks away."

"No way." He gave a sharp shake of his head. "Vivian made it clear how she feels. I'm not a glutton for punishment."

"If you ask me, the poor girl was just scared. After all, I think it's very hard not to bring our past hurts into our present situations." She gave Thomas a pointed look.

Wasn't that the truth? Hell, he had carried the resentment he felt towards his father throughout his entire life. Thomas wasn't even sure who he was without it. "I still don't know."

"I do. I am going to buy the store, and you're going to talk to Vivian. Listen to your mother."

Thomas gave his mom a small smile. "I don't think Vivian's uncle would sell at this point anyway. Pulling out so late in the deal could seriously hurt his reputation in the business."

"Trust me, sweetheart. I'm going to make him the offer of a lifetime. He won't think twice about it. You know just how deep the Becker pockets are." His mother smiled confidently. "Now that we've sorted out your personal life, should we tackle the restaurant next?"

Thomas chuckled and shook his head. "You make it seem so easy. I'm still stuck on the part where I talk to Vivian." He rubbed the back of his neck. "What if it doesn't work, Mom?

What if I lose Vivian and the restaurant and I have nothing left?"

"Or what if it all works out and you're happier than you've ever been?"

*You both deserve to be happy.*

Thomas's throat grew thick. His time with Vivian had been the happiest of his life. And no matter what she said, his heart believed she felt the same way. Maybe his mom was right. Maybe Vivian had been scared.

After all, hadn't Thomas been scared too? All his life, he had never felt like enough. He had craved approval, especially from his father. Perhaps Thomas would never get that from anyone.

For the first time, Thomas realized that the trust could change the number in his bank account. But it wouldn't change anything about how he felt inside. There was no amount of money that would make Thomas feel worthy. Only he could give that to himself.

Maybe it had never been that he wasn't enough for Vivian but that he believed he wasn't enough. They both deserved to be happy, yes. But it was more than that. It was that they both deserved each other. They were both worthy of being loved completely for exactly the people they were.

He lifted the corner of his mouth. "Do you have time to come to the restaurant right now? Tell me what to do there next?"

His mother beamed. "I'd love to. I find the best way to solve a problem is to tackle it head-on." She pulled her phone from her purse. "But first things first, I have a store to buy."

Thomas wrinkled his forehead. "What will Dad think about you buying the store? Will he be mad?"

"Oh no, not at all." She smiled knowingly. "He knows that love doesn't make sense."

Thomas laughed. The restaurant needed serious attention. Thomas had almost no money left. And all he could think about was a woman who told him she wasn't interested anymore. Yet here Thomas was ready to offer her everything he had. Again.

His heart squeezed. No, love made no sense at all. Because the last thing Thomas expected was that he would learn to love himself by loving someone else.

# CHAPTER TWENTY-SEVEN

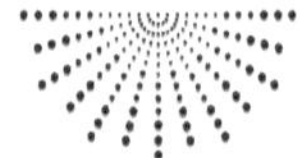

VIVIAN

Vivian wandered the store like a ghost, Trixie following at her heels. Desperate for a distraction, she had offered to work while her parents finished packing up the apartment. They only had one more week left before they had to move out.

But she wasn't able to get away from her memories down here either. Not when this was the last place she had seen Thomas.

Guilt curled in her stomach. She wanted to hate Thomas. It would be easier to hate him. But the only person Vivian hated was herself.

If only she hadn't panicked when Thomas had offered her things she hadn't dared dream of in years. After everything had happened with her dad, after Vivian had broken up with Philippe, after she had lost her restaurant, she had decided keeping everything the same was better than anything else life could offer. Vivian had given up on everything she wanted, and in order to survive, she had stopped dreaming.

She took a shaky breath. Now here she was, feeling so much worse than she had after Philippe. The truth bubbled up in her stomach. It hurt even more because she loved Thomas so much more.

Thomas was annoying and spoiled and everything she should stay far away from. But he also reminded her of who she was. Before Thomas, Vivian had been so focused on holding her life together she hadn't realized how much of herself she had lost.

Her eyes burned, and Vivian blinked furiously. The last thing she needed was for someone to pop in the store and catch her bawling her eyes out. Vivian could have a breakdown later. After they had left. Wherever they ended up.

The plan right now was to put everything in a storage unit and live minimally in a long-term rental in Minneapolis. Her mom was still set on seeing the Twin Cities, and her dad agreed, though he had mentioned a couple of times that he wasn't wild about the prospect of a Minnesota winter.

Vivian smiled in spite of herself. No matter what had happened between her parents all those years ago, she didn't doubt that her mom and dad loved each other completely. Too bad it had taken their lives in Darling falling apart for Vivian to finally see her dad in a new light.

She drifted past the chest freezer, eyeing a chocolate ice cream bar. It was her absolute favorite. But she couldn't have eaten a single bite right now if someone paid her to.

Ever since Thomas had left, Vivian struggled to enjoy anything she used to. She didn't want to bake. Chocolate tasted like dirt. Not even Trixie was able to cheer up Vivian. It was as if someone had drained all the color from the world. If she needed a reminder that love was a miserable experience, well, she got it.

As if summoned by the thought of ice cream, the door swung open, and Natasha stepped inside the store. "Oh, wonderful. You're still here. Did you get the card? Charlotte said she would give it to you."

Goose bumps popped up along Vivian's arms. She still hadn't figured out how Natasha had gotten the card back after giving it to Vivian the first time, so she chose to believe that there was more than one Wheel of Fortune card floating around Darling. It was less spooky that way. "I did. Thank you."

Natasha smiled brightly. "And? How are you feeling?"

Vivian's chest constricted. Even though the store being sold was common knowledge in Darling, she didn't like thinking about it any more than when it had been a secret. "I'm fine. We're going to Minnesota…"

"No, not about the store." Natasha waved her hand. "About the *card*. About all the changes."

"I, uh…I had thought you meant good changes. Instead, everything got worse." Vivian wrapped her arms around herself. As much as it scared her to be vulnerable, there was no point in lying to a psychic. "That's one thing that didn't change. My luck."

Natasha knit her graying brows together. "My dear. It has nothing to do with luck. It has to do with how you choose to see the world."

"How I see the world," Vivian repeated dryly. As if that would change anything. Her life was being turned upside down, and so were the lives of her parents. They had to leave their home. Vivian had pushed Thomas away. She would never have a restaurant. Those were facts. How she chose to see things had nothing to do with it.

The door opened again, and Mac stepped inside. Though Vivian wasn't in a social mood and Mac was the least social person on the planet even if she were, she was relieved to see the grumpy pilot. Maybe that would put an end to the confusing conversation with Natasha.

He nodded to Natasha and Vivian before hefting up a canvas bag. "Got some mail here."

"Thanks." Vivian took the bag from him. The store held mail for people on the remote areas of the island and those who Mac didn't run into on his way to drop it off at the store.

Natasha giggled, floating out of the store. "The wheel comes up, and the wheel comes down…"

Once the door closed behind her, Mac looked at Vivian, an auburn eyebrow cocked. "What was that about?"

"No idea. Any guesses?"

"Nah, I don't guess when it comes to Natasha. Sure as hell don't ask her a question you don't want an answer to." Mac bent down to scratch Trixie's ears before heading to the Driftwood for an afternoon caffeine fix.

Vivian opened the bag, sorting out the mail. Maybe getting away from Darling would do her good. Small towns didn't seem to be conducive to sanity. Or privacy.

She picked up the next letter in the pile, squinting at the envelope.

Her breath caught. It was addressed to her, postmarked in New York, from Simone Becker. Why was Thomas's mom writing to her?

Glancing around, Vivian worked the flap open, her heart pounding.

Simone had bought the store from Uncle Robert. And the deed was now in Vivian's name.

Her head spun. This had to be a dream. Maybe she was hallucinating? Isn't that what happened when a person went too long without eating and sleeping?

She read the letter again. And again. Hands shaking, she set the letter down and paced the store. Trixie trotted behind her, her nails tapping rapidly on the wooden floor,

Vivian looked down at the small dog. "What am I supposed to do now, girl?"

But Trixie just stared at her.

Closing her eyes, Vivian tried to think about anything other than Thomas. The way he made her feel. The way he made her laugh. His sandalwood scent and dark eyes that she dreamed about no matter how hard she tried to forget every detail about him.

The simple, undeniable, honest-to-God truth was that she felt more alive with him than she ever had. She felt happy. Excited about life. Heck, he made her wonder about life outside of Darling, outside of the fortress she had built for herself.

Thomas made her dream dreams she hadn't even known she had anymore. Maybe she did want to be in love. Or open a restaurant again. Or a million other things she had never let herself think about. Thomas had seen what no one else had seen. Vivian didn't have a wall up between herself and other people. She had a wall up between herself and her own heart. Thomas had put tiny cracks in that wall and reminded Vivian of the ache of wanting something. But the ache was more gratifying than feeling nothing at all.

He had reminded Vivian she was alive.

All this time, Vivian had told herself it was too late. That things could never be the same between her and Thomas. But then again, look how wrong she had been about everything else. Vivian had thought making this deal with Thomas would keep her safe. That nothing would change. But it was impossible to go back to her life the way it had been. Vivian knew the difference between being alive and living now.

She walked over to the staircase that led to the apartment. "Mom! Dad! I'm going to need you to watch Trixie! I'm going out of town!"

# CHAPTER TWENTY-EIGHT

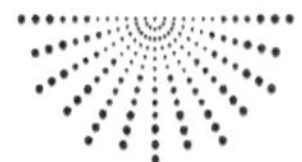

THOMAS

Thomas tapped the pen against his desk, glancing at the clock again. Only twenty-two hours until his flight to Alaska. Plenty of time to outline everything that needed to be done at the restaurant in the next week. The new manager was more than capable of running the show in his absence, but Thomas didn't want to leave without a firm plan in place. He had learned his lesson the last time.

He took a deep breath. Thomas was going to do things differently in Alaska this time too. Since his talk with his mom more than a week ago, all Thomas could think about was seeing Vivian again. He would've been in Darling already, except he needed time. Time to sort things out at the restaurant. Time for his mom to buy the store. And time to figure out exactly what he was going to say to Vivian.

Thomas had spent every spare second perfecting his speech. Her stance on their relationship might not have changed, but Thomas at least wanted her to know how he felt. To make sure he kept a clear head, he had even booked a connecting flight from Ketchikan through a different pilot. The Darling gossip mill was legendary, and Thomas and Vivian hadn't parted under the best of circumstances. Mac might not be a gossip, but the last thing Thomas needed was for Mac to give him the stink eye for the entire flight and rattle Thomas's nerves. They were rattled enough already.

A knock came at the door, and Thomas gritted his teeth. So much for coming in early to get some work done. But it was his fault. He had spent too much time thinking about his upcoming reunion with Vivian and not enough time actually getting ready to leave. Hopefully, this would be a quick interruption because then Thomas really did have to focus, or he wouldn't have everything ready before going to Darling tomorrow. And nothing, not even the restaurant, would keep him from getting on that plane to Alaska. "Come in!"

The door eased open, and his new manager, Alan, stuck his head in the office. "There's someone here asking if we're hiring a new pastry chef. I didn't realize we had even posted a position."

Interruption averted. He could wrap this up in two seconds and be back to work in no time. "We didn't. Whoever it is, just take a resume and suggest keeping a look out for future openings."

"That's what I thought, but she insisted. She said to tell you that she makes the best banana cream pie." Alan chuckled. "Odd to point out at a French restaurant, don't you think? Now, crème brûlée—"

Thomas sat up. "Bring her back, please."

"Are you sure?" Alan scrunched his pale blond brows.

"Yes. Now, please."

The door closed softly, and Thomas stood, pacing the small room. It couldn't be. Why would Vivian have come all the way here? To the restaurant where not one but two of her exes worked? But if not her, then who else?

A couple of minutes later, Vivian was ushered into the office. She gave him a shy smile. "So, no openings, huh?"

Thomas's heart pounded, each *thump* erasing another line of his carefully rehearsed speech from his memory. She was as gorgeous as ever. Gorgeous and in New York. "What are you doing here?"

"Guess I deserved that." Vivian winced, apparently mistaking his shock for anger.

He shook his head. "I'm sorry, I didn't mean it like that. I'm just surprised you're here. I was going to see you in Darling. Tomorrow, actually."

"You were?" Her green eyes rounded. "Oh, Thomas. I'm the one who is sorry. I should've never asked you to pick between me and the restaurant. That wasn't fair. And your trust…"

"It's fine." He swallowed, his throat thick. "Did you…did my mom tell you about the store?"

Vivian nodded, her eyes glistening. "Thank you. You didn't have to do that. We can pay her back over time—"

"No, don't. I'm glad you got what you wanted." He held her gaze, his voice a whisper. "That's all I ever wanted, you know. To make you happy. To make all your dreams come true."

A tear rolled down her cheek, and it took everything he had not to go to her. But if Vivian didn't return his feelings, until he was sure, he kept his distance. Otherwise, it would hurt all the more if she rejected him a final time. "There's only one thing I really want."

Thomas almost forgot how to breathe, wanting so badly to be right about what she wanted and being terrified he was wrong. But Vivian wouldn't come all this way just to apologize, would she? She could call or text or talk to him the next time he was in Darling. She wouldn't fly to New York and risk seeing Philippe at the restaurant just to tell Thomas that she was sorry. "And what is that?"

"I want you, Thomas." Her voice cracked, jerking on his heartstrings. "I'm beyond in love with you. I can't imagine life without you. Before you came along, I had stopped living altogether. You made me feel alive again. Like I could do anything. But I don't want to do any of it unless you're with me."

His heart slammed into his ribs. He had planned to go to Darling and ask Vivian to give him the chance to make her happy. Prove to her that he was worth it, now that he finally actually believed he was. Instead, Vivian had faced her worst fears and come to him.

*You both deserve to be happy.*

"Vivian, you are the most aggravating, annoying, impossible person I have ever met." He paused for a moment, her green eyes growing wide. "And you're also the best person I have ever met. I haven't ever stopped thinking about you since that night at the Buck."

Her shoulders sagged, and the corner of her mouth tipped up. "Finally getting me back for chewing you out over that pie, huh?"

"Never." Thomas walked up to her, tucking a strand of hair behind her ear. He eased his arm around her waist, holding her close. "That pie was what hooked me in the first place. But the sass is what kept me around."

She looked up at him, her green gaze searching his. "And what if the sass isn't enough? What if I'm not enough?"

"You're all I need. Because I'm beyond in love with you too." Thomas lowered his head, gently touching his lips to hers. Vivian wrapped her arms around his neck, leaving no space between them. His heart sighed as he melted into her, feeling perfectly at home for the first time since he had last held her.

They broke apart, and Vivian smiled up at him. "Speaking of pie, that's how I paid for my plane ticket here." She cocked a dark brow. "See? It's a good thing I didn't stop selling baked goods after all."

"Just when I thought I couldn't love pie more." Thomas kissed her nose. "Guess I'm not going to Darling tomorrow."

"In that case, want to get married instead?"

Thomas blinked at her, his head spinning. "Am I dreaming? I must be dreaming." He felt her arms up. "Hmm, you feel real."

She slipped out of his grasp, giggling. "I'm serious. That way, you can still get the trust."

Thomas smiled. He had waited his entire life for that money, for the chance to be independent. To finally feel like enough. But that was before he realized his peace of mind was not dependent on a certain number in his bank account. If they ever did get married, which he wasn't opposed to, it would be because they were both completely ready, not to meet a deadline. "Vivian, that's really sweet. But—"

She held up a finger. "You haven't heard my terms yet. I will only do it on one condition. It's *not* a business deal." Vivian pursed her lips. "Okay, two conditions. If your apartment isn't dog-friendly, we're going to have to move. I think Trixie will love going for walks in Central Park."

Thomas's heart stretched in his chest. Vivian was serious. She wasn't just marrying him so he could gain access to the trust. She wasn't just trying to pay him back for his help with the store. Vivian actually wanted to build a life together.

He sighed dramatically. "I guess we're moving."

"Luckily, we have plenty of time. Someone promised me a trip to Europe."

Thomas threw his hands in the air. "*Now* you want to go? Do you always have to have a crazy plan in place or something?"

"Of course. We got engaged before we fell in love. I think it's only fitting if we go on the honeymoon before we have a home. Like you said before, who cares if we do things out of order? That's our style."

"Whatever you want. As long as I'm with you." He pressed a kiss to her forehead.

"How about we start with a tour of your restaurant? I promise I won't try to fire Philippe."

Thomas barked a laugh. "Actually, you're too late. I already did. Yesterday was his last day."

Her jaw dropped. "You're kidding."

"Nope. Turns out you were right. The guy sucks." Thomas filled Vivian in on everything that had happened at the restaurant the month he was in Darling, including all the changes Philippe had made without consulting Thomas. "He should've been here today to start training the replacement chef, but Philippe no-showed and isn't answering his phone."

Vivian shook her head, properly dismayed. "I'm so sorry, Thomas. I wish I had been wrong about him. But he is impossible to work with and always has been. Just takes people a while to catch on."

"Thank God my mom could help me buy him out of his shares. If he was like that as a business partner and employee, I can only imagine how awful it must be to date him. Good riddance." Thomas made a face. "The new chef is really promising. Now, if I could just find a good pastry chef..."

"I thought you weren't hiring." She shot him a teasing smile.

Thomas chuckled. "You are more than welcome to spend as much time at the restaurant as you want. But there are a million other restaurants in New York. Or you can start your own place. This restaurant is my dream. It doesn't have to be yours."

Vivian wrapped her arms around Thomas, gazing up at

him with so much love and warmth that he wondered what he had done to deserve all this. Then he remembered they *both* deserved it. "I want to do something together. That's my dream."

"Then it seems this worked out for the best." Thomas smiled, his heart full. For the first time in his life, he had enough. "Because you happen to be my dream too."

# EPILOGUE

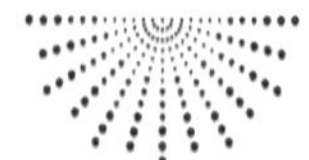

VIVIAN

"I think this is the first family holiday that I am actually looking forward to."

"Be nice." Marina poked her brother in the ribs. "I'm standing right here."

"Hey!" Thomas clutched his side. "I was *trying* to be nice."

Trixie danced around their feet, yapping at the horseplay.

"You know, it's hard enough baking three kinds of pie dealing with jet lag, let alone a boxing match." Vivian pointed a wooden spoon at Thomas. "Back to peeling apples, mister."

"Yes, ma'am." He fought a laugh. "Though I wouldn't consider the time difference between New York and Alaska jet lag. It was way harder when we came back from Europe."

"I am glad to hear our honeymoon was so difficult for you." Vivian stuck her tongue out at him. They had spent three weeks traveling around Italy, France, and Austria. Vivian had loved every minute of it, and Thomas promised they could go back as often as she wanted. He considered staying up to date on European pastry one of her most important job duties as the restaurant's pastry chef.

But Vivian didn't want to go back as soon as she thought she would. She was enjoying work too much. The restaurant was big and clean and modern. Vivian could spend all day there, whipping up recipes and losing track of time. Anyone else might have gotten frustrated with how much time she dedicated to work, but Thomas was right there with her every step of the way.

They had bought a new apartment too, one that allowed dogs and was closer to the restaurant. That way, they could check on Trixie and take her for quick walks throughout the day. The new place didn't have a garage, so Thomas had sold his car. They walked to and from work together, discussing recipes and tasting menus and daily specials. Every day, Vivian got to wake up to a life that was better than any she had ever dreamed about.

"If I really thought our honeymoon was that bad, do you think I would be bugging you about a second one all the time?" He waggled his eyebrows.

"No more, please." Marina covered her ears with her hands. "Love you both, but I have my limits. I think I am going to start visiting Darling on my own."

"Turkey delivery." An accented voice came from the doorway in the kitchen. They turned to see Wolfie holding a giant foil-covered dome. It was either a way to communicate with extraterrestrial beings or the biggest turkey that Vivian had ever seen. "It shouldn't need to go into the oven right now. It's still warm."

"Perfect. Because we're behind on the pies." Vivian gave Thomas a pointed look before looking back at Wolfie. "You can set the turkey on the counter for now, by the pecan and pumpkin pies. I set out some trivets already."

Charlotte bustled into the kitchen next, giving Thomas and Marina loud smacking kisses on their cheeks.

"Charlotte," Thomas mumbled as she smooshed his face. "We just saw you. This *morning*."

"Shush. I'm happy every time I see you."

Vivian bit back a smile at the pleased look on Thomas's face. She wasn't laughing at him. But he was so obviously happy that it made her feel happy too.

Her family and Thomas's relatives were celebrating Thanksgiving two days early to give them a day to finish preparing for actual Thanksgiving at the Buck. Anyone and everyone in Darling was invited, and almost the entire town showed up every year. The Buck would provide the turkey and, as usual, the beer. The rest of the meal was made up of a hodgepodge of potluck dishes. Vivian would be baking pies, of course, including one banana cream per her husband's request.

They had also invited Thomas's parents, but they had declined a return visit to Darling. However, Vivian and Thomas had celebrated their thirtieth birthdays with the Beckers in New York. Even Thomas's dad had managed to put on a smile, though he had grumbled more than once about finally signing over the trust.

Thomas's mom had gifted Thomas the shares of the restaurant she had bought from Philippe, joking she had been tempted to hold on to them and create another Becker family business. Thomas had thanked her and then immediately given the shares to Vivian, deciding he did like the idea of it being a family business after all.

Vivian's mom came upstairs with a bottle of wine, squishing into the already packed kitchen. "Henry is just closing up for the day, and then he'll join us. But in the meantime, I thought we could enjoy the benefits of living over a grocery store." She lifted the bottle of wine. "Who would like a drink?"

She opened the bottle and handed out glasses. Everyone but Vivian and Thomas went to the living room to chat. Trixie stayed behind at first, but once Vivian's dad walked through the kitchen to join the others, she trotted out on his heels.

Vivian grabbed a peeler, joining Thomas at the sink with the apples. "Need a hand?"

"I am supposed to be helping *you*." He puffed out his chest. "I'm your sous-chef."

She giggled. "Well, sous-chef, I have finished everything else except these apples. And they are all that stand between those hungry people in there and Thanksgiving dinner."

"Shit." Thomas started peeling faster. "Did Wolfie and Charlotte get here early or something? They weren't supposed to bring the turkey over until four."

"Careful. There's no need to rush." She gave him a reassuring smile. "Although it is after four."

Thomas stopped peeling long enough to lean over and give her a kiss. "That is why you're the one who runs the kitchen in our house. And I just pay the bills."

Vivian kissed him back. "You are very good at that."

He stuck his lip out in a mock pout. "Just with me for my money, huh?"

"And what's so wrong with that? You're just with me for my pies." Vivian winked.

Thomas barked a laugh. "Exactly. You seduced me with your baked goods."

They finished peeling the apples, and Vivian expertly assembled the pie, taking the time to crimp the crust just so. She slid it into the oven, clapping her hands together. "I think we're done for now."

Thomas wrapped his arms around Vivian, pulling her

close and nuzzling her neck. "Perfect. Because I was thinking we could have dessert before dinner."

"Seriously, Thomas. My parents are in the other room. This is a *family* holiday." But Vivian had realized long ago how futile it was to resist him. It was impossible. Instead, she only fell deeper and deeper in love.

"Mm-hmm. And you're my family, remember?"

"How could I ever forget?" Vivian leaned back and waggled her ring finger at him. She had kept the fake diamond from Ketchikan. She had to take it off so often when at work that Vivian worried about losing something more valuable, even though they had more than enough money to last them a lifetime. Besides, the ring was a memory of the day she had realized that she was seriously falling for him. Nothing could be better than that.

Thomas frowned. "You know what I've been thinking? We need to upgrade that ring of yours. I still feel bad that I didn't get you something better before we got married."

"There wasn't time." The wedding had been a rush affair, to say the least. Marina was the only person who had been able to attend the quick city hall ceremony. Instead of a reception, Thomas had arranged a private car to take Vivian and him around the city, tasting all kinds of desserts. It was her kind of night out. "Seriously, don't worry about it. This ring is perfect."

He shook his head. "But it's not real."

Vivian arched an eyebrow. "You know as well as I can it can become real."

"And you know as well as I do that things can always get better." Thomas reached into his back pocket and held his hand out to Vivian.

She gasped. There in his palm was a gold ring with a jade inset. "Thomas. It's beautiful."

"I know it's not the fanciest. I used the jade bracelet I bought you in Ketchikan. It's a good memory for me."

She held it up to the light. "I love it."

"That's a relief. You aren't always the most agreeable person, you know."

Vivian made a face. "How are you so attractive, yet so annoying?"

"It's part of my charm." He grinned.

She couldn't help but smile back. As she leaned in to kiss him, his stomach let out a roaring growl. Vivian giggled. "I think your stomach just gave Trixie a run for her money. It was *almost* as loud as her snoring."

He gave her a sheepish smile. "I am kind of hungry."

Vivian walked over to check the pie. Perfect. "Then you're in luck. Because it's almost time to eat." She slid it from the oven, replacing it with the turkey. "Want to let everyone know it should be ready in about fifteen minutes?"

While Thomas went to the living room, she fixed up the food on the counter in a buffet style. When the timer for the turkey dinged, the group filed through the kitchen, fixing a plate before they sat down at the table.

Charlotte scooped up a bite of mashed potatoes. "What are you making at the restaurant these days, Vivian? Any great new recipes?"

Vivian stuck her fork in a brussels sprout. "Actually, we've added a banana brûlée to the menu."

"*Banana* brûlée?" Charlotte's graying brows pinched together. "Is that, um, traditional?"

Thomas took Vivian's hand, giving it a squeeze. "It is for us."

Marina rolled her eyes. "Please, I'm trying to enjoy my meal."

Her comment earned a chuckle from the table. Then, the

group fell into easy conversation as they savored Thanksgiving dinner.

As Vivian glanced at her loved ones around the table, it occurred to her how different her life was compared to only earlier this year. Back then, she didn't need change. She hadn't wanted it. As far as Vivian was concerned, the only good thing was for life to stay the same.

Yet, despite her best intentions, things had changed. Now, they were so much better. Vivian was deeply in love. She had achieved some of her biggest dreams. With Thomas's help, she had been able to secure her parents' future. Vivian even had the sister she had always wanted.

*You make your own luck.*

Vivian looked at her husband, and Thomas smiled back at her. Her heart stretched in her chest. Vivian had no idea exactly how life would go. How many changes lay ahead. But she knew one thing for sure.

The best was yet to come.

# A NOTE FROM THE AUTHOR

Thank you for taking the time to read my book. I hope you had as much fun reading it as I did writing it.

If you did enjoy it, and want to help other people discover Thomas and Vivian's story, please consider leaving a review at the retailer where you purchased this book. It would absolutely make my day (especially if share who your favorite character is!).

Thank you kindly.

# ACKNOWLEDGMENTS

This is always the hardest part of the book to write. So many incredible people contributed to the story you are holding, and I don't how to even begin thanking them. Or maybe I do…margaritas for all!

To Sarah, for your invaluable feedback and wicked sense of style. Thank you for everything, including the most clever title! You made this book a story.

To Sandra, for her proofreading magic. Thank you for making the book perfect once again!

To the team at Best Page Forward, for both the gorgeous cover and wonderful description. Thank you for helping this story find the right readers.

To my mom, who helped me through every page. Thank you.

To being yourself. Sometimes that's really hard. But it's even harder not to be.

Thank you all.

# ABOUT THE AUTHOR

Lark Holiday is the author of feel-good and funny romances. She lives in California with her opinionated dogs and her human family. When she's not writing, she spends her time going for walks, vacuuming dog hair, and feeling like she should probably be writing.

Though Lark is based in California now, she lived in Alaska many times over the past few decades. Her time in The Last Frontier inspired the Darling Men series.